A FORLORN HOPE

L. J. STUBBS

This is a work of fiction. Names, characters, places, and incidents are products of the author's imagination or are used fictitiously and are not to be construed as real. Any resemblance to actual events, locations, organizations, or persons, living or dead, is entirely coincidental.

World Castle Publishing, LLC

Pensacola, Florida

Copyright © L. J. Stubbs 2022
Hardback ISBN: 9798365732407
Paperback ISBN: 9781958336960
eBook ISBN: 9781958336977
First Edition World Castle Publishing, LLC, December 12, 2022
http://www.worldcastlepublishing.com

Licensing Notes

Cover: L. J. Stubbs
Editor: Karen Fuller

DEDICATION

For my sons. I hope you like it.

CHAPTER 1

Life to this point had been a confusing array of training and conditioning. G39's earliest memories were a blurry vision of a female scientist in a lab coat disconnecting his feeding tube and injecting him with something that made the blurry vision turn dark. He didn't know at the time what she had said. After all, he had just been born. He learned later that the words she'd used were "G39's good. Let's move to 40."

Mechanical words. No emotion. Emotion was something he was forbidden to have, or at least if he did, they would deem him "defective" and "reallocate resources to a fresh unit." Mechanical words to describe his execution.

They couldn't force him not to feel emotion. They had tried, he had been told, but eliminating emotion in the test subject's genes, invariably rendered the unit brain dead.

Still, they did everything possible to limit and discourage emotion among the mobile infantry units. Each unit was integrated with a control device at the base of the skull that read, to a small degree, a unit's emotions and even thoughts, and when proper correction was needed, the device delivered either punishment or pleasure.

G39 had never felt anything more than a slight pinch in the back of his head, but he did see a unit be "exterminated" by the device when the unit punched a drill instructor. Actually, the unit never made contact. He was twitching on the floor before the act of defiance could be carried through.

The emotion that was most common for G39 was frustration.

Frustration was different than anger. At least the device treated them differently. Somehow the device could interpret frustration at one's own failings as acceptable, but frustration toward a superior was instantly corrected. The correction was gradual in its intensity for most infractions, but for others.... instantaneous and severe.

Most of G39's training was what the instructors called "book smarts," which consisted of being plugged into an upload port and receiving instant knowledge. The process was extremely painful, and so the uploads were reserved for only the most basic combat functions. The instructors, combat vets all, thought the uploads were a poor substitute for actual battle experience. None of the instructors had their "mother," as they called the control device and liked to flaunt their freedom at times. He supposed that most drill instructors would be a pile of blubbering meat if their constant yelling and obvious anger were corrected. Distinguished service could qualify you for promotion which could mean the removal of mother.

G39 wished for the day when he could be free of the device and instantly felt a tight throb at the back of his head.

He breathed in sharply and then took control and cleared his mind. It didn't take long for a unit to learn how to end the discomfort, at least for most. Some never seemed to get the knack of dissolving errant thoughts. Those washed out sooner or later, and the "resources were reallocated to other units."

Language had been one of his first uploads, walking, running, basic motor function, all learned within the first few days of "birth." He was not "born" in the traditional sense. Not in the way that the uploads described as the natural way. The way humans had given birth for thousands of years until Terran needed a new breed of soldier.

He had been grown in an amniotic sack and had a feeding tube giving him nutrients and complex growth hormones that would grant him added speed and strength. His very genome was altered to make life in space more tolerable. The gene engineers had given him, and all mobile infantry units, mental acuity to increase responsiveness and facilitate physical agility. He was given optimal stamina and dense bones that could support more of the stresses that combat on diverse worlds might demand.

G39 felt the deck plating beneath his feet tremble and could only assume that it indicated entry into the planet's atmosphere. He was aboard a troop transport awaiting deployment into his first warzone. He had been rushed through training. Training... not much, by way of that. They had taught him the basics, sure enough, but he felt hopelessly lost all the same. He didn't dare mention as much to his instructors or even his co-trainees for fear of being classified as defective.

G39 was part of Golf platoon in Charlie company, Lot 1286. The entire platoon had been "re-formed" after the entire unit was wiped out in a failed assault on a Grey base.

According to the upload that had all of the supposed relevant data that he would need, which 39 thought was completely inadequate, Greys were the longest lasting threat to his species, and unlike the perception that humans had of Greys early in humans exposure to them, they were not the benign appearing humanoids with oversized heads. At least the drones weren't. According to the data that Terra had on the Greys, the small creatures with large heads and uniformly black eyes were the leaders and decision makers among the species.

The other creatures, the warriors, were another story entirely. Massive, muscular brutes with armor plating. The Heaters, as they were called, while not stupid, relied heavily on the telepathic communication sent to them from the brains, the small humanoids with large heads. "Brains" and "Heaters" were not the names that the uploads gave them, but they are what stuck with the trainees and instructors alike. The true names were overly complicated, and they could get you killed if you took half an hour describing an engagement in the field.

In addition to the armor, the Heaters were armed in myriad ways, but by far, their most dangerous weapon was one built into the very anatomy of the Heater. When one was close to death or even wanted to commit suicide, it could build up a sort of plasma charge inside itself. If the Heater wasn't finished off before it was fully charged, then the explosion was like a plasma grenade. Their fluorescent blue blood, that would coat everything in the blast radius, was magma-hot and would melt anything it touched until it cooled into solid rock.

Nasty creatures, to say the least.

Despite all of their strengths, Terra had a resilience and ingenuity that the Greys had totally underestimated.

Terra and the Greys had been at war since the aliens showed up nearly two-hundred years ago when Terra was still called Earth. Things looked dire for Earth, but desperation breeds innovation, and with the new threat, countries who had up until that point only fought each other, united and pooled knowledge and resources. The first Terra fleet was formed. A pitiful thing by comparison with the fleet of today. But they got the job done.

The Greys finally retreated, giving Terra a fighting chance.

It was ironic to 39 that a lot of the tech that the Greys used against Terra was now being used to bring war to them.

"Don't piss your jump suit 39."

Lieutenant Maul was the only member of the toon that wasn't a trainee. He had been assigned this toon when he graduated from Westpoint. He was a commissioned officer and didn't have his mother. Only commissioned officers were without their mother in the Infantry units because they were true-born. If you were a Grunt, if you were "born" in an amniotic sac on a birthing ship, then you had a control device. Instructors were special cases, 39 was learning. Despite many of them only being sergeants, they could not operate as effectively with mother, so they were exempt.

"Don't worry, sir, I'll save some to put out the ashes of my first Grey man."

The Lieutenant liked this kind of talk, and 39 was smart enough to give his C.O. what he expected. Lieutenant Maul nodded his approval of the bravado and continued his circuit of the transport.

The ship shook, and 39 saw 23 wince and cup the back of his head. An errant thought clearly invited correction in the young man. Young. Did 39 look that young and scared?

39 wondered why they didn't try and correct the fear that was apparent on almost all of the trainees' faces. Not trainees. They were soldiers now, or at least would soon be.

He supposed that stabbing at a soldier's brain while he is legitimately scared for his life is a good way to get him killed.

The ship shimmied again, and 20 cursed.

20 was a female. It was hard for 39 to understand why she was so different from him. There were other females in the toon, of course, but from the uploads, 39 knew that females gave birth, not to soldiers like him, but back on Terra they did. Looking around the transport, 39 spotted the only other two females in the toon. All three were smaller than most of the men.

He didn't understand why the engineers allowed so much diversity in the program. Wouldn't it make more sense to apply the same superior genetics to each unit rather than allow this spectrum of genetic noise?

He had asked as much of one of the lab-coats that did weekly checkups during basic training. She shrugged it off and said it was needed for a strong pool, whatever that meant.

All of the toon member's feet hung above the floor except for 39's. He was the tallest in the toon and, therefore, carried a grenade launcher kit.

The launcher and its ammo weighed about a thousand pounds, and despite the increased strength they'd given him, he would never be able to pack all the gear around without the tech.

They each had exo-suits that were kind of an outer skeleton that supported and enhanced their movements. Each soldier hung in these, suspended from the ceiling of the jostled ship.

A deafening explosion sounded just outside the transport, and a piece of the wall broke in, eliciting a shriek from 42 as a piece of debris lodged itself in his bicep.

The toon was suddenly pitched sideways, hanging legs swinging violently in their exo-suits.

39 gripped his carbon fiber harness and feared that his pitifully short life would end so ignominiously. For some reason, he had always imagined that he would distinguish himself. The battlefield casualty statistics lent little to his hope. The numbers all indicated that he would die after a short engagement, maybe two. Seventy-one percent of all "fresh meat," as they were called, didn't survive first contact with the Grey Men.

The horrible numbers were why the genetic engineering was advanced. Terra needed soldiers, fodder for the war. Robotics and A.I. could only progress so far and were only used successfully when in concert with human support in the field.

The lighting flickered, and a rush of gas squelched into the hold. 39 searched the dim interior for the LT. Maul lay on his belly on the far side of the transport from him. A deep gash on his head oozed blood. He was motionless, unable to give orders. Alarms started blaring.

"Masks down!" 39 yelled with all of his breath.

This planet only had twelve percent oxygen, and it wouldn't take long for them to lose consciousness without their suit's rebreathing tech.

He was a little surprised when the others actually obeyed his order. "Only common sense," he told himself. He lowered his own. The rebreathers just covered their nose and mouth. If the gases of this world had been irritating to the eyes or skin, they would have had to lower their visors too.

He looked at a nav monitor to get a fix on their course and speed. The transports were drones; the pilots were safe back up in the control ship in high orbit. The monitor showed their trajectory was too steep for the intended flight plan. That would put them off their target landing zone by fifteen, maybe twenty miles. This was going to end with all aboard being crushed on impact and their corpses being burned to ash when the fuel tanks erupted unless someone did something.

39 hit his emergency release latch. The inertia of the twisting ship pulled him hard against the wall and then just as suddenly threw him to the ceiling.

He pulled himself toward the LT. It was the Lieutenant's responsibility to eject all of the toon in case of an emergency, and so he had the control protocols in his suit's computer. Using an officer's comp was strictly prohibited, and even the thought sent pain through his head.

39 reached Maul and pulled his C.O. close. There was no time to check for a pulse. 39 reached for Maul's arm screen, and a violent twist of the aircraft forced the two apart.

39 scrambled back over to the LT and grabbed the limp body again. This time, 39 grabbed his chest tether clip, used to fast rope down from the transport in dense foliage, and snapped it into that of his C.O.

Only after they were secured did 39 look at the screen. There was a crack through it, but it responded when he tapped its face. The pain grew worse. Stabbing from the control device forward, making his vision blurry. The screen flashed red in time with the blaring alarm overhead; the computer anticipated the need to eject, flashing the option, all but begging the unconscious LT to make the decision. 39 and the LT slid across the shaking floor. He looked up to the hanging toon above him.

"Prepare for emergency eject!" he yelled. The warning wasn't really needed. All of the toon members that could see him were already watching him with apprehension scrolled over their faces.

He hit the flashing button on the cracked screen. Nothing happened for a few seconds. Then the ceiling pieces above each hanging platoon member broke free from the aircraft one at a time with a percussive thud, and the soldier was shot out into the open air. More and more pieces of the aircraft were falling off of it, allowing in more of the bluish light peculiar to this planet's strange sunsets.

39 didn't wait until all were airborne but dragged his superior over to an open hook and, with the added strength that the exo-suit gave him, easily lifted the armored man into the opening. He grabbed the LT's helmet that hung next to the hook and jammed it onto Maul's head. "If he had been following regs, then he wouldn't have been knocked out," 39 thought and was instantly rewarded with a twinge of pain in the base of his skull.

He cursed one of the words that the instructors would bawl at him during training, and the pain increased slightly.

He grunted and punched the flashing green light next to the Lt's slot, and they were both launched from the transport. He was dragged upward with Maul, praying to every God that the uploads had ever mentioned that his chest clip would survive the stress. It was not designed with this in mind, 39 was sure.

The force of the ejection rockets firing him out of the transport sent his stomach into his feet. Just as his stomach began to travel back up to his mouth, blades shot out from the hook from which they hung and began to rotate with a whirring sound that slowed their descent considerably.

The transport slammed into the ground right beneath them, and the strange orange leafed trees snapped at the impact.

Dust and debris filled the air as momentum carried the ship deeper into the dense vegetation. Finally, it stopped with the loud protests of tortured metal.

39 and the Lt would come down too close to the downed aircraft for his comfort, but there was no steering the emergency descent. He quickly scanned the sky behind and above him, looking for his platoon members and saw them floating like seeds as they lazily drifted toward the ground.

He took a mental note of all he saw and the general direction he'd need to hunt for his team members.

They drifted over the top of the crash, and he felt the heat coming off of the downed craft. Explosion was a real fear for 39, and they came down in the orange trees too close to the burning wreckage.

Leaves and twigs fell in a shower around them as they broke through the canopy. Luckily they missed any of the larger branches or trunks.

With the added weight that he lent to the descent, they came down faster than they should have, but the shock absorbers in his exo-suit easily took the impact.

There were pieces of debris strewn all around them. Small fires dotted the vicinity.

He unclipped the Lt from his harness and disconnected him from the rotors, then laid him on the ground.

He kept searching the area for any sign of the enemy. Whoever had knocked them out of the sky could be coming to finish the job. He raised his grenade launcher in his right hand and opened his shield on his left arm. It was built from enhanced graphene and could collapse or open from the armor on his left forearm. With his torso protected, he did a quick reconnaissance of the surrounding forest, stashed the Lt behind a small rock promontory, then made for the transport.

Although the threat of explosion loomed, he had to get supplies, or he may not make it far on this foreign planet. As he approached, he looked for the comms antenna and was disappointed but not surprised to see it entirely crushed.

Protocol was not to use your suit's comms in situations like this, as the Grey Men could track it, but the transport's equipment could transmit shielded communiques back to the control ship. At least when it was functional.

He hurried on to where the supply lockers should be and wrenched one open. He grabbed as much as he could carry and ran back to the Lt.

He dumped the pile of supplies, a bunch of food of the M.R.E. variety, some purification tablets, canteens, a jug of water, a few flares, and a bunch of spare ammo for his sidearm, a 2211 Springfield Armory XD .50 cal. The gun was horribly inaccurate when shot without a suit on. It kicked like a mule and could barely be managed with two hands. They had been trained, of course, how to fire the weapon without the added strength of the suit just in case the exo-suit failed somehow.

There was a pack that he didn't bother looking in. He went to Maul and felt for a pulse. Alive, as he had suspected, but who knew when he would wake, and in the meantime, 39 could almost feel the enemy bearing down on their position.

CHAPTER 2

G20 scanned the forest beneath with her infrared scope. Nothing moved but some small lizards that barely registered as a heat source. One of Grey's biggest weaknesses was the intense heat that they put off. She clung to the thick trunk and slid down its smooth surface until she was ten feet above the ground and released, absorbing the impact of her landing with her exo-suit.

She was a scout sniper. There was nothing else. She knew nothing else. Sure the uploads attempted to give them a good base education, but there were no experiences past a few months ago. She moved silently through the forest, her massive railgun held at the ready.

The gun was two hundred and fifty pounds, and although her body was said to be a superb specimen of modern genetic engineering, she would never have been able to lift it without the help of her suit. Her exo-suit was a lot smaller than those of the other marines. She was the only scout in her toon, and so her training had been different. Her suit was different, her equipment was different. In an already short and traumatic existence, the small differences meant the world to G20.

The other toon members had kept her apart. The sense of camaraderie that they had begun to develop in the three months of training was not extended to 20. Her instructor told her that that would change once she saved one of their asses in the field, but until then, she had to withstand the solitude.

There was a part of her that felt safer on her own. She knew her duty was to link back up with the survivors of her platoon, but a group would be far easier for the enemy to pinpoint and annihilate than she would be by herself. She hoped that was true, at least for the time being.

Grey men would undoubtedly have a better understanding of the terrain on this planet than the Terrans did. It wasn't the Grey's planet any more than it was Terra's, but they had been here longer and had developed colonies here. Colonies and military installations if the egg heads back on Terra could be believed. Installations that were ideal for launching a full-scale invasion of the Grey's home planet, which was believed to be Tau Ceti F. Conversely, the Greys would also be able to use their new military installations to attack Terra, which is why this war was vital.

20 slid down the bank of a small gully. As silently as possible, she moved to the trickle of water at the bottom. The mud here was an orangey brown, not exactly the color of the foliage, but it was better than her light brown tan. She scooped up a handful and smeared it across her closed eyes and down over her rebreather, careful not to cover the vents. She proceeded to cover everywhere on her suit and helmet that she could reach.

She waited for the water's surface to still and studied her face in the reflection. Some of her blond hair poked out from under her helmet, and she matted it down with the mud and looked again. Satisfied, she moved off in the direction where the majority of her toon would have landed.

The Heaters didn't only use their eyes to hunt, but the camouflage would even help cover her scent and mask her body heat. Both were ways the enemy tracked humans.

She struggled with her decision to find her toon. This forest was too closed in. Despite all of her efforts with stealth, she could easily stumble into a bunch of Heaters and be dead before her brain registered the threat.

For the last few minutes, she had noticed a rise off to her right, its elevated vegetation making brief appearances as she walked. She made up her mind and, after only a short debate with herself, changed her bearing. She was a sniper, a lot of good she'd do from down here. Being in this confinement all but negated her only advantage.

After a quarter-hour climb, she reached what she decided must be the summit. The forest made it hard to tell. She climbed a tree, the ascent made easier by her suit's strength, but climbing this tree wouldn't have been hard without it. Sometimes she was annoyed by the suit. She felt like she depended too much on it. At times she wished she could go without it. Indeed she carried a stripped down rifle in her pack just in case the suit failed, and she was no longer strong enough to wield the railgun.

The other grunts in G platoon had made fun of her for that, but her instructors encouraged the behavior and applauded her paranoia. They assured her that, by far, the most expensive piece of military hardware that she would control was her own body. The genome project definitely made this type of war feasible, but it by no means meant it was cheap. With the mining of asteroid belts, rare-earth metals were no longer rare. That made all of the tech that was carried by marines like her cheap to produce. Time and knowledge were now currency.

Marines made a measly two chits for every hour of active duty, three for a firefight or an assault. The cost was directly related to uploads or leave. Two chits equaled twenty minutes of R and R or twenty credits of upload. It took a lot of credits to add up to anything worth learning. For example, it took one million credits to learn the English language. Luckily, the military thought it was a necessary upload, and 20 supposed they were right. It, and many others that she never received. She fought with her instructors about it. Not much of a fight with mother stabbing her every word. But there were uploads that would make her a force to be reckoned with in the field. They refused to invest more into her until she had proven that she could survive first contact with the enemy.

So here she was, scanning the distant clearings in the canopy for signs of her team. She was sweating under the caked mud, and some had run into her eyes, but she refused to wipe it away. Some discomforts were worth the benefits they provided, and if a Heater spotted her because of the exposed skin, she'd never live long enough to be disappointed in herself.

The sound of a Grey's troop ship reverberated over the trees, and 20 was glad for the dense canopy that still guarded her from the Greys as they passed directly overhead. The wash from the engines was strong enough to shake her tree, and she clenched the branch as it jostled and tossed back and forth.

The ship continued on to a clearing about three-quarters of a mile away, where it put down, and about five heaters ran out of the open rear and disappeared into the trees. She could only see two that remained behind with the ship. Seven or eight, then. That was plenty to take out a toon. Heaters were lethally efficient, especially if they got in close.

20's tree began to sway again as another ship passed overhead, but not as close as the last one. It moved in the direction of the downed Terran troop ship. Going to see if there were any mangled remains for them to experiment on. That was the rumor, anyway. Historically, Greys did experiments on humans way back when it was called Earth.

Sizing us up, 20 thought.

She couldn't see where the second Grey ship set down, her view blocked by dense tree cover.

She returned her attention to the ship she could see through her HUD's rangefinder. The device did far more than just report the range to the target. It gave her windage, temperature, humidity, and planet centrifugal forces. It even calculated the best shot path so that all she had to do was line up her crosshairs where the line began and pull the trigger. Well, that wasn't all, there was a whole lot of practice to even do that correctly, but the heads-up display made the process a lot easier. Again, she didn't need all of the data, but it did make her more efficient, and according to her instructors, every advantage would be needed against this enemy.

The railgun sent the shot downfield so fast that few adjustments were needed for this range. She could take out both Heaters without any risk, but it was a risk that she wasn't sure she needed to take.

An explosion sounded off to her left where the transport had crashed. She turned her attention to it and saw a fireball rise above the canopy. She looked back to the clearing and saw the forest come alive with flashes of small arms fire. As if the explosion was a signal both sides had agreed upon to start the murder, percussions diminished by distance sounded over the canopy.

The heater pilot was yelling something to the guard and gesticulating wildly. The guard started moving toward the far side of the clearing in the direction of the most intense fighting.

20 reacted instantly. She could not allow another heater into the fight. Time to do her part.

She sighted in on the pilot first, better to off the one that was most likely to be unnoticed by the other.

She controlled her breathing, and as she let out a slow breath, she waited until between heartbeats and then finished squeezing the trigger. The railgun jumped in her hands, and when it settled back on the pilot, she was pleased to see a gaping hole in the Heater's head. Its blue blood oozed out, melting into the control panel.

She quickly found the guard, who still stalked closer to the trees. She followed the same procedure with this one, making sure that the crosshairs lined up with her HUD. The gun fired its projectile at seventy-eight hundred miles per hour, and the impact of the round into the guard seemed instantaneous. The round itself was smaller than 20's pinky finger, but the hole it drilled through the Heater was bigger than her fist.

The rounds were designed to separate when hitting the Heater's extremely hard outer skin, and with the projectile's velocities, the result was impressive. It was the first time she had killed something. She didn't feel anything. For some reason, that disappointed her. She hadn't realized that she had anticipated... something. Some kind of emotion, but there was nothing. Maybe these hostile aliens didn't quite qualify in her psyche for an emotional response.

She scanned the perimeter of the clearing for additional enemies, and finding none, she lifted her head from the scope and used her HUD to search for heat signatures in the forest.

At a mile plus, she saw the overwhelming heat of the Heater bodies moving in and around the far fainter signatures of her team members.

She switched back to the railgun and switched to infrared. The IR came up and showed the huge body, common to Heaters, disemboweling a human. All she saw was the sudden intensifying of the heat as it left the Marine, but it was enough to elicit a growl from her.

She waited until other Marines were not in line with the creature. Since the round would continue on its deadly course long after killing the Heater, the threat of friendly-fire was real.

20 sent the round on its deadly course, taking the Heater from belly to head. The round had struck several trees and had flowered out into a mass of speeding splinters that tore through the Heater, spilling its caustic blood from a dozen wounds. The blood, a brilliant flash to her IR, signaled her success, and she scanned for the next target.

CHAPTER 3

The right arm of G39's suit had one of three different weapons activated at a time. He could switch between the M42 machine gun, the Springfield 50 cal, or the grenade launcher. He was classified as a "heavy" because of his size and given the bigger suit with a larger ammo reserve. With the added six inches of height that the heavy suit provided, he stood nearly seven feet tall, but he only came up to the shoulder of the Heaters that, even now, flooded out of their transport ship. They ran the short distance to the wrecked Terran ship and quickly began securing the perimeter.

If he didn't do something fast, he would lose the only advantage he had. They didn't know he was there, but after the wreckage was secured, they would fan out searching for survivors. He had maybe five minutes before he and the LT were discovered.

39 skirted the ridge of rock that blocked the LT from the Heaters and peeked around the trunk of a massive tree. As he had hoped, the view was beautiful. The fuel tanks spurted liquid hydrogen that pooled around the tanks. The pools evaporated quickly, but there was enough of a pool to combust brilliantly, and once what was left in the tanks went up…. He lowered his visor. 39 planted his feet. He lifted his grenade launcher and fired.

Unlike what the rest of the toon thought, it took skill to do what he did. They had taken to calling him the Hammer because he was as blunt a tool as the Marines had. The truth was a little more nuanced than that. It took more skill, in 39's estimation, to judge the lob of a grenade and apply the right amount of force behind it to hit your target than it did to simply point a rifle and fire.

His instructors would have been proud of that shot. The pool went up instantly.

He ran the few steps to the LT and crouched down behind the rocks, and covered Maul with his armored body. The secondary explosion of the tanks going up was intense. He could feel the heat on his back through his suit. Pieces of the transport rained down hundreds of yards out into the forest. Finally, he was able to, once again, peek at the wreckage. A crater dimpled the land where the hulking scrap metal and alien infantry had been.

39 supposed that he had earned his pay with that one. It was rare that new Marines killed a single Heater, let alone a dozen. Sure the liquid hydrogen helped.

He searched the blackened landscape for the enemy transport ship. They had set down on the far side of the wreckage, and the smoke that billowed from the hole obscured the far side, but if he had survived, being this close, surely any Heater that had been left in the transport did too.

They would be searching for whoever had launched that grenade. Unless they had assumed that it had gone up on its own. He couldn't risk it.

He turned to the LT and lifted him so that the rock supported him like some big chair, then he engaged the ring magnet in the front of his suit. He engaged his own in the rear of his suit and leaned back into the LT. With an electronic hum and a snap, the LT was secured to his heavy suit's back.

39 set off through the forest in the last direction he had seen the seedlings fall from their lofty heights. He went as silently as a Hammer was able.

He activated the rear-facing camera on his suit that gave him the feed through his HUD. He was worried that the Heaters from the ship were hunting them, and every sound of the forest sent his heart rate jumping.

The distant sound of a firefight added to his anxiety. He had adjusted his course toward the sounds of what must be the toon in a desperate fight against the Greys. They could probably really use a heavy right about now. He picked up his pace.

He pushed his way through a particularly thick hedge of dead branches and bushes. In his HUD, he saw a sudden flash of light, and he threw himself to the side. Landing and rolling, he disconnected the LT from his back and came up with his Springfield, somehow knowing that the Heater would already be in close. The plasma rifles that they used were not their preferred weapon. The Heaters enjoyed killing up close. They took a perverse pride in it. At least, that's what the uploads said. Maybe they just liked how much bigger they were than Terrans.

He fired at the charging Heater that was already too close to miss even with the fifty cal pistol. Large caliber or not, Heaters were hard to kill. Their armor was as strong as graphene, and once you got past that, you had to contend with their hide, which was like a rock.

His shots barely slowed the creature. As he closed, the alien pulled his blade. Each Heater had one, and according to the uploads, they had some ceremonial purposes as well.

39 engaged his shield, which extended, rapidly covering much of his body.

The sword bit into the graphene like it was made of wood. 39 twisted his shield in an attempt to wrest the blade from the alien's hands while simultaneously firing the Springfield into the Heater's midriff. One, two, three, four, five shots in exactly the same spot in rapid succession. The Heater let out a screech growl and ripped the blade free of the shield taking a chunk out of the graphene. The Heater backed and twisted the blade toward 39's throat with lightning speed. 39 raised the shield just in time to deflect the thrust, but barely.

The Heater growled in frustration and slammed into 39, any attempt at finesse now gone. 39 grunted with the impact. It felt like his ribs had been hit with a sledgehammer. They rolled on the ground, 39 using every advantage the suit would give him. The heavy was barely strong enough to keep the Heater from ripping out his throat.

Blue blood from the small wound that the Springfield had opened now dripped down onto 39's chest. It was armored, but it wouldn't be for long with that stuff on it. 39 fought desperately, trying to remove the Heater from atop him.

39 switched to the M42 and put all of his strength into bringing the barrel to bear on the Heater. Heat from the blood could now be felt through the armor. 39 lowered his visor and squeezed the trigger, and just kept squeezing. At one-thousand rounds per minute, the gun slammed slug after slug into the creature. The alien writhed, trying now to get away from the wrath of the machine gun. Blue blood began to splatter, but 39 kept the trigger depressed. Smoke rose from his suit. More and more heat cascaded over him with the blood. His body would soon feel like that of his writhing foe. He pushed the Heater from him and stood. He kept the gun firing, this time into the thing's head. He thought it must be dead, but you could never be too sure, so he put another hundred rounds into it.

The heat had turned to pain, and he toggled the liquid nitrogen sprayers and used his left hand sprayer to coat his suit. The Heater's blood hardened, and a cloud billowed around him as the liquid rapidly turned to gas.

He was sweating profusely under the visor, so he raised it. He could smell burnt chemical fumes through his mask.

He kicked the alien corpse. A chunk of hardened Heater blood fell from his suit with the movement. He scanned the forest. Nothing. This must have been the one left in the alien ship. It must have tracked him here. 39 sighed and attached the LT back to his back. He thought he heard his C.O. groan when he rose.

"LT. You there?"

Nothing.

He moved off in the direction of the continuing battle.

CHAPTER 4

"Where are my reinforcements?"

"The CS just messaged saying that they lost a transport and had to scrub the rest of the ships due to heavy fire, sir."

Colonel Santos growled at the news. This campaign had been nothing but problems. They barely had a foothold on the planet and were in threat of losing that if he didn't get fresh meat soon. He hoped that this batch lasted longer than the last one. Poor S.O.B. s didn't last through the first skirmish. Those that technically survived were completely gone mentally. They would probably have to be scrapped.

Not for the first time, Colonel Santos wondered what it must be like to be "born" like that. Out of a sac. Your whole existence mitigated by a device implanted into the base of your skull. He sometimes felt sympathy for the Grunts. But then he remembered that without them, real men would die. Men with families. With innovative careers and a white picket fence. Men with experiences more than uploads.

Colonel Santos didn't know what it was like because he had never experienced it. Commissioned officers came from Terra, not some birthing ship in the Terran fleet. He was born. Really born. He had a mother, a real mother, not a device in the back of his head.

"How long ago was the transport shot down?" he asked the comms officer.

"Forty-five minutes, sir," a hint of apology in the response.

"Forty-five minutes! What the hell took the CS so long to inform little old me?"

"Something about a distant ion storm, sir. To be honest, I didn't really understand the explanation."

The Colonel growled again.

"Those Grunts are, most likely, long gone," he said.

It had been meant to be a rhetorical comment, a way for him to come to terms with abandoning the toon, but the comms officer perked up.

"The CS reports heavy fighting around the crash site."

"You don't say." Santos thought for a moment.

"Does the Control Ship know what kind of enemy force they're facing?"

The comms officer tapped his wrist screen. Punching in the question.

"They say two drop ships, but one has been disabled already."

Colonel Santos slammed his fist into his palm.

"Maybe we have some real fighting men out there after all! Get me Major Grant. We have a platoon to rescue."

CHAPTER 5

39 worried about meeting another Heater alone out here in the forest. He was almost certain that an encounter like the last would end him. Something that he didn't want, but he didn't know why. What drives a person to survive? What makes them fight to live? It must not be a life of exceptional experiences that provided that drive because he wanted to live.

He slowed as he crested a hill, weaving through tree trunks and stopped.

Below him lay his toon. It had been a blood bath. Marines had been pulled apart, so it was hard to see exactly how many there were, but there seemed to be the full forty-one unaccounted for.

He crouched. More pieces of hardened Heater blood flaked off. There were two heater bodies. At least they went down fighting.

His heartbeat slowed little by little until it wasn't the only thing he could hear. Someone was still alive. The fighting hadn't stopped.

He launched himself forward, his suit giving him speed uncommon for objects as big as he.

39 crashed through a tangle of branches and saw a handful of the G platoon still alive. They poured lead into the trees surrounding them, few rounds actually hit the three Heaters that stalked the remaining soldiers. It was almost like they were toying with them.

G39 growled. How dare they? They were Devil Dogs!

They were Marines! He put on a burst of speed and closed with the closest of the Heaters. They wanted a fight. He would oblige them. He dismissed his M42 and grabbed his axe that was built into the right leg of his suit. Typically it was used for breaches where a grenade wasn't surgical enough. The thing was made of thick graphene wrapped in a tungsten sheath. The combination of the two metals made the breacher axe extremely strong.

The heavy suit gave him the strength to wield it one handed.

He hit the magnet release as he ran past the group of Marines, dropping the LT unceremoniously at their feet.

He extended his shield mere seconds before slamming it into the closest Heater. The alien stumbled back a few paces but snarled something and pulled his blade. The curved sword glinted in the failing light.

The Heater's eyes were that dead uniform black that so unnerved him. 39 didn't allow himself any time to think of what he was doing and how crazy it was. He pushed forward, swinging the axe wildly and roaring his frustration. The other Heaters just watched. Apparently, they didn't bother interfering. Maybe it was in their "code," the same reason they preferred close combat, or maybe they just didn't perceive him as a threat and so sat back to watch the entertainment. Whatever it was, it enraged 39. Their nonchalance was galling.

He swung the axe again, never intending to make contact, and used the momentum to circle the weapon back around into an overhand throw. He was only seven feet from the thing, and the axe made a single rotation in the air before it slammed into the Heater's chest.

39 had been advancing on it the entire time while the Heater gave ground, but when the axe head sunk into the chest, he launched himself at the much larger warrior.

In the air, 39 switched to the M42 and poured rounds into the beast's head.

The Heater fell backward under the fusillade and writhed,

much like the other he killed.

39 disengaged the M42 and wrenched the axe from the body before the head could be pocked by the magma-like blood.

He turned to the next Heater, who was enraged, but still, he put away his plasma rifle and pulled his sword. The other encouraged the Heater in their unintelligible speak but did nothing to help. Instead, he focused on killing the small force of Marines almost cowering forty feet away.

The Heater made the first move. It launched itself at 39, forcing him back step after step, and all he could do was barely fend off the thing as it stabbed and sliced at his shield and axe. His ribs ached fiercely, and his arm tingled with every blow to his shield. The Heater scored a slice that punched through his suit on his thigh. 39 swung wildly with his axe, trying to fend off the Heater as he stumbled backward, the hydraulics in his left leg giving way. This was not good. He was about to drop the axe and switch to his grenade launcher regardless of the proximity to the target.

39 was on one knee, gasping for breath and sweating rivulets. The Heater seemed not to have felt any of the exertion that he performed. The Heater smiled. The ugly thing actually smiled.

"Screw it," 39 said and switched to the launcher.

Just then, a hole appeared in the middle of the thing's face.

39 scrambled out of the way when a gout of blue arched toward him.

He turned, ready to hit the third Heater with a grenade which was a faint blue color. The color that emanated from the Heater's body pulsed in time with its heartbeat and grew brighter with each pulse.

This must be their failsafe ability that the uploads and his instructors warned them about. He raised his weary arm and readied his shield for the grenade's splash damage, but before he could pull the trigger, the Heater's head gained a third eye as the one moments before.

The blood that erupted from this corpse was markedly hotter and flowed across the ground with more liquidity. It didn't explode, though, thanks to G20. It had to be her, 39 realized. Thank the stars for that beautiful woman. 39 was shocked at his thought and even more shocked that he really believed it. 20 was beautiful.

A sharp stab of pain reminded him that such thoughts were strictly controlled by mother. The pain dimmed his vision slightly before he was able to clear the thought entirely.

39 hit the quick release and began extricating himself from his failing suit.

Epsilon Eridani B was bigger than Terra, and so, as he stepped out of his suit, the added gravity nearly brought him to his knees. His wounded leg trembled as he forced it to cooperate. He cinched a harness belt around the leg and began pilfering his suit's weaponry.

He pulled the M42 and the Springfield out of the suit's arm, grabbed an extra drum of ammo for the 42, and put it in a satchel that he slung on his back. He pulled the end of the ammo belt out of the drum and snaked it out so that he could reload easily, and he hoped that it would feed alright that way.

He clipped the Springfield to his belt and rushed over to the Marines. They seemed to be in shock, and based on what he saw, they had every right to be.

"We've got to move," he said.

They just stared at him or shot wild-eyed glances around the forest as if a Heater would come out of the deepening shadows at any moment. Which could be the case.

There were only five left. Other than he and 20. Seven, eight if you counted the LT, out of forty-three. And there had only been, maybe, five Heaters that had done it.

"Marines, move!" he yelled.

This had the desired effect. He supposed that their training, short as it had been, made up the majority of their worldly experiences, and this is how the instructors spoke to them. This was something known in a completely foreign environment.

They were finally looking at him and not through him.

Suddenly a ping sounded on his wrist computer and all of their suits. 39 rushed over to his suit and unclipped the screen from the armor, and looked at it. A waypoint.

The CS had finally gotten off their asses and given them a modicum of guidance. His head throbbed from the mother, but he was too engaged in the screen to give the dose of punishment any heed.

"We've got a bearing, men. Let's move! G10, pick up the LT. Let's go!"

He got up and slipped the computer's strap over his forearm and tightened it so that he could free up both hands and moved off in the direction that the screen indicated.

He was relieved when he heard the rest of the toon following.

They hadn't walked far when they came to a clearing. An enemy drop ship sat, silent and dark, in the center. He moved cautiously around the rear of the craft and came up on the pilot's side. He came to the armored window and shined a light in. A Heater, or what was left of one, still sat in the chair, but the remains of his head were everywhere, especially on the console where the body had slumped.

"30, take 19 and check the inside. Look for anything we could use. 12, follow in after they clear and set charges."

As on the transport ship, they didn't even question his orders and almost seemed relieved that he was giving them.

30 came out with a strength-assisted armload of alien weaponry.

"Got you some souvenirs, hammer," he said.

39 smiled at the nickname and at the souvenirs. The waypoint was only a few hundred feet from the alien ship, but no Terran transport was waiting for them.

They moved to the spot anyway, and 30 dropped his burden, and they sorted through the unfamiliar devices. 12 came out of the dropship and came over to the group.

"Sixty seconds," 12 said.

39 nodded. He set 12 and 24 on piquet 30 feet east, and G30 and 19 took the west and south. He and G10 took the north.

The LT still hung from the back of 10's suit. 10 wasn't as tall as 39. In fact, he wasn't as tall as the LT, so Lieutenant Maul's feet drug the ground. Boy, he wouldn't like to be the LT when he woke up. Well, he supposed that with his own wounds, his leg soaking his pants with blood, his painful ribs and parts of his torso burned from the overheated insides of his suit, he probably wouldn't want to be himself tomorrow either.

"I don't know what they are planning with the waypoint, and I don't want to break radio silence to ask. We could be in the shit when that drop ship goes up, so be ready."

As if on cue, the charges blew. A shockwave flattened the grass around it, and a brilliant fireball rose from the destroyed ship.

The explosion set everyone's nerves on end. They waited silently, scanning the forest's treeline for any movement. Their visors lowered of their own volition, and their HUDs switched to night vision automatically as it was now too dark to see clearly.

"20 will be coming in from some direction, maybe north, so don't light her up," he said loud enough for all to hear but directed at G10.

"I appreciate the thoughtfulness 39," came a voice from behind him.

39 cursed in surprise and spun but didn't see anyone. Then a figure stood up from the very spot around which they had arrayed themselves. To 39's reckoning, 20 had placed herself as close to the exact waypoint as was possible, and they had never seen her.

"How the hell did you get past us?" 39 said, somewhat annoyed with himself.

"You assume that I did get past you. Did you get me a souvenir 30?" she said.

"You were here the whole time?" 39 asked.

"When a waypoint says go, I go. I don't detour to blow crap up."

39 smiled.

"It was kinda on the way," 12 put in.

"Smooth," she said.

They settled back into watching the forest.

"Pretty sure we're clear," 20 said.

"Those Heaters light up the IR like nothing else, and I don't see any out there."

"I won't relax until I'm back in my bunk," said 10 as he scanned the shadows.

A low hum echoed through the valley.

Blue-lighted impulse engines flickered through the trees as they flew low over the canopy. Couldn't be Terran, as a Terran transport would have dual or quad rotors, not impulse. Only orbiting ships used Impulse engines in the Terran fleet.

G10 cursed and switched to his 8 gauge shotgun that was undoubtedly loaded with cold shot. Cold shot was a solid graphene load that was kept extremely cold by his suit's liquid nitrogen reserve. The cold seemed to affect the Heaters the most, and cold shot became known among Marines as screamers for what they did to the Heaters.

The hum became louder as it approached their location.

As they watched, a bright light fell from the dark sky and fell right toward the blue lights of the Grey ship. When the light hit the ship, a deafening explosion shook the valley. The shockwave tore leaves and branches from trees that fell among the Marines, who must have been cheering as he was because he saw their exuberant faces but heard nothing. The control ship and the Terran Navy orbited the planet, forming a blockade that could rain down targeted hellfire when necessary, and 39 was extremely grateful that the brass had deemed this a "necessary" occasion.

They would have sensed the approach of the rotors if they

could hear. They would have beamed at the Major's words of congratulations on their survival if they could hear. Despite their muffled ears, they were all smiles as they slapped each other's backs and boarded the transport.

39 smiled down at the dark blue sunset, now faintly visible as they rose into the air. According to the mission upload, it would be eleven Terran days before this planet's sun, Epsilon Eridani, rose again. It really was a beautiful planet, and he couldn't wait to see its sunrise.

CHAPTER 6

Fort McIntyre was immense. The engineers had been busy. It was almost full dark by the time they reached the fort, but 39 could make out the concrete bulwarks with graphene sheeting that reinforced the concrete walls. The fort sat atop a plateau with steep, cliff-like sides. Assault from the ground would be nearly impossible, but then 39 remembered who their enemy was.

Greys came from Tau Ceti F, which was about three and a half times the size of Terra. As a result, their physical strength had a commensurate increase when compared to humans. This planet, Eridani B, was about one and a half times the size of Terra. Despite his genetic advantages, the gravitational pull was wearing on him. Without his suit to buoy him up, he felt literally weighed down with fatigue. He supposed that the fighting had probably done a lot to sap his strength as well. The Greys would feel the opposite. He hoped that his body would climatize soon. The lab coats had said that they would become accustomed to the planet to some degree after only a couple weeks so that by the time he saw the sun again, he would, hopefully, feel better.

The transport set down on a large, raised platform where other ships, corsairs, copters and transports all waited to be called into action.

The Major shook each Marine's hand as they disembarked, congratulating them, once again, on surviving first contact with the Greys.

"Lost your tech, son? At least you kept your cover," he called to 39 over the sound of the rotors winding down.

"Yes, sir," 39 said, coming to attention.

"Looks like they gave you a going away present," he said, pointing at his leg. "Go with your team and get checked out by medical. Then someone will be by to get you all squared away."

"Aye, aye. Thank you, sir." 39 saluted and exited the aircraft.

He was the last of the toon off the transport and had to jog to catch up with the teched-out soldiers. 10 still carried the LT, and he led the pack to the hospital.

Some medics waited for them outside the entrance, and when they saw the LT, they unloaded him off of G10 and removed his suit. Then strapped him to a gurney and rushed him through the first of three doorways designed to keep a breathable atmosphere inside and the harsher gases outside. Only two grunts could fit through the doors at a time, their suits adding significant bulk.

39 waited for his turn in the rear of the toon, but one of the Marines at the front motioned him forward. "Hammer needs more help than any of us," 30 said.

He didn't think his leg was that bad, not as bad as his ribs anyway, or maybe the burns. Regardless, 30 was right, so he didn't argue, and he moved to the front. Each member of the tiny platoon nodded as he passed. Respectful. This small act made all of his pain worth it, almost. The disinfectant spray washed over him in the first breezeway. It was meant to kill foreign bacteria that our immune systems and scientists hadn't developed a good enough defense against yet, but its effect on his open wounds was instantaneous. He groaned and clutched at the wall for support.

A Marine waited on the inside of the door and took his weapons. A nurse came and showed him to a room, where they ran full diagnostics on him. Lab coats injected him with a number of pain-inducing drugs that would help his ribs heal faster and antibiotics. They cut away the burned skin that was too damaged to heal on its own. They then printed him some new skin and graphed it to those spots. They made sure that the slice in his thigh would heal without surgery and then glued it shut.

All in all, the Doctors and nurses worked mechanically, efficient yes, but devoid of emotion or sympathy for the pain they caused. They saw him as anyone else did. Another Grunter with an artificial mother. Soulless. He tried to justify the treatment. He told himself that they did it because if they didn't, they would become too attached to the fodder of this war, and the mass death would drive them mad. These were not people, after all. If they were people, they would have a mother. A real mother.

The Major. He had been kind. One of the kindest people he had ever met, granted, that list was rather short. At least he was the nicest officer or non-Grunt he had ever met.

Most officers treated them like robots.

Again, he rationalized that they had to separate themselves from the mass death somehow.

When he was finally done with the lab coats, he was told to report to his new barracks, and a waypoint was added to his wrist computer.

There was a sergeant cleaning his tech when 39 entered.

"Fresh meat?" he asked.

"I suppose so, sir," 39 answered.

"Don't 'sir' me. G39 right? The rest of your toon is over there. What's left of them. Had a rough entry, huh?"

"You might say that."

"Well, it'll only get worse from there. Go get some rack time with your team. You'll be put through your paces soon enough. The days are all screwy on this heap, so we all just grab some z's when we can."

"Aye, aye."

He found an open bed by G12 and passed out almost instantly.

Next thing he knew, he was being shaken awake.

It was the sergeant. The number on his jacket said E25.

"Come on, sleeping beauty, the Colonel wants to see you. Don't look at me like that. I'm as surprised as you. You and 20 are to come with me."

G20 was already awake and didn't look nearly as tired as he felt. He couldn't have had more than a couple hours of sleep.

They followed E25 down into a network of underground tunnels that connected the above ground buildings. In this way, they were able to keep the whole complex filled with breathable air. There were bulkheads and hatches every so often that would automatically close in case of a breach. Notwithstanding the measures, it was regulation to keep a mask with your person at all times, just in case.

They made several turns in both directions, passing Marines, laborers and engineers. Finally, they reached a sealed passage guarded by two nasty-looking veterans. Both were scared and not smiling.

"G39 and G20 from Charlie Company, here at the Colonel's orders," E25 said.

One of the guards nodded and punched in an access code, opening the door.

"You can find your way back?" the sergeant asked.

39 was suddenly considering looking like a fool and admitting that he hadn't paid close enough attention. Better that than looking like a bigger fool later when he got lost.

"Yes, we can," 20 piped up.

"You're not going in with us?" he asked E25.

"I was not included in the orders past conveying you here. Good luck," he said, with a hint of a smile.

Another pair of sentries stood inside the thick metal blast door. One of them took them to the Colonel. He was sitting at a desk in a room that was far smaller than 39 would have anticipated the commander of the ground forces on Eridani B having. The Major that rescued them, Major Grant, was sitting in the corner.

Both 39 and 20 came to attention in front of the Colonel's desk.

"Privates G20 and G39, reporting as ordered," G39 said. Was that what he was supposed to say? He was so nervous. Too bad they hadn't engineered him not to feel like this.

"G39, the Major has reviewed the vids from your recent engagement and has brought something troubling to my attention," the Colonel opined.

39's stomach fell. This was a bad way to start.

"Are you a commissioned officer, private?" 39 was confused by the question, surely he was being rhetorical, and yet the Colonel waited for a response.

"No, sir."

"No, you are not. I am confused then how you were able to order the emergency ejection of your toon. The lab coats tell me that your mother is fully functional. Did it not punish the action?"

"It did, sir." 39 was sure now that he would be executed. The regs were clear on this, but for some reason, he had never given any thought to the repercussions.

"I imagine that it gave quite a painful correction."

"It did, sir."

"Then why did you persist?"

"The toon, sir. I had to get them out. It wasn't fair for them to die that way, with no way to fight back."

"Indeed." Colonel Santos eased back in his chair, studying 39.

"I dare say you gave them that opportunity."

39 remembered the killing field of Marines spread out in front of him on the forest floor. So much blood.

"Yes, sir."

"Situations like this demand that I terminate you. Send you off to heaven or hell on some eternal voyage for the damned if you believe in that sort of thing. The top brass would have me do just that. They can not have mere grunts making the decisions set aside for their betters. Why, if all of you were allowed such latitude, the whole military would be in chaos. Still, I take a slightly different view on it."

Colonel Santos glanced at Major Grant.

"You took initiative that not only showed that you viewed the safety of your toon above that of yourself, you also saved the life of your C.O. That can not be overlooked. Add to that your exemplary actions on the planet's surface, the killing of a grand total of nine Heaters is extraordinary. As the remainder of your toon can attest, most fresh meat cower and cringe in their first engagement when faced with the primal destruction a Heater can exhibit. You did not. I need more men like you." The colonel steepled his fingers and blew through them lightly, thinking.

"Despite all of that, my hands are tied. You will be given fifty lashes for your usurpation of command to be administered as soon as the company can muster. If you survive the punishment, you will be raised to the rank of corporal, and I have put you in for a bronze star for your actions. Hopefully, it will not be awarded posthumously."

39 was shocked. Of all the underhanded compliments. How could this be? Mother didn't like the track his thoughts were going down and started to correct it at once. He grimaced with the pain and hoped it would be read as self-loathing.

Emotion warred with the calming thoughts he had grown accustomed to installing as soon as mother activated. Slowly he forced out the emotion and realized, with relief, they had moved on to G20.

"Textbook use of your weapon, private," Colonel Santos praised.

"Why, without you, G39 here wouldn't be with us."

"I felt I had to even the score, sir. He did save my life as well," she said brazenly.

"Quite," Santos said icily.

He glanced at 39 as if he had put her up to it. 39 just stared six inches above Santos' head.

"I have put you in for a Bronze Star as well, Private. I am also awarding you the rank of Lance Corporal. We expect great things from you." Colonel Santos stood and handed her the arm patch and collar pin signifying the advancement.

Lance Corporal. 39 would out-rank her, but barely. *That is if I survive.*

CHAPTER 7

Major Grant led G39 from the small office. Just outside, two sentries, having been forewarned, waited to accompany them to a concrete room eight feet by eight feet.

They stripped him and washed him. Then a lab coat came in to examine him and make sure he was fit enough to be punished, notwithstanding his broken ribs, which gave the doc a moment's pause. They passed him. 39 was glad. The wait would have been torturous if they made him wait the week it would take for his bones to re-knit.

Major Grant surprised him by staying with him the entire time. Maybe it was reg to do so, but he chose to believe that the man wanted to comfort 39 in some small measure. What surprised him, even more, was that it worked. The Major had a way about him. He seemed incapable of making the wrong decision, and 39 was grateful that this man was in charge of his company, or would be if this didn't kill him.

The reason why fifty lashes are so devastating to a grunt isn't the pain from the whip or even the loss of blood, but the pain from mother. Invariably, the subject begins to feel feelings that are restricted by mother. Anger, hatred, even mutinous thoughts. During the duration of a prolonged punishment, mother could inflict pain so excruciating that the grunt dies. It happened more times than it didn't, in fact. 39 wasn't sure how long it took to administer fifty lashes, but it had to be a long time. Plenty of time for mother to do her worst. Even now, he struggled to keep his thoughts above board.

Major Grant seemed to be able to read his thoughts.

"I've seen many lashings, son. The worst thing you can do is try to repress what you're feeling. At some point, that resolve to be calm will break, and so will you." The major sat backward in a metal chair, the only furnishing in the small room. He saw 39's look of confusion.

"I know, it's counter to everything you have learned to this point when it comes to mother, but let me ask you, what does mother do if you have disgruntled thoughts directed at an officer?"

39 was unsure how to respond, and so he didn't, but the major continued by answering his own question.

"The bitch kicks you in your teeth, that's what. So, instead, you need to channel your inevitable thoughts away from the brass. What does mother do if you are angry at, say, a Heater?"

"Nothing, sir."

"That's right. So if you can picture one of those blue-blooded bastards clearly enough and vent all of your pain and anger toward that, mother will be content, even praising. What I suggest is not easy, but those that survive this punishment do so because they were able to do as I have said."

39 wondered what the upper brass would say if they heard what the major was saying.

"Ultimately, you are the master of your own mind."

The upper brass would be appalled, 39 decided.

"Sir, may I ask you a question?"

"Of course, son."

"Why are you helping me."

Officers didn't help Grunts. It was a universal truth. Even the instructors who had once had mothers themselves kept themselves apart from grunts. It was hard for 39 to comprehend someone as high ranking as this taking the time to teach him how to survive. Death of Grunts was so common that it had lost all of its humanity to the officers. At least, that was the impression that he had had up until this point.

"I need good men, and you have already proven yourself as good as they come these days. Survive this, and you'll be commanding a squad, and who knows, maybe you'll make sergeant someday. The colonel gave you some hope. Use it." He stood and slid the chair back into the corner. He crossed the room and patted 39's shoulder before exiting the room.

He waited alone in the cell because that was what it was. Sure, the brig was something of the past, what mother couldn't correct, the threat of lashes all but decimated. There were only a few cases that required punishment. Cases like his. Cases that didn't really deserve it.

Mother laid into him, a stab so fierce he had to put his hands on his knees and breathe calming breaths as feeling slowly returned to his hands.

He recovered slowly and straightened. He was too nervous to sit as he waited, presumably, for his company to muster. The same company he had not even met. That he had not served with them didn't change the fact that they would stand and witness his pain. It was meant to dissuade any infringing behavior.

A lieutenant entered, and 39 stiffened to attention.

"Do I need to issue restraints, or will you come willingly?" The man's voice was high, and he had an air of superiority common to those of his class.

"No restraints needed, sir."

"Very well, follow me." He looked almost disappointed at his compliance.

They left the cell and picked up four more guards just outside the room that hemmed him in. They obviously didn't trust the word of a grunt too far.

Charlie Company was under-strength, and only about eighty Marines stood at attention in a large subsurface garage meant for a motor pool, but except for the company, it was empty.

They all faced the direction from which he entered, and he could see the six familiar faces of his platoon front and center.

Colonel Santos and Major Grant faced him as he entered.

There was a whipping post next to them, blood, now brown with age, spotted the floor around the post. He suspected they had intentionally left the blood as a reminder to all grunts passing by.

A lab coat stood behind the brass, there just to lend the proceedings a modicum of humanity.

39 winced. He really needed to watch his thoughts. This already wasn't going well.

He decided to try what Major Grant had advised.

A man with a hood over his head to protect his identity from the company trussed 39's hands over his head. His face was mere inches from the post. Nerves had made him sweat, and now it ran slowly toward his eyes.

He waited. The Colonel stepped forward and recited his charge and the punishment. He was tied so that if he looked to his right, he could see his platoon looking on. At the "usurpation of command," all of the platoon except G20 winced and visibly worked to calm their disgruntled thoughts.

Santos moved back and motioned for the lashings to commence. The hooded man wound up and laid a well-practiced slash of fire across 39's back.

"One!" Major Grant called.

The pain was intense, but 39 decided not to give them the satisfaction of hearing him scream. Mother interpreted his thought as rebellious, and he felt a spike of fire in his head more intense than the lash. He grunted and tried to visualize the Heater he had killed in the forest.

Another slap of spiked leather welted his back horribly.

"Two!"

He grimaced and focused on the Heater, feeding the image the pain from his back and the rage he felt surging inside him. Mother quieted noticeably, only giving slight corrections as it tried to interpret and catalog the storm of emotion in 39.

Another stinging blow. Another. His skin had broken and began to drip blood.

He gritted his teeth and thought of the Heater as he fought, rolling on the ground, sure he would be killed by this…thing.

Another.

Its blue blood dripped on him. That's what this pain was from.

Another.

39 began to lose count. He had a hard time distinguishing one from the other.

The pain. It was so intense. Fire couldn't be a worse death. He thought.

All he'd done was eject the toon!

A new level of pain washed through him.

He knew he had to do something. Something to ease the pain, but he couldn't think what it was. Something about Heaters. Oh, how he hated them. What they were doing to him. He thought of the pile of dismembered corpses. Rage flooded his mind, driving out the pain.

Another.

Staring eyes. He had been too slow.

Another.

Was that yelling? Who was yelling something? Was that him?

No, Colonel Santos. 39 tried to focus. He looked at the Colonel.

"Attention! Stand to!" he yelled.

39 looked past Santos as another blow fell.

His platoon, what was left of them, all six were kneeling on the floor, holding their heads. Someone had been sick all over the floor. As he looked, others, not of his platoon, grimaced in half-concealed agony.

The colonel's command only increased the agony of those unable to complete the command. 39 felt the impact of another hit, but the pain was some distant thing. A window seemed to open to him. He found he could observe what was going on and not be impacted by it. He no longer needed to distract himself with the Heater. He saw his team. He saw 20, and he felt immense sympathy, but it was like it was happening to someone else. Like a story related after traversing multiple tellings. He was buffered from it all.

He smiled. Not at what was happening. Nothing here was amusing. He smiled because the pain, at once so severe, was now a distant thing.

Men in the ranks started whispering to one another. Causing the Colonel to rage and turn to see what had caused the commotion. Santos scowled, bewildered at the sight of this man beaten near to death, smiling.

"Halt!" he called.

The hooded man stopped mid-swing and stood to attention, breathing hard from his exertions.

"Doc, check his control device," he called to the lab coat.

She scurried over and pushed a few buttons, checking that mother was still operational.

"It's functioning perfectly, sir," she said.

"Is he brain-dead?" he asked.

She came around to the front of him and shone a light in his eyes. She snapped her fingers and asked him for his number.

"G39, ma'am. Charlie Company, the best-damned company in the universe!" he said, loud enough for the entire company to hear.

"Oorah!" came the thunderous response from nearly every Marine.

Santos squinted at 39, thinking. Finally, he told the hooded man to finish his sentence. Only five more fell, and G39 looked at Colonel Santos the whole time. A faint smile on his lips.

They untied him, and he staggered under his own weight but shrugged off the guard's hands that tried to steady him. He looked down at the pool of fresh blood that had puddled beneath the post. He felt it soaking the back of his trousers.

Colonel Santos approached him and seemed surprised that he not only lived but was standing on his own.

"I must say, Private, you do put on a show." He seemed annoyed.

"I seem to have survived, sir."

Santos took his meaning and smiled. He turned to Charlie Company.

"G20, would you come forward?"

20 looked startled. The platoon had mostly recovered from mother's discipline and stood at attention, but at the Colonel's words, 20 walked stiffly toward them.

"I have petitioned and have received confirmation from brass to award the bronze star to Marines G20 and G39. They showed exceptional intuition on the battlefield. Together, they killed a combined thirteen Heaters."

Subdued conversation broke out at the number. Santos raised a hand for silence.

"Privates no more. I would like to introduce Corporal G39 and Lance Corporal G20 to Charlie Company."

"Oorah!" reverberated through the motor pool.

Santos took two bronze stars from his pocket and handed the medals over with a handshake for each.

39 was starting to come down off of whatever mountain top he'd been on mentally, and the pain was starting to break through into consciousness. Luckily the company was dismissed, and so he walked the short distance to the lab coat who waited with a wheelchair and slumped into the seat, exhausted.

CHAPTER 8

It had been five days since 39 was flogged. Five Terran days, meaning it was still dark on Eridani B. 20 pounded out the laps. This was her tenth, and she was breathing hard, but it felt great. This was her first time running outside, and it was luxurious. What would it be like to run on Terra? To be able to smell the scents and breathe the cool air straight into her lungs without needing a rebreather.

She looked out into the dark. She ran atop the massive defensive wall that surrounded the huge fort. She couldn't wait until Epsilon rose once again in the sky and illuminated her view.

Solar winds were strong in this area of space, and so the atmosphere was thin and, according to the uploads, the atmosphere was, at times, swept nearly entirely away. It was a testament to the hardiness of the vegetation that there was any at all, let alone the thriving forest landscape she had fought the Heaters in five days ago.

Because of the thin atmosphere, the stars seemed as though she could reach out and touch them, and the moon, that was just peeking over the horizon, was massive and bright.

She could see the lights of the CS and its supporting fleet in Geosynchronous orbit directly above Fort McIntyre. It was a comforting thing, knowing that you were watched over by the control ship. The ship was massive. It lived up to its name in that it controlled everything in a military operation like this. Top brass would be aboard, receiving constant feeds, keeping an eye on the troops. They could order strikes on locations nearly instantly upon viewing reconnaissance vids from scouts or drones.

Surprisingly, the planet didn't have much of a Grey fleet protecting it when they had arrived, and the pitiful resistance was easily swept aside by the Control Ship's massive guns and the more agile support craft in the Terran fleet.

All of this was before she had been "born," but she knew it from uploads. She knew a lot from the uploads, but there was far more that she was lacking. She knew what air was, but this was the first time she had felt the cool night breeze caress her sweat-glistened skin. She knew what a moon was, but this was the first time she looked up at a moon's crater-pocked surface and saw the bright reflection shine dimly over the trees. The moon's borrowed light illuminated the tops of hills but left the low places dark. She paused her run and leaned against the killstep, a step that ran round the inside of the parapet for defenders to fight from.

She looked out at the view that the moon opened to her. The breeze rustled orange foliage made gray by the low light. She looked down at her P.T.s and looked at the Lance Corporal insignia on the sleeve. It was nothing, really. Just above PFC, she would barely qualify for a respectful tone from the majority of Grunts. All the same, it felt nice. She was proud of it.

"You make my head hurt." came a voice from behind her.

She spun and saw a Marine walk by, looking her up and down and massaging the back of his head. That passed for a flirtation among Grunts. Commenting that a woman or man made one's head hurt meant that that person made the other's thoughts carry into prohibited territory.

She just shook her head and looked back out at the view.

A patrol drone zoomed by, continuing its scan of the outer defenses. The things went on constant patrol and could read the heat signatures of Heaters and would notify command if the enemy was sensed near the fort.

"G20?" came another voice behind her.

20 turned. A Marine Private stood maybe five foot six. Shorter than her.

"Yes?" she said.

"Major Grant wants to see you," he said.

She swore. Of course it had to be the one time she'd left her wrist computer for IT to check over while she went for a run. It had been blacking out, and she decided that it wouldn't hurt anything for her to go for a run while it was being worked on.

"You'd better hurry, ma'am. It took me a while to find you," he said, annoyed.

She sighed and set out at a run toward the company HQ.

When she arrived, a lean Gunnery Sergeant with C30 stenciled on his uniform was already there, standing just outside the doors to the Major's office.

He smiled at her when she approached. Sweating and forcing her rebreather to work hard to keep up with her rapid breaths, she slid to a stop in front of him.

"How late am I?" she asked.

"Very," he said.

She sighed.

He motioned for her to precede him.

The automatic doors slid open with a hiss as they entered. The next set opened after the first set closed, and then they were in a dimly lit antechamber of sorts. The Major's secretary sat at a desk and nodded for them to continue into Grant's office. They both pulled down their masks and moved to the door.

The major sat at his desk, swiping through documents on his board. She and C30 approached the desk and stood at attention. They waited for the Major to notice their presence. He finished skimming the document he was on and returned the salute she and the gunny gave him.

Major Grant was not fat. Anyone that called him that would have been mistaken. What could appear, upon first glimpse, as fat was, in fact, sturdy muscle. He was square-shaped and looked like he could hold his own with a bear if the bear had the high ground. Yet his eyes were almost gray like his hair, and they had a kindly sparkle.

"Why don't you two have a seat?" He motioned with his large hand at the chairs in front of the desk.

G20 glanced at the gunny as they sat.

What was he doing here? She had never seen the Gunnery Sergeant before, but it was uncommon for a Grunt to live long enough to become a sergeant, let alone a Gunny. He was lean, and she could see rope-like muscle working under his fatigues. He looked old, ten, maybe twelve years old. That was an exceptionally long life for a Grunt. His short-cropped hair was combed back and had a touch of gray at the temples. Maybe fifteen years old.

20 felt self-conscious in her P.T. garb. Maybe she should have gone back to the barracks and changed before coming here. No. When an officer beckoned, you ran. She brushed her short blonde hair self-consciously.

"You already know the terrain, Gunny, so you'll have to bear with me as I explain the situation to 20."

Uh oh, here it comes, she thought.

"The Greys have a strong defensive location on this planet. Their fort is more like a walled city five or six times the size of Fort McIntyre. As you may know, the Greys have shields, not physical ones like we have, but energy shields. Tech that our lab coats can't figure out and have yet to design a weapon that can penetrate."

Major Grant leaned back in his chair.

"These energy shields guard their fort-city. The energy being produced to keep the shields up must be incredible. Our lab coats assure me that a living thing should be able to walk right through the shield without any difficulty, but anything with an electronic signature is zapped."

He paused. Pursed his lips.

"We need recon of the fort and specifically the shield generators. Those generators are the key. They're keeping the CS from blasting that base to smithereens. If you and the Gunny here can get inside the fort and pick out the exact coordinates of the generators, then we can mount a targeted ground assault on the installation."

20 looked at the gunny and tried to gauge if he was as disconcerted as she was. He looked excited. Great, was she the only one here with any brains? Mother stabbed her. The pain was sudden and intense. Implying that the Major was less than a genius was not the best idea. Her hand went involuntarily to the base of her skull. Her body instinctively sought to soothe the source of the agony. The control device was cold to her touch. She slowed her breathing and forced her mind clear.

"Do you have misgivings, Corporal?"

She looked up at the Major. His eyes showed concern.

"You may speak freely," he said after her hesitation.

"The Gunny and I are to do this alone, sir?"

"It was determined that two trained snipers on their own would be safer than a squad or platoon, as was evidenced by your recent engagement with the Heaters. Do you disagree with that assessment?"

Saying yes would probably cause another correction from mother.

"Not generally, no. But I can't help but wonder if we will be able to breach the Heater patrols. Surely, they have just as efficient advanced warning measures as we do, maybe more so. How are we going to get past them, sir?"

"Honestly, I don't know. I'm sorry that we don't have a detailed plan for you to follow, hell, a plan at all, but the lack of information that we have on the fort is a testament to why we need recon in the area. According to your instructors, you show the most promise of any scout they have trained. I don't tell you this to swell your head. I tell you this so that you know why we chose you. You and the gunny are the best in the business. If anyone can do this, it's you two. And don't worry too much, 20, gunny's used to accomplishing the impossible. Isn't that right, gunny?"

"I don't know about that, sir, but you can count on us to

get the info or die try'n."

20 felt a little frustrated at being spoken for but knew better than to say so. Instead, she nodded her head in acceptance and agreement with the statement.

CHAPTER 9

G20 stood naked, waiting to enter the pool of viscous liquid that was somehow aided in the upload process. She knew that bodies during uploads thrashed uncontrollably. Perhaps the liquid made that involuntary movement easier. Maybe it helped the nerves conduct the flow of rapid-fire signals throughout the body. She didn't know, but neither did she care, only the stuff stunk. She would stink for a week after this mission upload.

A nerdy lab-coat tech sat behind the control panel for this upload station. He was true-born, as all lab coats were. Being True-born, mother did not correct his leer and his clearly inappropriate thoughts. The tech probably volunteered for this post. She crossed her arms over her chest and turned away from the disgusting man-child.

Mother didn't like her derision when directed at a true-born. It didn't correct her as harshly as it would have if the pimple-faced lab coat had been an officer, but it was still unpleasant.

After what seemed like an eternity, the upload station was free. She slowly descended into the pool. The temperature was exactly attuned to that of her body. She laid back, and the tech fastened mother's port to the headgear. She tried not to think about all the other people who had used this machine.

She tried to relax, but she knew the pain would come shortly, and she couldn't help but tense as the tech sat back down in his chair. There was no warning. No count-down. No time to prepare. Just sudden and intense pain. Images flashed through her mind like a kaleidoscope of thoughts, each having its own intense detail. She could, vaguely, feel her body jerk and shake in the pool, but it was distant, eclipsed by the blinding pain of pure knowledge forcing its way into her brain's gray matter. New folds formed, and synapsis fired. After what felt like hours, but what she knew was only minutes, she was done. The tech unhooked her, and she climbed shakily to her feet.

There was a risk that your brain just couldn't take the upload, and you'd short out. That's what the lab coats called it. Shorting out, like a circuit. One minute you are there and can think, speak and move. The next, you're brain-dead. Despite the inherent risk, 20 wanted more. She always wanted more. She didn't know why she wanted more uploads. Maybe it was that she thought the more knowledge she could get, the closer she'd feel to a true-born. The more she'd be treated like one. At least, she hoped. Secretly.

She went straight in and took a shower, got dressed and went back to the barracks. When she got there, Golf platoon was gathered in the back around one of the bunks. As 20 came closer, she saw that it was 39. He must have just been released from medical. He was smiling as 30 recounted some embellished story. The type of story he was known for. She felt herself smile.

Her instructor had been right. Once she had saved one of their asses, their attitude toward her changed. She had been accepted. More than accepted. She wondered if this was a glimmer into the relationship that a true-born had for his family.

They saw her approach and made a hole for her. They laughed at some punchline 20 didn't catch, but she chuckled anyway.

39 looked at her and smiled.

"Word is that you have some top-secret mission from the brass." It wasn't a question. How had he found out?

"Uh. Well, you know, they have to keep the talent busy," she said.

"So you're leaving me then. I see," he said dejectedly. His eyes still smiled. He had nice eyes.

"I'm gone first thing in the morning, well, whatever passes for morning on this place." She hadn't been specifically told not to share that tidbit, and they'd have found out soon enough anyway, she rationalized.

"Whatever it is, it's big enough that they gave you an upload for it," 12 said.

Was nothing secret in this fort?

"How do you know that?" she asked.

12 wrinkled his nose.

"You stink," he said.

20 felt her face heat, and she surreptitiously smelled her forearm.

The group laughed, and the heat in her face worsened.

"I'm surprised you could smell anything other than your own breath," she retorted. It was a childish thing to say, but it was expected of her, as evidenced by the renewed laughter.

"Anyway, I'll take as much as they can give me," she said.

"Not me," said 30. "I'm spending my chits on R and R."

"That's evident to anyone who sees you 30," 20 jabbed.

"What does that mean?" he said.

"It means you really need some beauty sleep," she said.

Everyone laughed, even 30. This is something that they must all crave. A sense of belonging. Uploads told of the importance of camaraderie. Brothers in arms, fighting a common foe. Strength in unity. But they didn't come close to describing how it felt.

10 slapped her on her back as he laughed. Maybe the laughter was more than the joke deserved, but it felt good to laugh. To forget their lot. To forget that about eighty-five percent of the toon was gone. Wiped out in a single engagement. An engagement in which they all should have died in. The fact was not lost on them. They knew that the probability of their dying in the next action was high.

10 continued to laugh after all others had stopped. He was bent double now, and sweat prickled his skin. 30 started to laugh,

not at the joke, but at 10.

"You alright, 10? She's not that funny," he said.

10 started to choke between laughter, coughing and gasping for air, then laughing some more.

Something was wrong.

20 patted his back, trying to soothe him. His shirt was wet with perspiration. He was burning hot.

"He's burning up," she said.

10 dropped to the cold concrete floor and shook. Foam came from his mouth, and his eyes rolled back in his head, showing bloodshot whites.

20 tapped her wrist computer and spoke into it.

"Medical to barrack 30. Medical emergency, G10 is seizing."

"Medical on route, G20. Hold tight," came the response almost instantly.

"Hold his head," she said.

39 knelt by 10's writhing form and encircled him in his big arms, protecting him somewhat from self-injury.

The odd thing was that 10 still had intermittent bouts of manic laughter that would come exploding out amidst the chaos of the seizure, foam spittle flying. It was disturbing to watch.

A team of corpsmen rushed in and pushed 39 away from 10. They held him face down on the floor as one of the medics took out a powered screwdriver and undid a panel on the back of his control device. He then got a strange-looking hooked tool and fished around inside 10's mother. A few more strange tools came out before, finally, the corpsman swore and jerked out a wire in frustration.

10 stopped moving instantly. He lay, face down, motionless.

"Is he?" 20 was afraid to ask the question that burned inside her.

The corpsman ignored her.

"We'll take him back to the lab and see if we can jump-start him, but I bet he's fried," the corpsman said to his colleagues. His callous words stung the toon like a slap to the face of each Marine. 20 felt her cheek. It was wet. She was crying. She'd never cried before, but she knew what this was. She knew from the uploads. But the uploads left so much unsaid. They didn't describe this. How could they?

39 circled her shoulder with one of his massive arms. It felt nice. She couldn't explain why. It was a strange feeling. Comforting, she supposed.

She rested her head against his chest and let the sobs come. This felt right. Natural somehow.

CHAPTER 10

39 opened his eyes and immediately turned to 20's bunk. She was already gone. He didn't feel good about it. What mission would she need to go on that would exclude them? Somehow, he felt nervous for her. He had seen her as part of his squad. Major Grant folded Golf Platoon into Bravo platoon and made them a squad which he was over. Five guys. Four now that 10 was gone, not counting 20.

It had been a shock to them all when a few hours after 10's seizure, they got word over their wrist comps that he didn't make it. None of them had slept well that night, and he didn't envy 20 having to suit up so early. He hoped that she would be alright and that she could keep her head in the game. He knew that he would have had a hard time staying focused after last night.

His back twinged as he rolled out of bed. The lights were still out. A look at his wrist told him it was still twenty minutes til reveille. Just enough time to take a shower and hit the head.

The water felt good on his sore back. The wounds were partly healed already. Open wounds were easy to heal within a few days with the regeneration injections that the lab coats administered, but wounds caused by disciplinary action were left to heal, more or less, the old-fashioned way. His genetic advantages made it so that he was an unnaturally fast healer, but the wounds seemed to take an eternity to heal by his perspective. He supposed that that was the point. A lot of good discipline would do if he wasn't made to recall it often. And he had. Painful memories that conflicted with mother.

In the five days...wait, was it six days? It was difficult to tell. The fort had to have round-the-clock defenses and patrols, so there was always a buzz. Six days, he decided. In the six days since the flogging, he had experienced a punishment that bordered on torture. Mother, in all her devastating, computed, and wholly logical judgement, deemed the majority of his thoughts to be treasonous, or at the very least, they were worthy of some pain correction. It was hard to view what he had done in rescuing this toon as a bad thing. In fact, as long as he only thought of it in general terms, he was okay. It was when he thought of the action of commandeering the L.T.'s wrist comp that he felt mother kick in.

The pulsing throb was there, as it had been, in some form or another, for days. He couldn't say he was getting used to it because he didn't think that was possible short of madness, but the constant pain made the moments when he could banish all thoughts of wrongdoing feel like a blissful paradise.

He forced his mind clear and let the water cascade over him. He luxuriated as mother eased and the heat of the water seeped into his sore muscles.

He finished his shower and was suited up in time for reveille. His squad was prompt as well, already veterans in the eyes of most grunts. They strutted along the top of the wall. Anybody who survived first contact with Heaters was a vet. The stats proved that even these, not yet four months old, were battle-hardened. His squad more than most, in fact.

It was their company's turn on the walls, and his squad patrolled the South East quadrant between markers 20 and 25. They had full battle suits, ready for anything. 24 nodded respectfully as they passed each other. They kept doing that. It was kind of annoying to 39. He knew he was their squad leader, but did they have to nod every time they passed each other on the wall? He had put a stop to the salutes. That was just embarrassing. Each member would slam a closed fist against their armored chest in a display that 39 was sure would bring some kind of mockery from the other squad leaders in the toon.

12 was in front of him and had stopped his circuit to look out over the moonlit nightscape. 39 stopped at marker 23 and looked out over the edge of the wall. Trees dotted the approach to the base of the plateau, but from the little 39 had seen of this planet, it was pretty open. They would be able to see an enemy approach for miles. He was about to proceed in his circuit when something caught his eye. It was like a shimmer, a wavy distortion like what the uploads described as a heat haze. 39 had never seen one, but the images in his head fit this description. Because of the dark, it was harder to see when he looked right at it, but somehow a little easier when just looking at it in his vision's periphery. He felt the hairs prickle on the back of his neck. This could just be some strange phenomenon native to this planet. Deity only knew how many things he'd seen here that the uploads didn't even touch on.

He looked toward 12 and saw that he was looking down, close to the wall's edge as he was, but closer in. 39 tried to spot what he was looking at and could just make out a similar haze.

"What the...."

A blade of air severed 12's leg just above the knee. He fell screaming onto the reinforced concrete. Blood streamed from his leg.

"Corpsman!" 39 yelled into his wrist.

12's suit should automatically apply a tourniquet at the thigh junction, but with a wound like that, he'd need help fast.

39 engaged his shield and grabbed his axe from its spot at his leg. Whatever the hell this was, firearms would do little good against something invisible.

He swung the axe in front of him, sure that whatever it was, was bearing down on its next victim. The blade had sliced so easily through 12's suit that 39 wondered if his shield and axe would do anything to protect him.

He kept swinging the axe and called for backup over his squad channel. He then switched to the platoon channel and reported the assault of an unknown enemy. His new L.T. sounded annoyed that 39 couldn't give any specifics.

"I don't know, sir. They're just...invisible."

Something struck his axes, pushing it to the side, and there was a follow-up strike to his shield that he had just gotten up in time to block the blow from hitting his face. He could see the dimple in the graphene in front of his eyes.

39 yelled, some unintelligible cry, venting his rage at the suddenly heated air. Sweat ran down his face. Heat.... He switched to his IR. A bright silhouette of a humanoid crouched in front of him, preparing for another series of strikes. 39 took a swing in the wrong direction. Goading the creature into thinking that he still couldn't see.

"Switch to IR!" he said to the entire company.

The feint had worked. The thing moved forward lightning fast, but 39 expected the move and swung his axe down to meet the head of the thing. The yellow of the creature, in his IR, turned bright white at the point of impact, and a wave of searing heat hit 39, staggering him. He raised his shield to block the heat and stepped out of its intensity.

He scanned the wall's top and saw sporadic attacks along the wall. Men were down, but he didn't see any bright spots like the one he'd killed. Then an explosion. So bright and intense in his IR that he had to switch back to normal vision. Then another. And another. All along the wall, explosions of blue heater blood engulfed defensive turrets and anti-air batteries. They were targeting the automated defenses. This was not good.

39 turned his attention back to his squad.

He walked to 12.

"To me!" he called, as he bent down to inspect 12's injury.

24, 19 and 30 came running over. 24 was missing his right hand. His suit had applied the tourniquet, but his face was contorted in agony.

"24, take 12 with you to medical. You'll need to go to the hospital, I'm afraid. The Corpsmen will have their hands full. 30

and 19, stay close. We need to make sure that any attack in our quarter is repulsed. They're not as hard to kill as Heaters once you can see them."

12 groaned when 39 bent over and picked him up. He patted his cheek.

"We'll repay the bastards for you." He smiled.

His casual promise of retribution seemed to encourage 30, who nodded his agreement as he kept an IR-assisted eye on the wall.

24 took 12 around the waist and helped him down the staircase on the inside of the wall. Already, other companies were making their way to the defenses, and the wounded Marines had to navigate their way past fresh meat who looked at the horrific injuries with undisguised dread.

Alarms sounded throughout the fort, calling for Marines to get to the defenses.

39 turned and looked out over the nightscape once again. He had thought they would have gotten plenty of warning in the advent of an assault, but as he saw the army approaching through the darkened landscape, he felt as naive as a child. He was one, in a way. He couldn't help wondering if 20 was okay. If she had made it safely past all of that. He didn't see how it was possible. The army seemed to shimmer into being from thin air as it came closer to the plateau. Bigger and bigger as more and more units spilled out of the forest.

CHAPTER 11

G20 met Gunny at the south gate two hours before reveille. She had been told that her genetic makeup was ideal for long campaigns on little rest. She stifled a yawn as they passed through the dark gateway into the shadow that the moon cast on the southeast side of the plateau. They had chosen this gateway for that reason, hoping the shadow would mask their exit. Really, the only fear they had was of outside observers. No Terran would collude with Greys. The thought was laughable.

Despite that fact, they took great pains to move stealthily among the boulders and ledge rock that formed the steep slopes of the plateau. Twisted trees fought to exist among the harsh terrain. They had muted their comms and wrist comps and communicated with hand signals only. Both of them understood the difficulty of this mission. She hesitated to call it an impossible task. Her short life gave her little bearing on her own personality, but she considered herself a realist, which was what a pessimist would call themselves while describing a mission like this as a death warrant intended only to give the brass something to do. Which she definitely wasn't doing. She just thought that it was a near impossible mission thought up by armchair soldiers, optimists all. Mother throbbed her judgement.

She scanned the terrain with IR and then switched back to normal view. They had reached the base of the plateau and hesitated, scanning for enemy scouts before making their way to the distant forest.

They crawled through strange wide-leafed grass that

covered the area. They went slow, and 20 would periodically switch to IR and scan their surroundings, careful not to raise her head above the grass.

They were only about a hundred yards from the forest's edge when she spotted a flash of heat coming toward them. She tapped Gunny on the shoulder, signaled that she had spotted an enemy contact and indicated the direction. He switched to IR and looked in that direction.

He spotted the enemy scout and motioned for her to get down. They lowered to their bellies and waited, hardly breathing. She listened intently for any sign of the Grey passing by. She heard a faint clicking sound and pointed her IR-enhanced vision in that direction. She slowly pushed the grass down in front of her and could see what looked like a particularly small Heater. It stood, looking up at the fort atop its earthen bastian and clicked into some type of small radio attached to its hand.

The thing wasn't far away and stood in the middle of the clearing for all to see. She switched to her regular view, curious to see how different this more petite version looked from the Brutes they had fought to this point in the war. Nothing. The thing was gone. She squinted. Trying to see some kind of camouflage that hid the scout, for this must be what they were. Scouts like herself. She switched back to IR, and the scout appeared again, this time looking right at her. She tensed.

She knew from her training that to move now was guaranteed death. She held her breath and trusted in her own camouflage that she had painstakingly created and draped over her exo-suit. She kicked herself for being too curious. What was that saying from the English upload? Curiosity killed the cat. She didn't know what a cat was, it being unnecessary data for a force recon scout sniper, but she imagined that the saying meant not to be too curious.

But she was a scout. Curiosity was a sought-after attribute in the field. However much she rationalized it, she knew she screwed up.

"Curiosity should always be tempered by the mission's priority." Had that been from an upload or from an instructor? She wasn't sure. It didn't matter. The thing was still looking at her.

Finally, after an age, the scout lifted the radio hand to his mouth and clicked. He slowly moved forward toward Fort McIntyre. Then up and down the edge of the forest, bright heat signatures crept out of the dense cover that the forest provided. This was no mere scouting mission. This looked like an assault. She, ever so slowly, shifted her head enough to see Gunny. The expression in his eyes was enough to see in the faint light of the moon, and he was every bit as shocked as she. They stayed in their scant cover and hoped that the enemy scouts would pass them by unnoticed.

Luckily that was just what happened. The scouts moved cautiously but stalwartly toward the fort. They had been commanded not to break radio silence short of transmitting the coordinates of the shield generators, and that was only if they couldn't get a messenger drone up to do it for them. The fort would be caught totally unawares. This new invisible threat would be devastating to the unsuspecting Terrans.

After the force had moved off, she flashed the hand sign for the radio to Gunny. He shook his head and motioned in front of him.

She nodded, knowing that would be his decision, and slowly crept after him. They entered the comforting concealment of the forest foliage and were able to make faster progress covering each other with IR enabled.

They came to a small clearing and started scanning the area for heat. Nothing. Just to be sure, she switched to regular vision and scanned the clearing. She was about to motion Gunny forward when she caught a glimpse of movement in the center.

It was like a portion of the grass covered ground lifted away, and out stepped a Heater. He glanced around, aiming his rifle ahead of his swiveling body. A second and third appeared.

Soon a steady stream exited the ground and began to cover each other, much as she and Gunny had moments before, as they moved in her direction. She waved Gunny back, and they moved out with all the haste they could stealthily perform. She followed close on Gunny's heels. They could no longer afford the time to cover one another properly.

Suddenly Gunny disappeared.

She slid to a stop at the edge of a crevice maybe three feet wide, but who knew how deep it was. She switched to IR and saw Gunny's heat signature about twenty feet down.

She looked behind her and saw an army materialize through the trees. They would spot her if she stayed here. She stepped forward off of the ledge. Her suit absorbed the impact of her fall without difficulty, but then she pitched forward, the uneven footing making the landing less than graceful. She cracked her face into the stone wall of the small canyon. Her helmet saved her from being concussed, but she felt blood trickle from a cut on her cheek.

She turned and saw Gunny. He was quietly placing loose stones and dirt over him, trying to mask his heat, she realized.

She lay down and began doing the same. They both lay on their back so that they could see the opening above.

Their suits were designed to mask much of their heat, but hopefully, the dirt and rock would break up their shape a little so that they resembled the small animal life that was so abundant in the forest rather than the scared Terrans that they were.

If the Greys didn't have their IR engaged, then they probably wouldn't see them in the deep dark of the chasm. 20 unwittingly held her breath as the first of the Greys crept forward. Their glowing bodies shone as they walked by. A dark canopy and distant stars was their backdrop.

20 was frozen, each muscle taut with tension. Movement suddenly caught her attention. Not movement from the distant rim, but something out of the corner of her eye, much closer.

Some type of snake protruded its sanguine, anfractuous

head from a dark recess in the rock next to her. Its body was bright red which was the only way she saw it in the shadows. Somehow her muscles tensed even more as the thing twisted out of its hiding place. Her suit protected most of her body from a bite. The vulnerabilities were her relatively unprotected hands. Since her visor was down, her face was protected. Despite the absurdity of being afraid of this thing while in her suit, she couldn't entirely banish some innate instinct that screamed inside her. The snake-eel thing slithered over her, somehow attracted to her body heat.

This planet had gotten more and more frigid as the long night continued. Most of the animals on Eridani B were reptilian in nature and would crave whatever heat they could find until the sun came again.

It coiled around her arms and chest, slowly squeezing. She could feel the pressure. Her suit sent messages to her body through its connection to mother and transferred that information to her senses. This is how the suits functioned so intuitively. When she walked, it walked. She didn't have to press any buttons or make any unnatural movements to function. It was all controlled by her through mother.

She knew that the snake was not hurting her, that it could not, yet the sensation was...disconcerting.

She focused her attention back to the real threat. The Heaters marched past the crevice in such numbers that she feared that there would be nothing left of Fort McIntyre when and if they accomplished their mission. A low rumble could be heard above, undoubtedly coming from mobile artillery moving into position to bombard the fort.

Finally, after what seemed like hours, the stream of enemy soldiers and equipment petered out, and the Gunny and she were left in silence.

CHAPTER 12

39 ripped his axe out of the head of a heater. He, 30, and 19 all had attacked the thing at once. Blue lava gushed from the wound. This was a full heater, bigger than the invisible ones but with less heat somehow. Maybe the others had charged up for greater destruction upon their suicidal death. Made sense.

The invisible Greys had wreaked havoc on their defensive batteries. Only a handful were still functional on 39's side of the fort. Flashes of heater incendiary artillery rounds lit up the fort in harsh contrast to the dark of the long night. Tracer rounds lit a path from the few remaining Terran batteries to incoming artillery rounds, intercepting and prematurely exploding them. More and more artillery fire blasted the wall. It was obvious that they were targeting the Terran guns, and 39 watched as a battery was hit with three explosions, one right after the other.

39 was surprised that the majority of the infantry had not approached the plateau. They seemed to be held back for some reason. Only a few small teams of Heaters had been sent forward at a time, drawing fire. The teams were suicidal. Those that had made it through the Marine's fire clambered up the wall as if it were a nuisance and nothing more, but the Marines on the walls far outnumbered the few that made it atop the walls, and they were finished off easily.

Why were they allowing this? The Greys had the advantage. With the defenses down, the enemy could completely overwhelm them if they came in a rush. The artillery fired again, ripping a hole in the wall not far from 39's marker. The blast made him stumble.

Something had to be done about that artillery.

And just as if his thought had conjured it, a light, like a falling star, descended from the Terran CS on overwatch. As it entered the atmosphere, 39 could see it split into three separate projectiles, each lanced down into the Grey army.

The bedraggled and bloodied Marines on the wall gave a cheer as three artillery cannons went up in a cloud of yellow and blue flame.

39 watched the Grey army turn and run.

The fort erupted with cheers and cajoling cat calls. 39 turned to 30 and 19. Their faces were exuberant.

Something wasn't right. Why would they amass such an army only to turn and run at the first salvo from the control ship?

Suddenly the horizon was filled with the light of hundreds of planetary defense missiles. They arced up toward the CS. 39's stomach fell.

Tracer rounds, visible from the planet's surface only because of their exceeding number, struck out at the incoming missiles with a fury. The missiles began exploding as the massive ship's defenses laid into the barrage.

Distance pops could be heard as the missiles flashed. The Marines in the fort stood spellbound, watching as their lifeline was threatened. 39 silently prayed, knowing that the odds were against the CS being able to fend off the incredible attack.

The pops and flashes crept closer and closer to the ship.

39 exhaled sharply as the first missile struck the control ship. The CS still fought like a wounded animal. It poured on the fire into the barrage. More missiles got through and slammed into it. Murmurs broke the silence around the wall as explosion after explosion erupted on the CS.

Disbelief painted the soldier's faces as the enormity of their sudden predicament became clear to them. The Control ship's defenses had all but stopped when the final missiles struck home and finished off the behemoth. Secondary explosions popped in the night sky, and then one massive blast, so bright that 39 had to avert his eyes.

Terran Marines dropped to their knees. One man bent over and vomited.

They were stranded on an alien planet, outnumbered, and outgunned, with no overwatch and little hope of reinforcements. The explosion spelled disaster to every Marine in the fort.

39 half expected weeping to break out among the soldiers. Instead, they hefted their weapons and looked on as the Grey army rematerialized from the distant trees.

Nothing would stop this host from decimating the fort and all those inside. Nothing, except the warriors that stood upon this wall with him. Something that 39 wondered before cropped into his mind.

"What makes a man want to live?" he said aloud.

He said it quietly, and he didn't notice when 30 shrugged his response.

"What makes a man want to live?" he yelled. He suddenly felt a fervor inside him. A desire to live. And a desire to pay back these blue-blooded demons for their savage attack on the Control Ship.

He looked around and saw eyes on him. Hundreds of eyes. Maybe thousands.

He suddenly questioned himself at the rapt attention he received.

"It is not the experiences that one has that make a man want to live. It is not a well-lived life, but the promise of a future that spurs us on."

Some of the Marines nodded. Others just looked at him with contempt. He steeled himself and continued.

"Hope. It is hope that drives us. Why, then, should we falter when this army is here, ready to assault? Our hope will see us through. Fight for your right to live! And show these bastards what Terran Marines can do."

39 was surprised when "oorah" rang out. It was a little

lackluster, but they did respond.

He turned to see that the enemy had already made it to the base of the plateau. A few of the dead among the enemy artillery were being piled on flatbed vehicles and ferried to the back of their lines somewhere. He switched to his grenade launcher and started lobbing the rounds down at the front ranks of Heaters as they scrambled up the side.

More heavies joined in, but there weren't enough. Once they had made it halfway up, they started converging on the breach in the wall. They would flood into the fort with little hindrance. There was a sergeant trying to form a battle line, but it looked miniscule by comparison with the tidal wave approaching.

39 turned and looked at the silent defense battery. Most of the 40 mm guns were melted or broken apart, but one still looked intact.

He turned and jumped across the gaping hole in the wall and ran to the battery, Marines dodging out of his way. He looked over the weapon for a manual override. He wasn't sure, but it looked like there was an emergency switch that could be flipped for manual targeting and firing.

He didn't know if this would work, but he had to give it a try.

The enemy artillery had gone silent, but the Terran artillery had picked up as the Heaters clumped together.

"Here goes nothing," he said, and ripped the 40mm gun off the mount. He flipped the switch, turned and jumped down into the gap in the wall. Right in front of the crazed front ranks of Heaters. 39 was tempted to close his eyes. He knew he had just gambled everything on getting this hunk of metal to fire.

He depressed the trigger, and a satisfying recoil pushed the weapon back as a volley of shrapnel shot, mixed with armor piercing and tracer rounds, sped from the barrel. The rounds came so fast that he had spent fifty before he could brace himself for the recoil and correct his aim. At this range, though, he was still wiping out rank upon rank of Heaters. Blue blood geysered and bubbled with heat. The air in front of 39 was like an oven. Sweat poured down his face as he fired. Within minutes, he had taken out fifteen or twenty. The unexpected resistance stalled the assault. The Heaters started to slow their headlong charge, and an especially tall heater started pointing and yelling at the others. "An officer if ever I've seen one."

39 directed his fire at the leader and smiled when the heater's head was torn from its body. Suddenly, the 40 mm gun clicked, and the sudden silence encouraged the Heaters.

"Get me another drum of ammo for this!" he yelled over his shoulder. "And get some cold tanks up on the wall!"

He didn't turn to see if his orders were being carried out.

He switched to his grenade launcher and pounded the heaters as they charged closer. The Heaters made up the ground they had lost during the chaos that the 40 mm caused, and the concussion from the grenades exploding so closely hurt 39's whole body. He poured on the fire, regardless and managed, just barely, to hold the Heaters back.

The blood, now thick and smoking on the ground, still blue with heat, slowed the Heaters. They trudged through the gore of their own kind. Suddenly a blue flash slammed into the broken wall next to him and sprayed chunks of concrete. They were changing their tact.

A group of Heaters behind the main sword-bearing force used their rifles to try and remove 39 from his perch. Others clambered up the sides of the wall instead of trying to come through the gap. 39 could hear the desperate fighting above him, but he couldn't spare the attention.

He was getting low on grenades.

"Where's my drum!" he yelled.

"Here, sir." It was 19 and 30. They had been busy. At their feet lay a dozen of the ammo drums for the 40.

30 grunted as he picked up the 40 and slammed a new drum into the receiver.

"I can barely lift that thing, let alone fire it," he said as he handed it to 39.

The Heaters were closer than they had ever been, and 39 dodged a sword swing while laying into the thing with the 40 cutting it in half and splattering blood onto his suit. One Heater managed to slam a steaming, blood-covered hand into 39's chest, pushing him backward. He managed to keep his feet and finished off the wounded Heater.

At least the press of Heaters kept the shooters from picking him off. There was now a bog of blue blood that the Heaters waded through. 39 took a second to see if anyone had gotten cold tanks into place above the gap. They were there. 30 was up there now, ready to pour the liquid nitrogen down into the gap.

"Good man." 30 had anticipated him.

39 raised his left hand and jumped backward, still firing the 40.

"Now!" he yelled.

30 tipped the tank over. A cloud of gas exploded over the ground, obscuring the enemy for a terrifying minute.

When, finally, the vapor dissipated, thirty or so heaters stood, trapped in the hardened blood. 39 smiled and moved forward.

"Forward!" 39 yelled.

He led the way and charged at the vulnerable aliens. He dropped the 40 and pulled his axe, wanting to feel this. Wanting to send a message to the enemy. They could destroy a ship, but they couldn't destroy him.

He rained blow after blow into the enemy. He had his shield up as he broke through the last of the trapped enemy. Marines whooped and screamed crazed war cries behind him.

He had expected to be lit up as he broke through into the fresh Heaters coming up the slope of the plateau, but there was nothing.

They were in retreat. 39 switched back to his grenade launcher and used up the last of its ammo to hurry the enemy on its way.

Finally, he looked at the exhausted faces around him. Faces that just hours ago were so mournful were now ebullient. They slapped him on the back and shook his hand.

"Calm down," he said. "We'd better get back into the Fort before those guns open up on us and wipe those smiles off your faces."

They laughed, but did as he suggested. The artillery fire didn't come. Instead, the Greys decided to cut their losses and head home.

39's section of wall had been hardest, it turned out, but the Fort's defenses had suffered grievously. Up and down the wall, smoke billowed. Smoldering piles of Heater corpses lay atop and under those of Terran Marines. 39 wondered what the brass would come up with to get them out of this horrible situation.

CHAPTER 13

"Do you think he's up for the challenge?"

"I'm not sure there's much he wouldn't be ready for. Did you see the vids?"

Major Grant shook his head.

"Haven't found the time, sir," he said.

The colonel nodded his understanding.

"The past few days have been trying in the extreme, I don't blame you for missing them, but he was recommended for promotion from three Lieutenants, one Captain, and one Major. Upon reviewing the vids, I have to say, they're convincing."

Major Grant nodded, but Santos could tell that something bothered him.

"Spit it out, George. What's eating at you?"

"Well, sir. He's a newborn, sir. He's only been on the planet for ten days. It would be putting a lot on his shoulders."

Santos tapped his desk, considering the Major's concern.

"He all but single-handedly filled the hole in our wall with the enemy dead. I'd say that he's already taken the responsibility of the entire fort's safety on his shoulders and proven himself capable, but if you have someone else in mind, let's hear it."

"I don't, sir. No one that fits the bill. We don't have enough officers to head it up, and if we did, I'm not sure a True-born would be the best route in this case."

Colonel Santos' eyebrow lifted at the Major's use of the Grunt's vernacular for those born on Terra.

The Major rushed to explain.

"I like him, don't get me wrong, it's just the enormity of the mission...."

Colonel Santos understood why a Grunt was preferable to lead the mission. It had taken some hard knocks early on in his career to learn that Grunts were especially apt to act when a "True-born" would deliberate and hesitate. Maybe the Grunts didn't have enough to live for. Or the True-born had too much. What they needed now, however, was action. They needed destruction incarnate.

"I get it, George, but nothing about our situation is ideal. In all honesty, he's the most sure part of this plan in my mind."

Santos tapped his wrist computer, and a moment later, G39 stepped into the office. Big didn't describe G39. He was massive. He had to stoop to enter the small office. It was ironic that the last time this Grunt had graced this office, he was being summarily punished. G39 stood stiffly at attention.

"Thank you for coming, Corporal. Take a seat."

He sat next to his company commander and waited nervously for one of them to speak.

"Your actions in the defense of Fort McIntyre have not gone unnoticed, and as is always the case following a bloody engagement, there are openings in the chain of command. You have been recommended for promotion."

Santos couldn't help but smile at the Corporal's genuine surprise.

"It's unusual for someone as young as you to rise so quickly in the ranks, but your actions were equally unusual and quite extraordinary. I reviewed the vids, and while you were recommended for Sergeant, I disagree."

This was an evil way to phrase it, and Santos couldn't resist. G39's face fell subtly at the news.

"I believe that you should be raised to Gunnery Sergeant. Unfortunately, with the loss of the CS and all of the top brass, you will have to wait for approval from Terra for the medal I put you in for."

Santos reached across the desk and shook the big man's hand.

"Thank you, sir," he said with what seemed like genuine gratitude.

Major Grant shook his hand as well and patted the big man on the back.

"I'm sorry to cut your celebration short, but we don't have time for frivolities. As you know, Gunny, we're in quite a pickle. The CS was destroyed and what ships are left in the fleet are under heavy attack with every orbital insertion. We can't count on many reinforcements, if any, and our defenses will take weeks to get back into working order. That is time that I fear the Greys will not afford us. They will come again, and they will come soon. Questions?"

"Sir, I saw the Greys picking up their dead. I had thought them to be beyond any of that. Beyond any emotional attachment to the dead anyway. Do you know why they do it?" 39 seemed embarrassed by his question after he was done, and he looked down.

"Sorry, sir. It's a stupid question," 39 said.

"Nothing stupid about it. Our intelligence folks asked the same question during their invasion on Terra. The short answer is we don't know why they take the bodies. But we do know where. There is always a single building in their settlements that house their dead. The theory is that they incinerate them since the building would be full of the dead in no time. But we don't know why."

Santos understood 39's interest in the subject. Terra never had ceremonies or funerals, he supposed they were called for Grunts. Sometimes they'd lift a glass for a fallen comrade, but there were simply too many deaths to commemorate them all.

"If this is of interest to you, I'll requisition an upload for you of all the data we have on the subject," Santos said.

"Thank you, sir. I'd like that."

He paused and sat back in his chair.

"Our defenses are down, and we need to even the odds. If we can knock out theirs, namely their base's shields, it will force them into a less aggressive stance and might give us the breather we need."

G39 was nodding at the assessment. Good, he could think.

"We want you to lead the assault on the shield batteries. We don't have the forces necessary to do this in any way other than surgically. We already have assets en route to the enemy's Fort. Their last ping put them a day's march out. We need you to follow close on their heels and link up with them. I believe you know one of the snipers in the team we sent."

G39 nodded and looked relieved of all things.

"Once you link up, the recon team will inform you of the location of the shield batteries, then you and ten picked men will destroy the batteries. Any questions?"

Santos was afraid of this. The Grunt looked like he was about to malfunction.

"Go ahead, Gunny, speak freely."

G39 hesitated, then sat forward a little. "Sir, I don't know where to start."

39's face contorted in pain and then relaxed. Mother in action. Poor bastard.

"How is a force of only eleven men supposed to get into the Fort?"

"I'm not going to lie to you, son. It's a shit heap if ever I saw one, but we are desperate. We have drone recon photos that show two possible entries, but it will be hairy any way you cut it,"

Santos paused, then looked at Major Grant.

"Which is why I'm implementing the ancient practice of a forlorn hope. Do you know what that is, soldier?"

G39 shook his head.

"It means that for any man who makes it through this mission, and if the mission is successful, that man will be raised to an officer."

The look on his face was priceless. It was sad how much the mere hope of this reward lightened this man's heart. Which was the point. He needed these men to do the impossible, and to accomplish that, he had to promise them the unattainable.

G39's hand went to mother.

"Does that mean...."

"Yes, son. You'd have mother removed, and you'd be a lieutenant.

CHAPTER 14

Tomorrow would be morning on this planet. This was the coldest part of the night, the day before dawn. This was the most dangerous part of their journey to the enemy fort for two reasons. It was so cold that their faint heat signatures, which their suits couldn't mask, would glow like a beacon among the frost-crusted plants and rocks, and they were getting close to the enemy fort.

They had to be on a constant lookout for roving bands of heaters. More than once, she was sure of being discovered. Heaters would come within a dozen feet of their prone forms, pause, look right at them, then move off. Maybe their eyesight wasn't as keen as had been thought. Or maybe the Heaters saw what they expected to see, not what was really there. Complacent patrols, unused to actually finding Terran infiltrators on their marches, probably contributed to their luck.

They were both prone as they slowly crept over the crest of a small rise, Gunny first, then her. As she did, she saw the enemy fort in the distance and sucked in a breath. It was huge. She had expected a fort similar in size to that of Fort McIntyre, but this. This was immense.

A knot formed in the pit of her stomach as she realized the inherent difficulty of the task ahead of them. The lights from hundreds of buildings shone through the night. The city, for that's what this truly was, illuminated the horizon like a rising sun. They made their way to within a mile of the walls without being detected and rested in a hollow pocket made by two trees. It was a small space for two suited Marines, but it was the safest location they'd found since leaving Fort McIntyre.

They ate dried rations from their packs and silently watched the city fort. Their pocket was about twenty feet in the air and gave them a good vantage of the comings and goings. They spoke little and whispered when they did. The sound of a whisper was still too loud to her ears after days of silence.

"How are we going to find the shield battery in a place like that?" she said.

"I don't know. We will need to split up. There's no way for us to find it this year if we don't."

She nodded. She had made the same assessment, but she didn't want to split. In the days of their stealthy journey, she had grown used to the man's presence, almost comforted by it. She had, originally, been of the mind that she would do better on her own, but as they stalked the darkness together, she learned more than the uploads could ever teach. The man was incredible. From the way he brushed aside a blade of grass to how he could sense the way the land in front of them would lay and cross it along the bottom of every low spot or shadowed route. He was fluid. He moved like he was a part of the environment.

The thought of leaving him worried her. Did she know enough? She felt completely out of her element at the prospect of entering the alien city by herself, but she didn't dare say the fact to Gunny.

"Do you think we're safe to ping in there?"

Pinging was a way that the Terran command had learned to communicate with its assets in the field. It was a short burst of comms that couldn't be tracked. Data packages of limited size could be sent in a ping as well. Packages that could contain the location of the shield batteries.

"I'd say only ping if you have run out of options. If you have found the batteries but can't get back out of the fort, then send one up. It's better that they have the location at the very least, but we'll try to meet back up here and exchange notes."

Gunny looked down at her and smiled.

"Don't be too brave. If you see an impossible mission in there, then don't try and tackle it yourself. Meet back here, and we'll come up with a plan."

"Just getting in the city seems like an impossible mission."

"That will be the easy part. Once you get in, find something you can camouflage with, our suits will stick out like a sore thumb how they are now."

She nodded.

"We've got to get a move on. It's gonna be dawn too soon. We need to see if we can find this thing before then. I'll circle the city and come at it from the opposite side. We'll meet back here at thirteen hundred hours."

He must have seen the apprehension on her face because he smiled again. It was a reassuring smile, not a mocking one.

"You've got this 20. I've never seen someone as naturally talented as you. You'll be fine."

With that, he leaned forward and wiggled out of the pocket in the trees. Moments later, he was gone, another shadow in the dark forest.

She made a waypoint on her wrist computer and followed soon after, making sure no patrols were close before making her way to the wall.

As she got closer, the sheer size of the fort became more apparent. This is why they needed recon done, she realized. The Grey fort could swallow all of the Terran ground forces in an assault without difficulty. The Terrans needed an exact location so that a surgical assault could be performed. Anything else would be completely ineffective.

She kept an eye out for drones or cameras that would alert the Greys to her presence. She crept along about a hundred yards out from the wall, making sure that any sentries above weren't present as she moved. She scanned the wall for any breaks or handholds. Anything that she could use to gain entry. She came to a small lake that butted up against the wall and was about to turn back and head in the other direction when she paused.

Small ripples in the water caught her attention. She lay prone in the tall reeds that surrounded the lake. She watched the surface of the water. The ripples spread from the center of the lake, where the wall met the water. Could it be?

She lowered her visor and crawled into the water.

As her head dipped below the surface, her HUD informed her of the change in the breathing conditions and automatically switched to full backup air supply. She crawled forward through the murk, unable to see more than a foot in front of her and unable to turn on any lights for fear of giving up the game. She did her best at heading straight toward the wall, but navigation seemed impossible down here.

When she judged that the water was deep enough, she stood and was able to walk upright on the lake bottom without any difficulty.

G20 was not prone to panic. She felt that she could handle most situations better than the majority of men she knew. But this. This was eerie. The murky water seemed to stifle her. Her whole world had been shrunk down to this one-foot buffer.

The debris in the water seemed, suddenly, to shift and swirl ahead of her. She hadn't caused that, had she? She felt her heart race a bit at the thought of some alien creature down here just waiting for a tasty Terran to come along. She thought of the snake in the crevice and shuddered.

Something slid past her. This time she knew it wasn't her. Something was down here with her. She pulled her K-Bar. The knife was a special Marine issue and was massive for an unsuited Terran, but wearing her suit, the thing seemed proportional. It had a wicked saw edge on the spine and was razor sharp.

She waited for more movement, but none came. Slowly she forced herself to keep moving. One step in front of the other, she came closer to the wall. At least, she hoped she was. After a distance she thought must be past the wall, she decided to risk the light from her nav computer. Surely the murky water above her would hide the weak light from the computer.

She looked at her wrist. She had definitely gone off course. She had made almost a half circle and would need to bear hard to starboard to reach the wall.

She let the computer screen go dark again and waited for her eyesight to try and readjust to the darkness. Suddenly something gripped her leg in a grip so strong that she gasped in pain before realizing that the suit had taken most of the force. What she was feeling was just the suit triggering mother to inform her of the danger.

She looked down and saw only a cloud of mud and debris. Suddenly the thing wrenched to the side and ripped her from her feet. Fear gripped her heart.

She was dragged along the bottom of the lake while she tried to reach the thing with her knife. She swiped at the sinewy thing wrapping her leg. The grip loosened slightly, but not enough to free her. She reversed the grip on her knife and started stabbing down. A satisfying cloud of the animal's blood obscured the water around her, and she was free. She climbed to her feet and looked at her nav computer again. She judged her new bearing and switched the computer off, afraid the light might attract the thing again.

She moved out, not keen on staying down here any longer than she had to be.

She almost bumped into the wall before she knew it was there.

20 felt along the wall walking in one direction until the lake floor began to rise toward the shore. She stopped and turned around. She retraced her steps, feeling the wall with her right hand as she walked. Just as she started to despair, she felt it. An opening in the smooth stone of the fort's wall just big enough for her to fit through. Not her and her suit, just her.

She undid the air rebreather on the back of her suit and then began removing it. It took a terrifying quarter-hour to extricate herself from the armored exo-suit. There was an emergency eject that she could trigger, but that would spread pieces of her suit all over the lake bottom. She tried to keep a wary eye out for the monster that stalked these murky depths. She was scared to even think of what that thing would do to an unarmored leg or arm. She finished, then pulled the broken down fifty cal rifle out of her cargo pocket on the back of her suit, and she fastened the rebreather to her back. She used the sniper rifle's sling to secure it to her front, then pushed into the small opening. This had to be some kind of drain. She only hoped that the murk in this lake wasn't caused by alien excrement. The thought made her cringe.

Once she'd gone a good distance into the tunnel, she switched on a light that was attached to her wrist and switched it to the red light, which was harder to see from a distance. At least, that was true for humans. Maybe Greys were the opposite. She hoped not. She crawled through the tunnel a few inches at a time. There wasn't much room for her to move and so her progress was limited to what her toes could propel her with each flex.

She soon came to a metal grate. She swore to herself, but she had expected this. She flicked on the cutting torch that she carried in her right hand. It was a small unit and didn't have endless fuel. She hoped this stuff wasn't some alien equivalent to graphene or titanium, or she'd definitely need the spare fuel cartridges in her suit.

Surprisingly the stuff cut easily. She now only feared that some unseen sensor was informing the Greys of her intrusion. She'd know soon enough.

The end of the tunnel came into view, so she switched off her light and pulled herself to the lip of the opening. This side was just as muddy as the other, and she couldn't see much beyond a foot or two. She wondered if there was a creature on this side as on the other, but she couldn't imagine such a threatening creature being left alive inside the fort.

She was afraid, of course, she was afraid. Not having her suit made her feel small and weak, but it would do little to protect her if she was found out. The only thing she really missed was her railgun. The fifty was formidable, especially with the cold slugs she'd brought, but the rail was devastating, even for Heaters.

She pulled herself out into the open water and used her hands to backstroke so that her feet would come down into the slick muddy bottom. She knew the principles behind swimming, an academic knowledge, really. The uploads gave her a sense like she had done it before, but she knew she hadn't. Feeling the water envelope her was humbling. It felt strange. She decided it would be better to surface next to the wall, so she skirted it and rose toward the lake shore.

She could make out the light above her, faintly filtering through the murk. She undid the fifty and assembled it under the water. She mounted the scope and chambered a round, clipped the sling to her chest clip and shouldered the weapon. She rose ever so slowly from the water, making as little disturbance as possible. Once the top half of her body was out of the water, she scanned the area through her scope. The fifty had a silencer on it, but there was no way to silence a fifty. The thing kicked like a mule and sounded like a thunderclap. But if she had to, she would use it.

She saw no telltale heat signatures and so climbed out of the water, rifle at the ready. She quickly moved into the shadows. The water had been cold, and the night air was even colder. She shivered and concentrated on regulating her breathing. She slowly made her way down a narrow alley between two tall four-story buildings that looked like they might be warehouses of some kind.

She came to a door in the right hand building's wall and stopped. There was no knob. She could see a control panel on the wall by the door. There was only one button. She mentally shrugged and pressed it.

The door slid open noiselessly. The interior was pitch dark and smelled of, well, she didn't know what it smelled like, but it definitely smelled. Something organic, she decided and walked in. Her left arm burned with the desire to drop the fifty. The frame was a lightweight composite, but the barrel's twenty-six-inch length felt like it weighed a ton after a few minutes.

She switched the rifle to her left shoulder. She had trained with both, so her left arm could get a break while the right supported the majority of the weight. After she cleared the doorway, it slid shut behind her. The darkness was complete. Paused and listened to the darkness. She waited for any sound to betray the presence of some hidden enemy.

Silence. The IR was clear as well. She looked at her wrist computer, and it detected no electronic security. She relaxed and switched on her light. It was a warehouse. The smell was old foodstuffs of a sort that resembled grain. She searched the building for anything that would help disguise her but came up empty.

She exited the warehouse and back into the same alley she had been in. She continued up the alley and came to a door into the left hand building. This keypad had additional security. Instead of the single button, this one had twelve keys. She moved on down the alley. G20 came to the end of the alley. It opened into a larger street. She scanned through both IR and normal vision so as not to be surprised by one of those invisible heaters. She needed elevation. She couldn't see anything from the street.

She peeked around the corner of the building, looking left, then right.

She was about to sprint across the street when two Heaters came around a bend in the street off to her right. She backed down the alley and stepped into the niche created by the doorframe to the warehouse. Hopefully, those two weren't headed to this warehouse.

They passed by the mouth of the alley, conversing in their strange chittering language. The fact that these were the first she'd seen of the enemy gave her the impression that this city-fort was built for a much larger force than was now occupied it. She waited until she was sure that the Heaters were well out of the area and crept to the alley's opening again. She kept looking up as she went, trying to see something she could use as a perch.

She crossed the street and stayed in the shadows. She came to a courtyard of sorts. Probably a parade ground. There was a low wall that hemmed in one side of the large square. She used this for cover as she scanned the area. This must be night for the Greys. There was surprisingly little movement in the fort. She hoped that they were all in bed.

She spotted a tower in the distance. Its faint outline reflected the moon's wan light. She made for it, careful to stay out of the view of whoever may be inside the thing. She hoped it would be empty but decided it was too much to ask for. She had already enjoyed an abundance of luck.

She crept around the corner of a building and saw the tower's base. A guard sat on a crate by the door. He was small for a Heater. Not as small as the scouts she had seen through the IR, but definitely not front-line quality, she decided. The thing still stood twice as high as she did. It could rip her in half, so it was little consolation that this one was a subpar example of the species. She watched the thing from the cover of some barrels that were haphazardly stacked against the wall.

The guard was tired, she realized. It kept closing its eyes and then would stamp its feet and sway, then go still again, then its eyes would slowly close again. It seemed almost human in its behavior.

Somehow that buoyed her confidence a little, and she made up her mind. She had to find that shield battery, and if it meant that she had to go through this Heater, suited up or not, that was what she would do.

She slowly lowered her rifle and swung the length out of her way onto her back, then took out the K-Bar. It was more like a small sword in her unarmored hand, but it was light enough.

The uploads described what the lab coats had determined was the weakest spot on a heater's body, and she knew it would take a precise strike with all of her strength to accomplish the silent kill. Heater's skin was hard, almost like a leathery stone, but the weak spot was in the chest, just above where the sternum would be in a human. Right where the neck met the chest.

G20 crept forward. She was approaching from the left of the guard, and she hoped that Grey's peripheral vision was no better than human's.

She was sweating now, despite the cool air. As she came closer to the guard, doubt started to enter unbidden into her thoughts. If she missed, even by a little, she'd be dead. Nobody lives forever, she thought. She was by the door now and only feet from the Heater, who was asleep. It was asleep. She felt almost cheated.

She pushed the button on the door to the tower and crept in. She took the stairs once through and swung the rifle back in front of her, and shouldered it. As she neared what she determined must be the top of the tower, she slowed in her silent accent and peeked her rifle and head above the lip of the floor. IR was on her scope, but her HUD was set to normal vision. There was a white-hot figure in the scope and absolutely nothing in her HUD. She switched to IR in her HUD and slowly swung the rifle back around to her back, and drew her knife.

Hopefully, the anatomy of these scouts were similar enough to the Heaters that her strike would be enough. She slowly lifted herself up the last few stairs and crept forward.

She held the K-Bar in a white knuckle grip. She was only a couple of feet from the thing's back when it turned. It must have smelled her. The lake's stench was still strong in her own nose. She launched at the creature, knife held in front of her in a two-handed grip. The blade hit just to the side of the sweet spot and only went in an inch or so into the tough hide. She pulled it out and slammed it back in. This time the blade sunk in several inches, and the thing gave a cough of pain. It fell to its knees, and she used all of her leverage to force the blade all the way into the hilt. The choking cough cut off, and the IR went white hot at the wound as blood began to bubble out.

She twisted the knife free. She felt the thing, careful not to get any of its blood on her.

On its chest, about six inches below the wound, she felt a button and pressed it. A faint buzz sounded. She switched off her IR and saw the corpse. She pressed the button again, and the thing disappeared.

The thing wasn't that much bigger than she was. Maybe... She hurriedly removed the alien's armor before the blood could foul the thing. It took her twenty minutes just to figure out how to get the leggings on, but when she did, she felt them conform to her body's shape. She worked on the torso next and then the arms. The thing didn't wear a helmet, so she should be able to activate the invisibility function without sacrificing her HUD.

Once she had all the pieces on, she was about to press the button on her chest but hesitated. What if this armor only worked on Greys and had some biological failsafe that would protect the tech from being stolen. She imagined the thing electrocuting her. She shook the thought out of her mind and pressed the button.

She felt the entire suit vibrate and then go still. She looked down at her legs and arms. Nothing. It worked. Well, at least it worked on her body. Hopefully, it concealed her head. The thought of her floating head made her smile. She wiped her K-Bar clean on the dead Grey and held the knife up to look at herself in the reflection of the shiny metal, but the knife was gone. The suit must project out to conceal whatever was in the area or connected with it somehow. The Brass would be very interested in this tech.

Finally, she looked out from the tower at the fort. In the distance, a faint glow prophesied of the coming dawn. She had to hurry. She searched the scene before her for any sign of the shield batteries.

She knew from the mission upload that the batteries would have large transmission cables going in and out of whatever building they were in and so she searched for those lines.

There was a probability that the building would be in the geographical center of the fort to facilitate shunting power out to the defenses. She found what she figured must be the center of the fort and saw a large building. There was a communications tower on top of it. If she had to, she would bet that that was the building, but she needed to know for sure. She fixed the bearing in her mind and took the stairs two at a time.

CHAPTER 15

24 had a new hand. The lab coats had opted for a cybernetic one rather than organic. This meant that he was back into the ranks the next day. 12, on the other hand, needed a far more complicated surgery to replace the leg. They had almost decided to scrap him, but command said to save as many as they could since reinforcements would be long in coming. For that, at least, 39 was grateful.

They had pushed hard the first day. The most recent ping from 20 and C30 put them just outside the fort. Despite their need for stealth, 39 wanted to get into position as soon as possible. Brass had said that they hoped that after the attack, a strike against their facilities would be the last thing the Greys expected. If that were true, then the sooner they could hit back, the better.

A quadcopter gunship had dropped them in a canyon southeast of the enemy fort. The canyon was part of a drainage that came close to the fort. They had fast roped down, and the copter barely slowed. They wanted the enemy to just see a Terran patrol.

So far, any evidence that their insertion had been observed was nonexistent. They had made it to the point where they needed to climb out of the canyon and cross to the rendezvous with 20.

39 had chosen 19, 24, and 30, plus seven of the toughest veterans he could find. So far, they gave 39 the respect his rank afforded him. For some reason, 39 hadn't expected that. He had expected to have to fight for their obedience and prove himself worthy of their respect.

"C10, you're first. Your file says you have uploads and experience in climbing."

"That's right, Gunny," he said.

"You'll leave your packs here and set pitons for the rest of us."

"Aye, aye."

C10 set to his task while the rest of the squad rested.

30 came over to him and held out a canteen. He'd instructed the squad to drink from their canteens first and spare their hydro packs on their backs for the heat of battle. The rebreathers made drinking from canteens a process, but they managed without complaint. They'd need the hands-free hydration system later, 39 was sure of it.

39 took the proffered canteen and sucked down three big gulps. It was still night, but the sun had started its extremely slow rise in the west. A faint light illuminated the distant horizon. It would be almost a full Terran day before the sun was fully up.

E18 and G9 sat on the nuke crate, a large container the two men carried between them filled with three tactical nukes. The case protected the bombs and shielded the radiation from any sensors that the Greys may have that could detect the things.

"They admire you, sir," 30 said. Nodding toward the resting men.

"What makes you say that? And stop with the sir business."

"They keep asking us about you." 30 motioned to 24 and 19.

"They say they've never seen someone rise to Gunny so fast. They wanted to get the full story about why you were flogged."

"Well, they're easily entertained."

"I get the sense that they volunteered for this mission solely because of you. Sure, the forlorn hope spurred them on, but they wouldn't have been so keen had anyone else led it. They see you as invincible," 30 said.

39 turned angrily on 30.

"I'm anything but. I spent the first night on planet getting skin grafts. Then I spent a week recovering from that flogging. It still hurt 30. And every time I think about it, mother gives me a headache. You see this?" 39 pointed to his suit's chest plate. It still had the handprint from the dying Heater melted into it. He had painted it red. It was a symbol to him. It helped him realize that he could die at any time, but he'd take as many Heaters down with him as he could.

"This is how close I came to dying last time. Next time, I might not be so lucky."

"That's not what it means, Gunny. Begging your pardon, but you're wrong."

"I'm wrong about what something on my own chest means to me?" he asked in an incredulous tone.

"You're wrong about what it means to them," he said. Pointing to the group of men sitting in a half circle eating dry rations.

"Enlighten me then," 39 said, unconvinced.

"That red hand is a sign that we can be something more. We can escape this existence." He grimaced as mother, undoubtedly, attempted to correct his rebellious words.

"They're already calling themselves the Red Hands."

39 must have been wearing his thoughts on his face because 30 shrugged apologetically.

"Not very original, I know, but they asked me if they could paint their suits with similar marks."

39's knee-jerk reaction was to say no. He even opened his mouth to say so, but something stopped him. Hope...these men had it. Who was he to take that away from them, especially with the peril they were soon to find.

"Do you have paint?"

It took the Red Hand an hour to climb out of the canyon's depths. After they were all up, they hauled up the packs that were tied to the end of the line. 39 led the way through the dense foliage. They were trying to be stealthy, but by a scout sniper's standards, 39 knew they were cacophonous. Another hour of hiking brought them to the rendezvous. They were early, and neither of the snipers were there. He hoped that they had gotten the ping. If not, it would be near impossible to link up with them in this wilderness.

CHAPTER 16

Moving through the city was easier with the cloaking suit. So far, the most nerve-wracking moment was getting back past the sleeping guard at the base of the tower. She still moved with as much stealth as possible, trying to stay out of sight regardless of being visible or not. She hoped that any of the helmeted Greys she came across didn't have their IR enabled. If they did, her slinking, creeping behavior would be a red flag. Still, she gained confidence with every alien she passed.

She was getting close to the building she had seen from the tower, and she judged that she was only a block or two away when she came across a large bundle of cables. They ran next to the street she had turned down. These had to lead to the shield battery. The bundle was as thick as her waist. Even accounting for the insulation, the cables had to be massive.

She followed the cables and came to a walled compound. Inside was the tall building with the tower atop it. This had to be it. Heaters came and went through the wide gates, but all were scanned by the guards who were far from falling asleep.

Alarm klaxons started up. The sudden sound startled 20, and she spun nervously, sure she had been spotted.

She backed around the corner and made for a dark alley. They must have found the dead guard in the tower. The dark outline of a ladder stuck out from the wall of one of the buildings skirting the alley. She climbed it and slithered over the top rung onto the roof of a building. It gave a good view of the compound. She lay motionless atop the cool metal roof and looked through the scope of her rifle. Oddly the thing stayed invisible until it was close to her eye. Then she could see with the increased power that the scope provided. Heaters came and went, as did uncloaked scouts, and there was even a brain that came out of the building and talked with a tall Heater, then went back into the building.

After about twenty minutes, the alarm was turned off, and the alien's excited demeanor calmed. Then a squad of Heaters came out of the darkness on the other side of the compound, dragging a limp form. Gunny. They had captured Gunny. He was unconscious, maybe even dead. The blood dripping from his head was concerning, but the fact that they had brought him to this building gave some proof of life. Pieces of his suit hung off him, swinging like a disturbing pendulum. She told herself they wouldn't bring a corpse to what looked to be the hub of Grey command. It didn't matter, she decided. There was no hope of her, or anyone, getting him out. If he wasn't dead already, he might as well be.

She saw a message flash across her HUD. It was a priority ping from Terran command. It displayed a list of instructions and a set of coordinates to link up with a specialized assault team. The rendezvous time had already passed. She cursed and did the arithmetic. The message had been sent when she would have been on the bottom of a lake fighting some unseen monster. The message had waited for the next safe atmospheric window, which was now.

She slowly backed her way down the roof and climbed down the ladder. The sun was just cresting the distant horizon when she entered the lake from the city side. She crawled through the tunnel and hurried up to the bank furthest from the fort. She was careful to time her exit from the water so no wall guards would see, then crept to the closest tree. The rendezvous was well positioned to be out of the way of enemy traffic but was two miles away. She ran once safely blocked by the trees and didn't stop till two hundred yards from the waypoint. She spotted the spotters early and was able to skirt them without any difficulty.

She crept around a group of trees and saw the back of a giant with G39 stenciled on the back of his suit. She smiled to herself.

He was standing directly over the waypoint. She tapped him on the shoulder and hit the decloak button on her chest simultaneously. The surprised look on 39's face as he turned soon changed to dismay, then anger.

"How in the hell do you do that?"

Poor man had really tried to catch her.

"Oh, I'm sorry. Did you want me to go back out and let you see me first?"

He squinted his eyes and looked her up and down. His eyes on her made her feel... strange. Then, out of nowhere, mother pricked her brain. She cleared her mind of anything. Wait, had she really just felt that way about 39? It was a first for her. She knew guys struggled with this type of correction all the time, but she never had.

"You cheated!" he said.

He typed out a quick message on his wrist, undoubtedly informing his team that she had made the rendezvous.

He pointed at her chest.

"Where did you get that?" he asked.

"Do you like it?" she asked, giving him a twirl to show off her prize.

She hit the button and was pleased at his intake of breath.

"That is...That is perfect. How did you get it? Can you get more?"

She went over all that had happened to her from the point of leaving Fort McIntyre. He listened, spellbound, as she described her struggle with the hidden creature in the lake. 30 had come within hearing at some point and cursed when she talked of her knifing the scout in the tower. "You've got a pair on you. I'll give you that," 30 said.

She only smiled and continued her story up until Gunny's capture.

"Poor S.O.B.," 30 said. "They'll have killed him by now.

They don't keep prisoners alive, you know that, right?" 30 said. He was clearly troubled, thinking that she was expecting a rescue.

"For the love, 30. Of course, I know they don't keep prisoners," she said irritably.

He just nodded.

"30, set up a two-man watch rotation. I want everyone to get some rest before the assault. 20 and I will discuss the fort in greater detail and come up with a plan. Make sure everyone is clear on the radio silence. Only HUD coms from here on out."

30 saluted and moved out.

"Looks like you sure went up the ranks fast without me there to take your kills? What happened? You kill the whole Grey army or something?" She pointed to his insignia. "A Gunny already, huh?"

If she didn't know better, she would have said that 39 was blushing.

He just shrugged. "They were pretty hard up for someone to lead this suicide op, I guess. 20, they took out the CS."

Her stomach fell. She couldn't have heard that right.

"The Control Ship?" she asked, certain she'd heard wrong.

He nodded.

It all made sense now. The miniscule assault force sent after such a high-value target, the nonchalance of the Grey defenses.

"Wait, why didn't they wipe out McIntyre then?" she asked

"They tried," he said. "Damn near did. Those invisible Heaters or scouts, or whatever they are, took out almost all of our defensive batteries. Then their artillery started up, but they were coaxing out the Control Ship's exact location for their planetary defense missiles. After the CS dropped the hammer, the Greys lit up the CS like you wouldn't believe. You mean you didn't see any of that?"

"I was in a hole," she said simply. "How many men do you have for this assault?" she asked, scared of the answer. She already knew, based on the few she had seen, it wasn't enough.

"Ten. Twelve counting us," he said.

She laughed. It wasn't funny. Not really. But inside, something far darker threatened to explode out of her mouth, and so she laughed instead. 39 looked at her with confusion, and she laughed harder.

"You've got to be joking," she managed to get out between spells. "It's a city. A whole Grey city, and we're going to assault it with ten Marines?"

"Twelve," he countered.

She just looked at him, all laughter gone.

"We're gonna die," she said.

He didn't deny the statement. He looked down as if he couldn't look at her.

"What made you decide to lead this merry band? Don't tell me it was a misguided sense of pride in your new rank. They just waved a new patch in front of you, and you Aye Aye'd right out of there, didn't you?" The statement hurt. She knew it was the wrong thing to say before mother stabbed her stinging correction.

She sucked in a breath at mother's rebuke.

"A forlorn hope," he said. That was all it took.

20 felt her eyebrows raise and her heart catch.

"No. Really? Anyone?" she asked.

He nodded, not needing a more verbose question to know that she wanted...needed, to know if she qualified for the advancement.

"Anyone to survive," he said.

"Well. That would do it," she said. "It doesn't matter anyway. We're gonna die regardless."

"Well, with that attitude, I don't know how we could survive," he quipped.

CHAPTER 17

From a historical context, the pace at which they had come up with and implemented the first stages of a plan was break-neck, but it was in line with what 39 had come to expect from this life. It had been one hundred and eight days since he was cut from the amniotic sac and had mother plugged into his brain. Since that day, he had been rushed through training, had thousands of other people's experiences crammed into his mind, and been nearly killed three or four times. Action seemed as natural as breathing.

They sent off a ping containing their basic plan of attack and the coordinates for the suspected shield battery. Hopefully, the brass would be ready to take advantage of any break in the Grey's shields when and if they occurred.

The red hands, guided by G20, moved out while the shadows were still very long and dark. 20 kept watch when they were at the edge of the forest closest to the lake and signaled when a member of the red hand was clear to enter the lake. Once all were safely below its muddy surface, 20 followed.

Under the surface of the lake, they stayed close to each other and made for the drainage tunnel in the wall. Once they arrived, everyone stripped off their suits and half of the team squeezed through the tunnel. 39 was first since he was the biggest, and they needed to know if their plan needed to be revised because of his size, but he just managed to shove through. He had to remove his rebreather and push it in front of him, but he made it.

Once on the other side, he pulled his bundle of tech

through. He had tethered it to his leg and now pulled while 30 pushed. Finally, after many mumbled curses, they got the heavy's equipment through.

30 came next. He had little difficulty, and his smaller suit followed without a problem. E18 and G9 were both artillery units. Their suits were heavies as well but shaped differently. They were squat, short even, but wide. They had big howitzer cannons on their backs that would be central to their plans. All exo-suits were designed to be capable of being field-stripped, but doing it on the bottom of a murky lake was challenging. They had to remove the Howitzers and feed them through the tunnel separately. It took half an hour to feed all of the artillery pieces and the nuke crate through, but once all of the heavies were over, the following eight came smoothly.

20 was the last one through. She had insisted on bringing her railgun despite her not being able to carry it, and so 39 pulled the gun through and slung it on his shoulder. The thing felt light to him, but he knew it would be all she could do to carry it without her Terran exo-suit.

So far, so good. The team was in the fort. Now all they needed to do was destroy one building. The problem would come on the exfil. He knew they wouldn't have the time to do what they just did getting in. The best plan he had was to just blast a hole in the wall and hope they could fight their way to safety. Not much of a plan, but he had little to work with, and the team seemed to understand their lot. It spoke to the effectiveness of the forlorn hope. They all wanted to be free so badly that they would risk almost certain death to attain it.

To his knowledge, no one in modern times had won his freedom from a forlorn hope. It didn't change the fact that they all had, to a small degree, expected to be the first. 39 motioned for C10 to set up the scrambler and jammer. The devices would, hopefully, confuse their comms signals so that they could use them without becoming an instant target for the enemy. He had gotten assurances that the equipment would work below the surface of the lake before moving forward with this plan.

Once C10 gave him the thumbs up, 39 motioned for 20 to move out. She slowly walked forward. She hit the cloaking button before breaking the surface of the water, and 39 lost track of her progress soon after. That tech was amazing.

"All clear," came 20's voice over his coms.

The team moved forward, covering each other as they left the lake. They had to move fast. When 20 used the radio, she would have informed the Greys of their presence if not their location. The scrambler would bounce the message all over the place within a twenty-mile radius, and the jammer would do its best to block the actual origin of the message, but the Greys would be on the lookout.

39, C10 and G30 moved out with 20 who had uncloaked so she could lead them to her perch.

"Watchdog, you're clear to set up. Thumper, get into position," 39 said into his mic.

Watchdog consisted of A21 and D4, who carried an impressive array of sentry guns that they would set up to defend the stationary and vulnerable artillery units, or Thumper.

"Understood," came their response.

They were to move to a location 20 had indicated would be the best defensible location they could get to and set up without having to take on an army to do it. It was only a couple of blocks from the lakeshore, and the artillery should start in a matter of minutes.

39 held the railgun, deciding that he might as well use the thing if the situation demanded it while he carried it. Besides, he'd always wanted to shoot the thing. 20 had her more reasonably sized fifty held at the ready as she ghosted on silent feet around a corner.

39 followed.

He was surprised and elated that they hadn't seen any Heaters yet, and remembering there were other predators out there, he switched his view to IR and back to normal, just to be sure. They had gone several blocks before they ran into the first Grey patrol. 20 had spotted them before she had rounded a corner and ducked back behind the wall before they could see her.

"Five tangos." Was all she said before cloaking.

39 swore under his breath and backed down the narrow street they were on, motioning C10 and G30 back with his free hand. The sun was up now, but the shadows were long, and 39 hoped the darkened street would obscure their forms. He switched to IR and looked for 20. She had crossed the street and crouched, holding her knife. What was she going to do, kill all five Heaters with a knife?

The railgun was their best bet. It was quiet. Far quieter than 20's fifty or his M42.

39 heard a clicking noise and recognized it for the eerie alien speech of the Greys. They were close now. 39 brought the rifle to his eye and saw 20 bend over and pick something up. He couldn't see what it was with the IR. She threw it down her own alley.

The clatter of whatever it was seemed to excite the Heaters, who moved to her side without more than a cursory glance down his street. They passed her, following the noise. They had all soon entered the alley with their backs to 39. He was about to pull the trigger, deciding he couldn't ask for a better target, when 20 moved back into the main street and motioned for them to follow.

That was the smarter play, 39 realized. He slowly crept out of the shadows and rounded the corner, followed closely by C10. They hurried down the street, continuing as they had before. He was pleased to see that G30 was keeping a wary eye to their rear for the reappearance of the Heater patrol.

They approached the building 20 had previously chosen from the south and had to slide around the east side to find the doorway. Security was non-existent. There was only one button on the keypad by the door, and it slid open soundlessly when 20 pressed it. The inside was a warehouse full of boxes, as 20 had described it, but there were two more levels above the warehouse, making this building the tallest between Thumper's location and the Shield batteries. Perfect for what 20 intended.

"Thumper is ready to start the rain dance," G19 called over the radio.

"Wait one, overwatch getting into position," 39 responded.

39 took the metal stairs three at a time, and at the landing, he sent C10 and 30 off to clear the level. Ideally, he would go with the Marines to be able to cover each other better, but he was extremely low on personnel and time.

39 continued up to the top floor and swept through the empty rooms, making sure that 20 would be free to practice her art in relative safety.

He dragged a box over to the corner window that 20 indicated and placed the railgun down atop it.

"You sure you can manage it without your suit?" he asked.

"Yeah, I'm sure. We practice this in basic. I just would have sweat a little carrying it here. Thanks for that."

"No problem. C10 will stay at the top of the stairs to guard your back. Let him know if you need him."

"Will do. You'd better get going," she said, and winked at him.

Somehow that wink sent an unexpected warmth through him. His nervousness eased slightly.

"I'll be back to check on your work later." He smiled at her, and turned to the door.

"Sir," she said. He turned back to her.

"Yeah?"

"Take care of yourself...Don't be heroic."

"At this point, I don't think any of us can make that choice."

CHAPTER 18

It had been six minutes and forty-three seconds since the Red Hand walked out of the muck like their ancestors supposedly had millions of years ago, dripping and smelling of swamp scum. Thumper began its barrage.

39 heard the thunder of the twin Howitzers slamming their high-explosive rounds into the air. These first rounds were vitally important in determining the efficacy of any interior defenses the fort had. His hopes rose as he heard the rounds pass overhead without any intercepting fire from the Greys. Then, just as 39 anticipated the impact into the massive building, the rounds exploded.

A turret had appeared atop the building and fired some kind of laser at the projectiles just before the rounds could spend their payload effectively.

39 swore. The development wasn't surprising, but it was disappointing.

"Thumper, this is Rover. Cease your fire and reposition to the Alamo."

The Alamo was the location where A21 and D4 had set up with their sentry guns. It would be the team's defensive stronghold, or as much a one they could set up with the limited resources that they had. It would also be the team's fallback location, provided Overwatch and Rover survived that long. They had planned on the first salvo being intercepted, and so they launched it away from their ultimate base of operations to try and throw off the Grey's inevitable counter-attack.

Thumper should, even now, be running as fast as their suits could take them toward the Alamo. 39 couldn't see the artillery team from where he was, but as he feared, a missile streaked toward where Thumper had launched from. The Grey's response was commendable, but hopefully not fast enough.

"Thumper, this is Rover. Are you clear?"

"That's affirmative, Rover. We're clear," came G19's breathless response.

G19 wasn't an artillery unit, but he had been tasked with protecting Thumper as it doled out its heavy ordinance.

"Overwatch, can you take out that roof turret?"

20's voice was calm. "If it's not armored, I should be able to punch a few holes in it," she said.

"Do it," he said.

39 turned to 30 and motioned for him to move out.

He and 30 made up "Rover" their job was to try to sow chaos around the fort to try to relieve the pressure from Thumper and Watchdog. Their hit-and-run tactics would also, hopefully, keep the enemy from zeroing in on 20's location as she picked off Greys.

39 hit the twenty-second button on the explosive he had just set on a group of tanks that looked like they held some kind of fuel. He hoped this wouldn't destroy the whole base and his team with it.

39 and 30 ran from the scene just as a group of Heaters exited a building by the tanks. They chittered excitedly and started after the pair of Terrans. 39 pushed 30 down behind a low wall and braced as the explosion ripped over them. A secondary explosion rocked the ground, and 39 thought they were gonners. Stones and metal clanked off of his suit as it rained down.

Finally, the explosions subsided, and 39 and 30 began unburying themselves. Their helmets had automatic ear protection that saved their eardrums from almost certain rupture.

30 sat among the debris scattered around them.

"Maybe.... Maybe you should let me set the next one," he

said.

39 laughed. He couldn't help it. Something about the situation seemed comical. Maybe it was just the relief of being alive after a brush with death. 30 joined in. He slapped 30 on the back and helped the smaller man to his feet.

A Crater was all that was left of the storage tanks. There was no sign of the Heaters.

39 whistled at the devastation. "Alright, let's get going before all hell breaks loose," he said.

They made for the network of alleys that would mask their movements and keep them off of the main thoroughfares that would surely be used by the Grey's troops as they mustered to the defenses. Their next target was unknown to them as they ran through the narrow alleyways. Speed took priority over caution. The whole plan hinged on them being able to confuse the Grey's response.

30 was leading the way and took a right suddenly. 39 followed and slid to a stop, barely keeping from colliding with 30, who had stopped short. A small patrol of three Heaters stood, surprised, thirty feet away.

30 Swung his 8 gauge shotgun around and slammed a cold slug into the lead Heater. A large hole appeared in the thing's chest, blue with heat. Steam rose from the wound then the blue darkened as the cold of the liquid nitrogen was released. The Heater screamed a blood-chilling screech and clawed at his chest as if trying to rip the round from his chest.

The other two Heaters came forward in a rush. 30's second round caught the Heater on the right in the shoulder, but it closed the distance in two strides.

"Shields!" 39 called, engaging his own.

He then fired a grenade into the Heater on the left. The explosion broke huge chunks off the Heater, and the shock knocked the two wounded Heaters to the ground. 39 looked around his shield, surveying his work. None of the Heaters looked like they were going to get up.

39 turned to see 30 picking himself up off the ground.

"Would you stop blowing me up?"

"Sorry, 30. I'll try to be more considerate." 39 switched to his team channel. "Overwatch, how is that turret coming?"

"Just finishing up, Rover. Thumper should be good to resume bombardment."

"Thumper, this is Rover. Are you at the Alamo?"

"Affirmative, Rover. Ready to recommence."

"Give them hell Thumper."

39 and 30 started their pell-mell course through the roofless corridors until they came to a tall building with a ladder up one side. 39 stopped and called 30 back as he started climbing. "We need to take a quick look. We might as well try to make our next target count."

As 39 climbed, he heard the Howitzers start up again. A few seconds later, the distant thunder of the high-explosive rounds striking home made him smile as he climbed. Atop the building, 39 oriented himself and scanned the City for the shield battery building. Smoke rose from the building, but what little damage he could see was superficial.

"Lay it on, Thumper. Your aim is true," he said into his mic.

Another salvo sounded from the direction of the Alamo. 39 turned his attention to the surrounding buildings, searching for a distracting target that could draw off some of the forces that were undoubtedly closing on Thumper and Watchdog's position. He had to buy them as much time as he could.

The artillery rounds slammed into the shield battery, but 39 made himself focus on his current mission. Just as He was about to decide on a squat, windowless building off to their right, a missile launched from a gap in some buildings to his left. It was only a block and a half away from them, but he couldn't see the source of the missile.

The missile streaked through the air toward the Alamo, and 39 prayed that Watchdog's sentry guns would be able to intercept it.

39 watched it approach Thumper with apprehension. Then it exploded in the air, showering the buildings below with debris. Watchdog's sentry laser air defense was doing its work. Good. 39 Turned and started back down the ladder that 30 had just scaled.

"What the hell? I just got up here."

"We've got a target," 39 said. He put his hands and legs to the outside of the ladder and slid down it, allowing the force of the landing to be absorbed by his suit.

He led the way toward the origin of the missile's truncated flight. He turned a corner, and six Heaters stood in the street, on guard. He didn't even hesitate, knowing that to do so would only negate the one advantage he had, surprise. He kept running.

Grenade after grenade slammed into the unsuspecting Greys. After the first shot, all he could see of his foe were the occasional flash of blue among the billowing smoke and flashing explosions. He shot at any glimpse of movement within the cloud until he was sure that no Heater could be left living.

He had kept running throughout the attack and barreled through the wall of smoke, unsure what he would find on the other side. He felt heat all around him, intense heat. His boots slipped in the alien gore, but he kept his feet. He broke through the smoke and saw more Heaters. They had their guns up and fired as he came through the smoke. One shot went high, and two more went wide to his right. The Greys were protecting a strange looking device in the center of a courtyard. It was huge, as big as some of the smaller buildings they'd passed. The tips of missiles poked out of one side, hundreds of the things. Row upon row of deadly warheads sat menacingly in the massive turret.

If this thing fired multiple missiles at his team, there would be no way for Watchdog to hold them all off. The emotion once felt not long ago flooded him. Looking up into the night sky as a massive barrage of missiles, likely fired from missile banks like this one, streaked toward their lifeline, their hope.

39 juked to the left and fired a grenade. He was still moving. Not daring to stop. A distant part of his consciousness registered 30 bellowing a war cry behind him. 39 did the same.

As he ran, he pulled a charge from its compartment on his hip, hit the ten-second button and hurled it at the missile bank with his left hand. His right kept up a constant stream of grenades. 39 let another one go and turned to 30.

"Go!" he yelled, then pushed 30 to spur him on.

30 turned and sprinted for the relative safety of the alley they'd just come down. 39's wrist computer beeped its timer in his ear as they ran. When two seconds were left, he pushed 30 down and covered the smaller man with his body as the charge exploded. The initial blast sent a shockwave over them.

39 twisted to look behind them and saw huge portions of the buildings around the courtyard were gone. Fires burned on the turret. All of the Heaters in the courtyard were down.

"We have to move," 39 said. He got up and jerked 30 to his feet. "Move it, Marine."

They ran back through the smoke and didn't stop running until they'd gone three blocks. The sound of explosions tailed them the whole way. When finally, they stopped, 39 saw that 30 was favoring his left arm.

"You're wounded," 39 said.

"Very observant of you, sir," 30 said, through gritted teeth.

39 ignored the insubordinate jibe.

"What got you?" he said, as he took 30's arm and looked it over.

"One of those blue-blooded demons. They're really not very good with those rifles of theirs. They were just a spray'n and pray'n at you and managed to wing me."

"Well, thank the almighty for that," 39 smiled.

"You up for another campaign of destruction?"

"You bet."

"Let me check in first. Overwatch, how's the shield battery holding up?"

Nothing.

"Overwatch, this is Rover. Do you read me?"

Nothing.

"Thumper, this is Rover. What's your status?"

Silence. A silence so deep that it hurt. No crack of distant thunderous artillery. No distant explosions of Howitzer rounds crashing home. He wasn't sure when the guns had gone silent. Sometime during the attack on the missile turret, he thought.

"Watchdog. Do you read me?"

Despair gripped 39 as the reality of their situation settled into the holes in his heart.

CHAPTER 19

"We're pulling out, and that's the last time I'll say it. I know you don't like the idea, George, but you don't have to like it." Colonel Santos turned to face Major Grant, and his expression softened slightly.

"Do you really think that they had a snowball's chance in hell of pulling it off? We needed the diversion, George." Grant didn't like the Colonel's condescending tone.

"I understand the tactics, sir, but I still can't believe you left me out of it."

"George. Your poker face is...nonexistent. Even a newborn like G39 would have seen through any deception on your part." The Colonel placed a hand on Major Grant's shoulder. "Just get your gear and load up, we've got to use what time they buy us, or it is all in vain. Their sacrifice would be for nothing."

Grant knew that Santos didn't give a damn about the Grunts he'd sent to certain death any more than the thousands of Grunts he planned on marooning on the planet's surface, leaderless and subject to the whims of the vengeful Greys.

Grant understood the reasons. Without the control ship's massive barracks bays, the Marines would not all fit among the remaining ships of the Terran fleet. Logically, it made sense. They were Grunts, after all. Some of them weren't two months old. Grunts deemed unworthy of expensive training and uploads that had been sent to the planet to soak up enemy fire or perform menial labor of the sort the robots couldn't do well. Logic told him that these Grunts were, somehow, less than he. That, by being created in a lab, they were subhuman. His heart told him differently. He told himself that hard choices needed to be made in war and that there wasn't an alternative. The enemy would destroy them if they stayed, and it would be better if all of the Trueborn escaped than if all died together.

His concern must have shown on his face because Santos sighed.

"You allow yourself to get too attached to them. They are a tool, and just like any tool of worth, it is regrettable that we have to leave them, but to think of them as more than that is... dangerous."

Grant had heard this speech before. His father had said much the same thing to him many years ago. Terran society could not have made the leaps that it had without the genome harvesting project. After the Greys first attacked Earth, the human race knew the peril they were in and united in a way that had never been seen before. In a way, the Greys had given mankind a gift that would never have been possible before the invasion.

Earth's greatest minds dissected the Grey's technology, reverse-engineering it to develop the faster-than-light technology that expanded Human's reach and opened up the mining of asteroids, which in turn allowed the development of stronger alloys. The abundance of raw materials and the huge improvements in technology were key in the Terran offensive, but personnel were needed. Drone and robot tech was great for the automation of mining an asteroid belt, but nothing could match a human for instinctive, intuitive fighting spirit.

When Major Grant was still in the academy, he had stepped on quite a few toes. He had argued that the lab-born genetically engineered units were human and needed to be treated as such. The sentiment was unacceptable to command, and if his father hadn't stepped in, Grant would never have gotten any command at all.

Units were what they were, not human. It was a hard thing for him to remember. When looking into the face of a dying grunt, seeing the terror there, it was impossible to see anything but a human that feared the eternal blackness of death. A human that cared about life. A person that wanted to live.

He knew he was strange. Such emotional connections with mere grunts were unheard of, especially in the social pools his family swam in. The Empire was built on the backs of the genetically engineered slaves. That was what they were...slaves. The poor wretches were worse than slaves. The slaves of the distant past could, at least, think their own thoughts.

Major Grant was saved from having to respond by a comms officer.

"Sir, the fleet has cycled up their FTL drives."

"What?!" Colonel Santos growled. He turned to the Lieutenant with such anger in his eyes that the comms officer took a step back. The young man nervously looked at his wrist computer.

"They say there are multiple enemy contacts approaching the fleet, and there is no time to receive the transports." The Lieutenant looked like he was going to be sick and glanced back up at Santos before continuing.

"They say...Sorry."

"Sorry? They say sorry?" Santos' voice was dangerous.

A crash like thunder rumbled, and the men who recognized the sound looked up.

The Terran fleet, distant specks of reflected light against the backdrop of an early morning sky, began to disappear. One by one, amidst fresh rounds of thunder, the fleet fled, but not fast enough.

There were a handful of Terran ships left when the first of the Grey's ships appeared. A brief exchange of fire and a flash of light testified that at least one Terran ship was destroyed before it could escape. More and more ships appeared until the sky sparkled with the enemy craft.

Santos cursed the sky, pumping his fist in the air. The outburst was regrettable. Major Grant looked at the faces of the men around him. They looked at their leader with fear written plainly in their eyes.

"Colonel...sir, we need to get the defenses fully operational before they ready their missiles." Colonel Santos seemed to collect himself a little and turned to him. Major Grant could see tears in the man's eyes.

"Major. Take command here. I will be in my quarters." He turned on his heels and walked away.

"But, sir," Grant protested, but the Colonel kept walking.

Major Grant was the highest-ranking officer left on the planet's surface other than the Colonel. The other company commanders and most of the staff officers were transported to the fleet before it fled.

The men's despairing eyes were on him now.

He cleared his throat.

"We've got work to do."

CHAPTER 20

G20 had watched as the first of Thumper's salvos crashed into the building. The sturdy building seemed to absorb the force of the explosion, and when the dust cleared, only superficial damage could be seen. She saw a mass of grey warriors marching down the wide street toward the Alamo. The Greys were about half a mile distant, and she made minor calibrations to her HUD's targeting before going to work.

Her first shot knocked two Heaters out of the fight. It was a target-rich environment, and she couldn't miss as she laid into the column of troops.

It wasn't long before the Heaters had stalled, and the priority of attacking the Alamo gave way to their need to find cover. It was believed that enemy triangulation equipment couldn't track the rounds from a railgun, but 20's training told her that she should reposition before engaging another enemy unit in another direction.

"G10, can you come pick up this beast for me? We've got to reposition."

Nothing. No response. She looked at her wrist computer and swore when she remembered that she was cloaked and couldn't see her own arm.

If 10 was out of the game and she hadn't heard anything, then it had to have been...She switched to IR and moved to the window. No one was in the room with her yet, but it would only be a matter of seconds. She stepped out of the window onto the narrow ledge and shuffled down it so that she was out of view of anyone in the room. She waited, hardly daring to breathe.

The sound of a fire-fight erupted from the direction of the Alamo, but she couldn't see it from where she was. She strained her ears to hear anything over the concussive booms and the higher-pitched whine of ricochets as the unseen fight intensified. She thought she heard something inside the room she'd just vacated, but she couldn't be sure. Was she just being paranoid?

It was possible that the Greys had found some way to jam their comms, and that's why she had been unable to reach G10, but something, some instinct, told her to hold fast. She stood sixty feet in the air, perched precariously on the narrow ledge.

If she had had her Terran scout suit, she wouldn't have worried about the drop. The tech would have been able to handle the drop...probably. She looked over her shoulder at the street far below. This Grey suit, however, she wasn't sure about. She doubted the suit had the kind of built-in exoskeleton that the Terrans depended on. Greys were far stronger than humans, and so they didn't develop the kind of tech that Terrans needed to be in the fight. This suit would probably crumple upon impact, along with her bones.

Suddenly she didn't feel strong or independent. She didn't feel like the tough Marine that had become the centerpiece of her identity. She felt weak, scared, and alone. A jolt of reality hit her when she realized that she felt that way because she was, indeed, all of them.

No. She could not entertain those self-defeating thoughts. She was a Terran Marine, a force recon scout sniper. She brought her focus back to her environment, precarious as it was. She was alive, and that counted for something.

20 was worried that if there were Greys in the room, they would be searching for her in both regular and IR vision. By now, they had to know that one of their suits was missing. If they stuck their head out the window, she would be lit up like a Christmas tree.

What was a Christmas tree? She didn't know. The saying

was still a common enough phrase to be worthy of admittance into the English language upload. All she knew was that it was bright. It was a strange feeling, knowing something, and yet, not at the same time.

She shuffled back from the window as quietly as possible. A series of clicking emanated from the open window. She froze.

That was it then. 10 was dead. 10 was dead, and she was stuck on a ledge sixty feet up. 39 came over her com channel asking for a sit-rep. She remained silent, afraid that the Greys would hear her response.

The corner of the building was a few feet to her left, and she shuffled around it with all the stealth she could manage. On this side the edge of the roof was lower, and she reached up and gripped its lip.

20 was in peak physical condition. Her body was literally the ideal human specimen, but with the added weight of the fifty caliber rifle hanging on her back and the Grey suit, she struggled to lift herself over the edge. When, finally, she slid over the ledge onto the roof of the building, she lay for several minutes, calming her breathing.

She looked out over the city in the direction of the enemy column she had laid into with her railgun. The column had moved on, but their dead still littered the street. As she watched, a vehicle with a flatbed approached. It hovered above the surface of the street but kicked up little dust as it moved. It came to a stop at the first corpse, and two heaters jumped off of the back and began loading their fallen comrades onto it.

She brought her attention back to the Greys below her. They spoke freely now, their strange noises more discernible from the distant firefight. They must be looking over the railgun, examining it. After finding the gun, they would surely widen the search for the sniper who wielded it. It would only be a matter of time before they found her.

She pulled a frag grenade off her belt and crawled over and lay just above the window that she had climbed out of earlier.

The clicking was louder now. She pressed her thumb down on the switch three times for maximum yield and rolled to the edge of the roof, and swung her arm around. She couldn't see where the grenade landed. She just hoped that it had made it into the window. She rolled back from the edge and curled into the fetal position.

She wasn't sure if the maximum yield was too much or not. It was quite possible that the explosion would engulf the entire roof of the building. She wasn't spoiled for choices, though, and covered her head with her arms.

She felt the explosion before she heard it. It was like a giant hammer hit her, then the entire roof vibrated with the force of it. The sound came in a rush, and smoke and dust burst out of the window.

She decided that movement was her only defense now, and she rolled to the edge of the roof once more and gripped the edge, then swung through the window feet first. The heat was intense. Blue Heater or scout blood covered much of the interior of the room, and smoke crawled along the ceiling of the room, searching for an exit. She pulled a charge from her belt and dropped it on the ground as she ran. She went to the door and pulled her fifty around, ready for action.

Heaters charged up the stairs. 20 ran down the catwalk to the back of the warehouse, praying that the Greys didn't have their IR enabled. At the end of the elevated walkway, a metal column stood. The column not only supported the walkway but the roof as well. 20 swung the fifty back to her back and gripped the smooth metal in both hands, and slid down it to the next level.

She reached down and gripped the pole again and slid down it to the floor of the warehouse. She could see the bright heat signatures of the heaters as they filed into the room she had been in moments before. 20 smiled as she decloaked and looked at her wrist computer. The controls for the charge she had dropped flashed on the screen, pulsing. With each flash of green light, 20 felt the urge to detonate the charge grow, but she waited.

She watched as the last of the Heaters disappeared into the room.

She pressed the button and cloaked, then sprinted toward the rear door.

The explosion seemed massive. The building groaned from the force of it, and pieces of the catwalk and support beams crashed down around 20 as she ran.

Sudden heat radiated from above, and she glanced up. Heater blood from more than a dozen aliens was too much for the weakened ceiling. Blue lava-hot blood melted its way through the beams and dripped into the warehouse.

20 cursed as some splashed onto her shoulder. She dodged a metal beam that swung down from the roof and jumped out of the door. The feeling of freedom that rushed over her as she escaped the oppressive danger and heat of the crumbling warehouse was intense, and she had to force herself to keep moving and not luxuriate in the feeling.

She didn't look back as the sounds of the disintegrating building grew louder. Suddenly, in a crescendo of violence, the building fell in on itself and sent a torrent of dust over and around 20's fleeing form.

She had to stop and walk carefully while she was blinded. Her rebreather wouldn't last long in this cloud. The filters would soon clog, and she would suffocate. She pushed on down the alley as fast as she could, and soon the dust thinned, and she could see enough to navigate down a different alley that she hoped would take her to the Alamo and her comrades. She hoped that the other pieces of this plan were being implemented better than hers had been.

CHAPTER 21

39 looked at the screen on his wrist and sighed in relief. Contacts blinked on the area map indicating the active vital signs of at least some of his team. Other markers had gone dark, though, many others. It looked like the Alamo hadn't lasted as long as he'd hoped, and the few remaining team members from Thumper and Watchdog were moving in the direction of the giant main building. He envisioned them captive, being dragged or carried there much how 20 had described the Gunny's conveyance to incarceration.

20, where was she? An explosion, muted by distance, echoed from the direction of 20's perch. He watched the screen and saw her signal move suddenly. Moments later, he heard a larger explosion. His throat clenched in anticipation. He sighed again as he saw the blip continue to move from the probable source of the rumbles that continued to echo off of the surrounding buildings.

39 tapped 30's hip and moved off. 30 would move with him, covering their rear. He navigated the alien city, afraid to take the larger streets, and felt an eerie sense of impending doom. There was nothing to really blame the feeling on. It just was. Maybe the lack of anything was what was wrong. This city was far too large for its inhabitants.

The empty streets and buildings testified to a population far beyond what the recent Terran aggression could account for. There was no way that the Terrans had killed so many Heaters.

39 grew more and more uneasy as they moved. He felt like eyes watched his every move. He looked at the screen again and

judged where 20 would be, and took a left down a particularly narrow alley.

He tried sending a ping to 20, but there was no response. He supposed that if she was on the move, she'd be cloaked and not looking at her screen. He hoped that was the case and not that their comms were being jammed because that would mean that the only escape route he knew of had been cut off.

He looked at his wrist and stopped.

He signaled for 30 to hold up, and he took a knee behind a large container that he hoped didn't hold something particularly deadly. 30 took a knee behind him, still watching his six.

He waited for a count of twenty before whispering. "20."

A cloud of dust betrayed her presence before her body decloaked. She looked stunned and frightened. Well, if 20 could be frightened, he reasoned this was it. She held the fifty caliber sniper rifle at the ready but swung it around to her back when 39 stood up. The relief on her face as she recognized him swelled his heart. Surprisingly, she stepped forward and gripped him in a bear hug.

In his full-sized heavy suit, he was gigantic, especially when compared to her when she wore only the Grey's cloaking suit. Her hug was around his waist, but he patted her back as delicately as he could with the heavy suit.

"You're okay," he said.

She nodded and pulled free of the hug. She seemed suddenly self-conscious and attempted to cover her embarrassment with questions.

"Are you headed to the Alamo? I haven't heard anything from Thumper for a while. Are they still active?"

"Some." He looked down, unable to look into her eyes for some reason. It was like he feared that she would blame him for the deaths. He knew it was a suicidal mission to begin with and that he shouldn't be ashamed, at least not as ashamed as he felt.

"It looks like E-18 and A-21 were taken. The rest are SD." SD stood for Signal Dead, and 20 nodded solemnly at the news.

"What now, sir?" she asked.

That was the question that had been plaguing 39 since he deduced that the Alamo had been overrun. The plan had been to lay everything they had into protecting E18 and G9 while they rained fire down on the shield battery, but both Overwatch and Rover hadn't been enough to dissuade or confuse the enemy, and Watchdog obviously didn't last long against the mass of Heaters the Greys must have sent at the Alamo.

He contemplated retreat, and as he did, mother throbbed her sadistic disapproval. They must have set the mission parameters to S.O.D., succeed or die. True S.O.D. missions were rare since there were usually stipulations put into mother that allowed for a tactical retreat in the face of overwhelming odds. Mother either saw this as a redeemable mission, or it was set to S.O.D. Since 39 saw no way to redeem this near impossible mission, it had to be a succeed or die.

He cursed Colonel Santos and blacked out momentarily as an intense wave of nausea-inducing pain rooted itself in the base of his skull. He braced himself against the wall of the alley. He grabbed at his rebreather and fought it free of his face, then bent over and vomited on the tan stone ground.

"You alright, sir?" 30 asked.

"It's an S.O.D.," he managed between heaves.

30 cursed and was soon doubled over as well. 20 either managed the pain better than the two men, or she managed her thoughts better. She remained upright but couldn't hide the grimace on her face.

39 got a handle on his rebellious thoughts and stomach and stood, replacing the rebreather before his lungs began to burn from the alien gasses of this place.

30 shook his head as if he'd been hit.

"We need to get off the street," 39 said. He led the way around the corner until they came to a door with a window in it. He looked inside. The interior had a few pieces of dusty furniture but little else. He pressed the single button on the wall by the door, and it slid open. He scanned the interior for any security systems that he'd triggered with his entry, but his wrist comp showed that there were no active electronics in the room. He looked along the walls for any inactive cameras but didn't see anything obvious.

"This will do until we can decide how to proceed."

"With all due respect, sir, that's your job," 30 said.

39's reaction was, at first, defensive, but when he looked at his friend, he realized that the comment was not intended to be insubordinate in the least. The proof was the lack of any correction from mother. He was simply reminding his leader of his place over him. 39 suddenly made another revelation. He had thought of 30 as a friend, and as he thought about it, he decided that the sentiment was true.

This was his first friend. For some reason, that thrilled him. It was like a step in his development as a person had taken place, and he wasn't even sure at what point it had happened. It seemed childish to feel this way about making a friend, but then again, he was still considered a newborn. He slapped 30 on the back.

"Let's find a dark, defensible corner to hole up for a while. With luck, they'll think we moved on, then we can make a move."

The other man nodded.

They went down a dark corridor and turned into an empty room. 30 took up a guard position at the doorway without being asked, and 39 and 20 sat down in the corner, and 39 pulled a bundle of rations out of his pack. They ate in silence, pulling the rebreather down with each bite.

39 looked at 20 as she ate. She tore each bite free of the ration bar with her fingers, then popped them in her mouth, one at a time. 39 felt like an animal by comparison. He was starving and had to force himself to eat slowly and not take the huge bites that he wanted to. 39 tried to time his glances at her so he could see her face as she pulled the mask away with each bite. Mother throbbed her disapproval of his appraisal of his team member,

but he didn't care. The pain only seemed to make the furtive glances all the sweeter. It thrilled him in a wholly different way than he had felt moments ago. Forbidden though it was, he felt himself gain feelings for this beauty.

He was content to just sit and be next to her. After all, what would they have talked about? Their lives were somewhat parallel. Born at the same time. Pushed through training at the same rate, and although that training had been different, they had had enough contact, being toon mates, that little would have been learned from each other about that.

He stole a glance at her again, but this time 20 was already looking at him. He quickly looked away. He felt like a fool and looked at her again to see if she was still watching him. She was, with a smile on her face. He returned the smile, sheepishly.

His head was throbbing now, and he fought to clear it. He looked away and continued eating. His feelings of attraction for 20 were slowly replaced by anger for the Terran high command, for the engineer that had designed the first mother, and for Colonel Santos for sending them, as pawns, on an impossible mission, using the freedom that instinct told him should have been his since birth, as a dangled prize above their upturned faces. A dizzying array of punishment emanated from the bitch inside his skull, and he quickly changed the target of his ire to the enemy. The pain decreased, but he was no longer hungry.

"We need to get the nuke crate," he said, once the room stopped spinning.

One of the three nukes would have been captured with Thumper. The plan had been to launch the tactical nuke at the building once the first few salvos had been verified as on target, but clearly, Thumper had not had a chance. The remaining two nukes were, hopefully, still in the crate at the bottom of the lake inside the city fort's walls.

"How will we launch it? Thumper's been killed or captured," 20 said.

"That's the part you're not going to like."

CHAPTER 22

Grant had expended valuable surveillance drones on 39's team. Drones that he was sure to be reprimanded for if Santos ever found out, but he needed to know how the team was faring. The Greys had been able to pick out the drones and shoot them down periodically despite their tiny footprint. They were no bigger than a large insect, and after being cut off from their support fleet, their supply on all things was dwindling, so the loss of the tiny drones hurt. Still, Grant had enough footage to piece together the team's progress to this point.

He had rewound the vids and played them forward several times, watching as the city rocked with sporadic explosions, a quick burst of action and then nothing. He was surprised by how much damage the tiny team of Marines inflicted in such a short time, but they had been quieted quickly. As he cycled through the vids, he tried to pick out the Terrans to identify casualties and units that were still active.

He thought he had a handle on who remained within the city. He wondered why the three hadn't tried to retreat after the rest of the team was wiped out; maybe the lure of freedom from the control device was just too big of an incentive. He felt pity, once again, for the trapped team.

He wondered, not for the first time, whether Santos would make good on his promise to the team if, by some miracle, anyone survived. Given that the entire assault on the shield batteries was merely a diversion, a smoke cloud, that the Colonel had hoped to escape under, he doubted it.

Grant returned the feed to real-time and looked for any sign of his surviving Marines. They were his. His responsibility not just because they were members of his company but because guilt tied him to them more firmly than any duty of command could. Smoke still billowed from the Grey's city. Undoubtedly the Greys in the fleet that had just sent the Terran fleet scurrying away with its tail between its legs were quartered in the massive city fort. Suddenly the reason for the difference in the size of the fort relative to the size of the enemy garrison was painfully clear.

They were in deep. This engagement would end with his body being dissected by the Grey Brains. They would hypothesize and examine and try to determine if a commander was in any way different from those he commanded, as was the case in their species. They would find that they were indeed different. A great deal weaker, in fact. Probably not as smart either, but kept in check by the control device.

He saw no way out of this. He thought of his wife and child back on Terra. He would be ten now. She would look different, wouldn't she? He had received communiques from Terra with vids, but they were old by the time the signal was picked up by the fleet. He knew he had changed. He looked past the images of the live drone feeds to his reflection on the screen. He had definitely changed. His eyes had dark circles around them. Wrinkles, of the type he had once pigeonholed to the old, formed at the corners of his eyes and mouth.

What was he doing here? Eight years. That was how much of his life he had devoted to this mission. This campaign. This failed campaign. Had his wife been faithful? He wouldn't have blamed her if she hadn't. It was too much to ask of her. Too much to ask of anyone. A sudden red flash appeared on the screen, and he refocused his attention on it.

A ping. The team had sent off a ping. He opened it hurriedly and scanned through it. When he was done, he sat back in his chair, stunned. Then he began to laugh.

CHAPTER 23

"Are you sure it won't go off?" 30 whispered for the fifth time.

"60/40," 39 said. He put the odds closer to 70/30, but he took a devilish delight in seeing 30 go pale.

"Don't worry, if it goes, then you'll never know it."

"Not a comfort," 30 said. The irritation in his voice made his words clipped and harsh.

"Would you rather do my part?" he asked.

"But that is a comfort. What, would you say, are your chances?"

"I wouldn't even put a number to it," he said.

The talk seemed to make 20 uncomfortable. He noticed that she couldn't meet his gaze. They were hunkered down, about as close to the main building as they could get, without being seen among a pile of what looked like building supplies.

"You okay?" he directed at 20.

She shifted and only held his eyes for a second before looking away again.

"Fine," she said. "I just don't like to make a racket fit to raise the dead while trying to hide from Heaters. Unlike *some*, I hold a healthy fear of them." She imbued the word "some" with a surprising amount of disgust.

"I never said I wasn't afraid," he countered. "But what other options do we have?"

Her silence was her answer.

"Are you synced?" he asked. He knew he had asked this before, but, like 30, he tried to fill the nervous void with something familiar. 30 and 20 looked at their screens and nodded.

"If you get made, and I still haven't made it clear, then just blow it." This had been a sticking point in the plan, one of many. They had argued with him relentlessly the night before. Well, it wasn't "night," but they had slept, taking turns keeping an eye open for any patrols. At one point, while 20 was on watch, Heaters had passed by. They had made a cursory probe of the interior of the building. They had clearly made far too many searches that day, and their attempt was laughable. He and 30 hadn't even woken up during the "search."

20 and 30's faces showed their reluctant acceptance of the eventuality.

"Right. No use sitting around until a patrol stumbles onto us. Remember, absolute radio silence from this point."

They nodded again, and he stood and walked out into the street. He didn't turn to look at them, though he itched to do so. He felt their eyes on him as he went. 39 approached the two Heaters that stood guard, an outer piquet for the city's center. The Heaters sat at a guard post of sorts three building lengths down. One saw him and turned his rifle on him, and fired. The range was too great for the notoriously poor aim of the Heaters, and the blue orb of energy flashed past him.

39 pulled the axe from its spot at his leg and strode brazenly forward, a sure challenge to the Heaters. Both Heaters drew their swords and readied themselves for combat. One, the one that had seen him first, swung his sword through the air, testing his muscles or whatever they had. Warming up, 39 thought with a smile.

From his experience, he knew that these giant aliens had a strange sense of honor and would most likely fight him one at a time. At least, that had been what had happened before. Maybe here, now, their orders would change that. He lifted his axe and pointed it at the first of the Heaters. He hoped that that would ensure the contest, and he was rewarded with a war cry from it just before a savage lunge forward.

Perhaps pointing at it was a mistake. The thing seemed enraged, past the point of any Heater he'd ever seen. Even the fodder he'd piled in the gap at the wall didn't look this angry. The second Heater stood apart from the fight and watched, chittering its excitement.

39 dodged left and right as the giant swung his blade and just engaged his shield in time to stop a hammer blow that would have cut him in half. He was forced back, step by step, as the fury of the Heater emptied itself on him. He held his shield high now as the Heater slammed blow after blow down onto it. The constant strikes made standing difficult, and his left leg gave, followed by his right.

Through the chaos of the fight, he looked over to where the rest of his diminished team sat, hidden, watching his pitiful performance. His feet were under him so that he was crouching rather than kneeling, but the sword crashed down with such force that his shield was folding in on itself. The Graphene was an amazingly strong material, but the Heater's abuse could prove too much for it.

He had little opportunity to counter-attack. His shoulder ached, and the vibration made his arm numb. Was this it? It was not the first time he had asked this question in his hectic and short life. No. The fury that fueled his enemy seemed to be, finally, flagging while his built. He used the rage he'd felt upon learning of the succeed or die status of the mission. He used the frustration of having to keep his very thoughts in check. He used the unfairness he had experienced so far in his life. He looked once more at 20 and 30. They sat watching, apprehension in their eyes. 20 had her hand on 30's arm, reminding him of his duty to stay concealed.

39 bunched his legs, preparing them for action, and in the wake of another jolting blow, he launched himself upward and pushed his shield into the Heater's face. He had pushed off the ground with all of the exo-suit enhanced strength that he had, and the shield connected with a satisfying crunch.

The Heater stumbled back a few steps, but 39 didn't give it any time to recover. He pushed forward and hit it in the face with his axe. The blade gave the Heater a cut across its face, but the strength of the blow would have destroyed a Terran. It raised its sword to try to deflect the next swing, but 39 slammed his shield into the sword and got inside the giant's reach. Too close to use his axe effectively, he jabbed it into the Heater's midsection. He knew the jabs wouldn't seriously hurt it, but he needed time.

It was amazing how one's life, even one so short as his, came down to needing only a few microseconds.

He jabbed again, and the Heater snarled in rage. 39 bent his knees and launched upward again. This time he smashed the edge of his shield into the jaw of the Heater with such force that the impact crumpled the shield in on itself. The Heater was clearly dazed, and its all-black eyes blinked up at the sky.

39 smashed it again and again in the face with his misshapen shield. Blue blood sprayed and hissed through the air. Finally, the thing fell to the ground. 39 stood over the grievously wounded Heater, gasping for air through his rebreather.

He looked at the second Heater, then swung his axe into the neck of the prone figure. The blade only cut halfway into it, despite all the strength that he used. He swung again and again, and blue Heater blood bubbled up from the neck of the corpse.

He bent over and picked up the head with his left hand, and tossed it to the feet of the other Heater. It moved to attack, but 39 forestalled it with a raised hand. He threw the axe down at its feet, then knelt and put his hands on his head. A clear sign of surrender. It was plain that the Heater wanted to kill him regardless of his capitulation.

He knew, from the uploads, that captives were highly sought after by the Greys. He also knew that few of those prisoners survived a month in captivity. The Grey leaders, the Brains, took a keen interest in the study of human physiology, which amounted to little more than torture.

This Heater would probably have a standing order to

capture as many humans as possible. The drive to follow orders fought with the Heater's sense of honor. The battle of wills played clearly on its face. The thing looked at the head of his fallen comrade, then back at 39. It finally made a decision and stepped forward. 39 braced himself, unsure if the Heater would kill him or not. It walked to within a few steps and swung its huge arm. Blackness.

CHAPTER 24

39 woke up with a start. He looked around. Disoriented as he was, it was difficult to comprehend what he saw for several seconds. Blue light pulsed like a beating heart. Some kind of energy field shone in the distance. Closer, 39 recognized the bars of a jail cell. Strange how the tech for restraining humans hadn't changed much in the centuries of their existence. The bars were thick, square and sturdy looking. He tested them with a hesitant hand. At least they weren't electrified.

His cell was tiny. Barely five feet square. He had been sitting with his back against a stone wall with just enough room for him to straighten his legs. He was devoid of his suit, and he felt naked without it. In point of fact, he was naked, he realized, looking down. He still had his rebreather, but that was it.

He felt at his forehead, gently probing the goose egg that protruded there. He was lucky the Heater had done as he'd hoped and not killed him in anger. He looked around, trying to see the room outside his cell. It was huge, and judging by the lack of windows and the roughhewn stone, he deduced that he was underground. The blue glow emanated from hundreds of cylinders, maybe thousands. They were in neat rows whose brightness diminished with distance making it difficult to know exactly how many there were.

39 could see humanoid forms silhouetted in the cylinders closest to him. This, oddly, felt familiar. It was a birthing room, he realized. As he watched, carts of Heater corpses distributed bodies to empty and waiting cylinders. Maybe the availability

of a body jump-started the process so that they didn't need to regrow everything. Seemed like a plausible explanation but a complete stab in the dark. He knew nothing about the Terran process followed on the birthing ships, let alone the process going on down below.

39 looked to his left, then to his right. There were other cells. Hundreds of them. They were dug into the stone of the cavern, and the upper levels of cells had a metal catwalk that provided access to them. It looked like he was on the third level. He wondered why they had the cells here with the birthing cylinders.

The cavern thrummed. The clatter of tools, the inconsistent hum of a huge energy bank of some kind, and the indistinguishable chatter of alien and Terran voices all worked to generate an almost overwhelming cacophony of sound.

It might work.

He removed his shoulders from the straps to the rebreather and pulled it around in front of him. He felt at the seam in the pack that formed the exterior of the rebreather unit. It was still there. He smiled beneath the mask and began ripping at the fabric. The stitches he had made with the needle and thread from his med kit the night before came away without too much effort. He had feared that his poor sewing would be seen by his captors, but the Greys must not have noticed or cared if they had. After all, who would suspect poor stitches.

He pulled on the det-cord firmly but slowly, extricating it from the lining of the rebreather pack. The stuff shouldn't go off unless he pulled on the draw wire that he kept well away from his probing fingers. After about eight minutes, he had freed the explosive cord from the pack. He wrapped the wire around two bars, then ran it up a couple feet and wrapped it around the same bars. He didn't bother waiting. He couldn't see any guards, but they may be watching him on some hidden security camera. He had to move quickly in any case. He couldn't be sure how long he had been knocked out, but if 20 and 30 had done their jobs, then his time would be short.

He stood as far away from the det-cord as he could and still reach the draw wire. He gave it a sharp tug. The fuze was only a second long, and he turned his back to it and covered his ears. The explosion was not overly loud or fierce, but it felt like a thunderclap had sounded. The close confines of the tiny cell reverberated with the force of it. He cursed, then cursed again when an alarm sounded that was every bit as loud as had been the cord.

Lights above his cell flashed their betraying dance onto the catwalk. He shrugged inwardly and picked a direction at random. Right or left, he didn't think he was making it out of this one.

The cool subterranean air felt good on his skin, but despite the temperature, sweat covered him from head to toe. His heart thumped like a wild thing trapped in his chest. He couldn't picture a wild thing in particular since no animals were worthy of a Grunt's basic uploads, and yet he felt he understood their nature. He, somehow, knew that, in that moment, they probably looked and acted similar to him. Crazed eyes searching for danger, looking for an escape.

A drone's ominous whine sounded, and 39 moved with all the speed he could down the catwalk. He hoped that drones were the only guards he'd have to face. Voices started to call out to him, not the chittering speech of the Greys but Terran. He didn't even process what they were saying. He just had to move.

The end of the catwalk was in front of him, and he took the steps down to the next level, four and five at a time. The clatter and ping of projectiles ricocheting off the metal railing behind him spurred him onward. Maybe he wouldn't prefer the drones to the Heaters he'd expected.

The rough metal grates of the catwalk tore at his feet as he ran, but he moved as fast as he ever had. A drone flew down from the level above and zeroed in on him. He saw a support pole out of the corner of his eye, and he hooked it with his arm and jumped. He cleared the railing and rotated down. As he swung, he gripped the pole with his other hand and let the pole slide through his hands til he was on the floor of the massive cavern.

He turned to run from the drone that stalked him from the moment he'd stepped foot outside his cell and stopped. He stood three feet from a Brain. The first one he'd seen. He knew them from uploads for sure, but in person, they seemed far less threatening and far smaller than he imagined. It stood, staring at him from behind a kind of holographic control panel.

39 vaulted the short wall separating them and grabbed the alien in a firm grip. He spun the Brain around to face the oncoming drone. He crouched down so that it would shield him from the drone just in time. The drone stopped, hovering, but no shots came. Good. Certain niceties had to be maintained. No killing of the race's superior caste.

"Open the cells!" he yelled.

He knew that the thing probably didn't speak any of the same languages he did, but they were said to be able to communicate subtly through telepathy. 39 wrenched the thing's arm back, holding its wrist high up against its back. The thing made a small mewling sound. It sounded so pathetic that 39 was tempted to let it go.

"Open the cells," he repeated, pushing the thought at the alien.

He felt like he was barely putting any pressure on the arm, and yet the thing acted like he was torturing it. Its arms were frail feeling.

He felt something brush his consciousness. It was odd. Like a whisper. Like a faint breath on the back of his neck. It was a plea for mercy from the thing whose arm he held. He almost jerked away from the thing in disgust. It just felt...wrong somehow. Another whisper, this time it conveyed, subtly, the fear that it felt.

"I won't hurt you any more than I have to *if* you do what I say," he said. He wasn't sure if the thing could understand him, but he hoped it could.

Confusion mixed with fear flitted through his mind. Maybe it couldn't.

He tried to think of how to project his thoughts to it but rejected the idea. It seemed far too complicated to communicate that way. He pointed at the doors to the hundreds of cells over the thing's shoulder, and the drone shot him.

Searing pain spread from his left hand. He cursed and wrenched on the Brain's arm, lifting the miniature alien off the ground. He cursed again as more of the pain radiated from the wound. He looked at his hand and was shocked. Three of his fingers were missing. He stayed hunkered down behind the alien shield as well as he could.

The warbling cry of the Brain at the increased pressure on its arm far exceeded any show of pain he exhibited.

"Open the damn doors!" he yelled at it.

Suddenly the drone fell to the floor, then a second later, all of the cell doors swung open. Alarms started sounding from the control panel.

39 ignored them. He had to move. He turned and smacked the frail Brain's head against the control panel. He did his best not to kill it. He didn't expect the thing's head to be that fragile. He had meant to knock it out, but judging by the widening pool of black, he had failed.

Black. Why do Brains have black blood? None of the uploads he'd received addressed the question. Heaters and those invisible scouts both had lava-like blue blood. This was entirely different. There was no heat that emanated from the pool. No more than one would expect from a pool of fresh blood.

The thump of feet on the catwalk stairs above him reverberated through the cavern floor. He looked up and saw an onrush of humanity. Prisoners, naked all, poured out of the cells. Women and men both ran down the stairs. Here and there, he saw the back of some officer's unmarred head, but the vast majority of the Terrans were Grunts. He signaled for them to follow him.

Even though he didn't have the first clue where he was going, he knew they stood a better chance together than apart.

39 swung open a heavy manual door and blinked at the flood of light. A tunnel or corridor stretched off in both directions. He chose right and led the way down the hall at a jog. They would be torn apart if some truant Heater guards showed up. Odd that there weren't any. Automation must have seemed adequate for the captive population that didn't look like it had been outside their cells for months in some cases. Those struggled to walk and were helped by others that were more fit.

He wondered where his exo-suit had been taken. The dead Heater bodies in the cavern worried him. He hoped he could get some distance from the cavern and wherever his suit was. Would 20 and 30 wait?

CHAPTER 25

20 looked down at the melted butt of her fifty-cal sniper rifle. She had used it to push the nuke down into the corpse; its blood sizzled hot and loud on the bomb's surface as it slowly submerged below the blue gore of the beheaded Heater. She had closed her eyes at the sound, sure that the heat from the body would set off the bomb. It hadn't.

Now her only concern, besides 39's escape, was that the remote trigger mechanism didn't withstand the heat and that nothing would happen when she triggered the device. The second device was concealed within 39's suit, wrapped in the lead insulation from the crate to keep the bomb's radiation from apprising the Greys of the danger. She hoped that the Greys wouldn't inspect the suit too closely.

She looked through her HUD at the distant headquarter building. A group of Heaters ran into the main entrance.

"Looks like 39 poked the hornet's nest," she said to 30 without looking over her shoulder at him.

"He's good at that," he responded.

"But can he get himself out of it?" She was worried for him. More, perhaps, than was strictly allowed by Terran restrictions. Okay, she conceded inwardly, *definitely* more than the restrictions allowed.

Time seemed to crawl, and she glanced up at the countdown timer that was displayed prominently in her HUD. She looked at it probably one hundred times since 39 had killed the Heater and been taken captive and had stressed every second of it. Although time crawled, she felt like it was going too quickly. There was so much that could go wrong. She didn't honestly know if she would be able to push the button. 39 was the person with whom she felt the safest, despite the almost constant danger they seemed to find themselves in together. Mother, ever vigilant mother, shocked her scull in firm denunciation. 20 wasn't sure if the control device wasn't keen on her budding feelings for her senior commander or if it didn't like her hesitancy to perform as that senior commander had ordered and blow the bombs, whether he was clear or not.

She closed her eyes and embraced the pain momentarily. Its throbbing correction seemed to be more. For a few seconds, she let her feelings for 39 reside side-by-side with the pain, and for a while, they...complimented each other. Her respect for the man who was, even now, more bravely facing almost certain death than anyone any of the uploads told of grew with every day. When they spoke, their few words seemed to flow in a way she had never experienced before.

Heat spread to her face, and she hurriedly cleared her mind before mother could ramp up the punishment.

More Heaters ran toward the building. She clenched her fist and swore at the orders that 39 had given, restricting them from engaging the enemy and giving up concealment. They were the linchpin. Without them triggering the bombs, the whole plan would collapse. The idea was sound, she admitted to herself, but in reality, her conscience fought with mother's by-the-book enforcement of adherence to orders.

They sat atop a building close to the lake from which they had entered the city. They were covered with some metal roofing that they had pried up enough to climb under. She had cold-shot loaded into her fifty, and despite the melted stalk, she was sure she could hit what she needed at this range.

Instead of punching holes in the Heaters she saw running toward the building like she wanted to, she waited. 30 sighed next to her, undoubtedly feeling some of the same helplessness.

She looked up at the countdown flashing down in her HUD again and echoed 30's sigh with her own.

CHAPTER 26

The stench of hundreds of Terrans that had been left unwashed in their tiny cells for months was significant. It was a legitimate concern for him that the Heaters would smell the group long before they saw them. At each staircase 39 went up, searching for an exit to this subterranean network of tunnels. They came to a large room that felt like a furnace. A Heater stood at the open door to what looked like....a furnace. Blue fire danced beyond the startled Heater. A loud hum reverberated around the room.

The Terrans, upon seeing the Heater, stopped and stared at the alien. 39 looked around the room hurriedly. He spotted a metal tool of some kind, three feet long with a wedge shape at the one end. He grabbed it and held its comforting weight in his right hand. His left was beyond the ability after the drone had blasted it.

The Heater must have been a worker since no weapons were in evidence. Still, the thing would be able to bring down a score of humans. It stood on the balls of its feet, ready to leap into action.

39 let out a war cry and ran forward, holding the metal bar ready to swing. The Terrans behind him followed suit, perhaps understanding that little was gained by standing around. Most would probably prefer death than to be hauled back to their tiny jail cells. The crowd rushed the Heater and fell upon the alien with a level of savagery that 39 was surprised at.

Though none of them had weapons except him, they pulled on the giant alien and struck at it with bare hands. Two

Terrans went down when the Heater swung a huge arm at them, but the crowd quickly replaced the front ranks with fresh troops. The Heater was chittering angrily as it swung. The bare hands of the Terrans would do little against the tough rock-like skin of the Heater, but the bar was taking its toll, and the Heater concentrated its fury on 39. It swung, and 39 dodged to one side, barely getting out of the arc in time. A Terran with jet-black hair to his left wasn't so lucky and went down with a sickening crunch.

39 pushed the bar out in front of him and tried to push the Heater back. Those behind him must have seen what he was attempting and began helping. 39 felt hands pushing on his shoulders, helping sustain him. Others worked on pushing the Heater with bare hands.

The Heater took a step back, then another, and finally, running out of space, the Heater screamed as the Heat from the furnace began to be too much for even it. Those pushing with bare hands stopped as the pain of their burning skin was too much to bear. 39 gave another cry and brought the bar back and then forward with all the strength he had.

It was enough to tip the Heater back into the furnace. The chittering turned to a screeching that hurt 39's unprotected ears. The alien's kicking legs finally stilled. 39 looked around at the faces of the men and women that had helped. They were all looking at him.

"What now?" someone yelled.

He looked at their hopeful faces. They obviously thought he had this all planned out, or at least they hoped that he did. He couldn't bring himself to tell them that he was lost in here. Someone moved to the front of the group and grabbed 39's shoulder. It was A21, then a stocky man that had been standing next to him holding his burned hands looked up and 39 recognized E18. His hands were burned so badly that the skin had sloughed off, leaving them bloody.

39 wasn't sure what to do, what to say. They all looked at him with such hope in their eyes. He smiled at his fellow

comrades and put his hands on both their shoulders.

E18 clinched his right fist and then pressed it against his chest. The mark of the red hand. This time it was made from the blood of his men. His men. Not Terra's, not Marines. His. And no pain shoved into his head could dissuade him from that sentiment. These men were his. He would take responsibility for them since Terra clearly had given them up for dead.

39 patted E18's sweaty shoulder.

"Follow me," he said. The Terrans parted for him, and he led the way onward, where to, he had no idea. All he had now was onward.

As 39 went, he started to think that he would never reach the surface. They had been jogging through tunnels that would have been low for a Heater but were comfortably large for the average Terran for close to half an hour. He had no clock or way to tell how much time he had before the nukes were detonated, but an inner sense of urgency told him that it was imminent. They had gone far enough down the corridor that he thought they might be safe from the explosion, but he really had little confidence in his guess.

They came to a ladder leading up, and 39 climbed up and slowly opened the door at the top, peeking through. Fresh air hit him in the face. The outside. He looked around as best he could, still in the city. He wasn't sure where, but he saw the feet of Heaters as they ran past, undoubtedly on their way to recapture the fugitive Terrans.

He climbed back down the ladder and saw that a man was waiting for him. He stood proudly, despite his nakedness and despite his flab. He didn't have a control device. An officer then.

"What, may I ask, is your designation?" he said. His voice was nasally and high, and he spoke with a strange accent. He also had a scowl on his face. Apparently, the portly officer had gained enough assurance of their situation to assert his authority. 39 stood at attention at the base of the ladder.

"Gunnery Sergeant G39, sir," he said.

"You look a little young to be a Gunny. I bet you still have a mark from the feeding tube, am I right?"

They didn't have time for this.

"Sir, I…Affirmative, sir," he said.

"Well, I'll tell you that you have done a fine job up until this point, but I can take it from here," the officer said, poking out his chest.

"Sir, there is a nuke…."

"A nuke, where? Damn it."

39 fought his frustration with this conversation and plowed on.

"There is a nuke stashed in a Heater corpse that, I'm assuming, should be making its way to the cavern where we were and another wherever they stowed my exo-suit." The officer's eyes widened. 39 continued. "Since I have lost my helmet, I have no way of knowing what the countdown is at now since I was knocked unconscious when they took me," he paused and waited for the officer to say something, but surprisingly, he remained silent but for his somewhat labored breathing. "Should we continue, sir?" 39 prompted.

The officer fluttered his eyes as if he was coming awake again.

"Yes, by all means, Gunny, let's get the hell out of here. Lead the way."

39 was relieved. He turned and pushed on, leading the prisoners down the dark tunnel.

As they jogged, 39 noticed that the tunnel walls had taken on an unfinished quality. Jagged angles of protruding stone replaced smoothly polished surfaces. Scars from the teeth of heavy machinery shone brightly among the dark stone and dirt walls. The tunnel was lit with the occasional weak lamp that hung from the ceiling.

Roots began to show, here and there, among the rock and dirt. They must be outside the city's walls. Next ladder up, they were home free.

They came to a small room with doors in the walls that resembled lockers. He judged that they were probably out of the blast radius of the bombs, so he stopped and tried to open one, but the lock was engaged. He used the bar to pry the thing open. There was a plasma rifle inside. He crowed with delight and handed the bar to A21, who used it to pry open the other lockers.

Soon, and without much instruction, the group had prized out the contents of the small closets and distributed them. 39 was large enough to almost fit into a pair of Heater leggings. He tied them around his waist with a cord he'd found. Most of the Terrans were still completely naked save for the rebreathers, but a few wore the overly-large articles from the lockers to try and maintain some semblance of decency.

They started off again, down the tunnel, and 39 tried to figure out how to fire the plasma rifle as he ran, slowing down when he was under a lamp so that he could see. He finally thought he had the thing figured out. When the sound of a plasma rifle reverberated through the tunnel. He had thought that he had accidentally fired his for a second but then heard screaming from behind.

39 turned and saw a group of Heaters bearing down on them.

"Keep them running!" 39 yelled at E18, "I'll hold them off."

39 and two other Terrans that were armed with the alien weapons ran back to the rear of the column. He should have set some rear guards. Stupid. And now the person that had been hit in the initial shots was writhing on the ground far to the rear, the Heaters practically upon him.

39 hit the button that he figured must fire the weapon, and the thing jumped in his hands. The pulse of energy that he released on its errant trajectory sped past the Heater's heads. No wonder Heaters weren't known for their accuracy. These things kicked like a mule.

39 held the butt of the weapon against his shoulder and

leaned far into the shot as he hit the button. This time the shot struck a Heater in the shoulder. The Heater barely reacted. It came on, hardly pausing. 39 fired two more shots. The other two Terrans opened up as well, figuring out how to fire the rifles from watching 39, and all of the rounds that struck did little to dissuade the oncoming Heaters.

This wasn't working. He scanned the interior of the tunnel between them and the Heaters. There. A concrete support column and header stood not ten feet from him.

"Fall back!" he yelled to the two Terrans and suited his words to action. Once he'd moved back thirty or so feet, he turned and poured fire into the beam that ran the width of the tunnel. Explosions of rock and concrete proved the shot's effectiveness. He shot a few into the surrounding rock and dirt of the tunnel ceiling. He spared a glance for the Heaters, who were too close. If the beam didn't give soon.... A boulder suddenly cracked and crashed to the tunnel floor. Dust made seeing the Heaters impossible. He heard more of the ceiling cave-in and saw light through the dust, and felt a stir of air.

The cave-in had opened up to the outside. 39 waited in the dust-filled tunnel for any sign of the Heaters. Nothing. Either they had been crushed in the cave-in, or it had blocked the tunnel. There was no sign of the enemy. He turned to one of the men that had helped him defend the column of Terrans.

"Catch up to them and let them know we have a way out."

CHAPTER 27

Heaters ran into the Grey's main building, but no one came out, least way, no Terrans came out. As time ran out for 39, 20's heart rate increased. Where was he? When the Heater had dragged him off, 39 was limp and looked unconscious. She feared that he hadn't woken up despite the chaos around the building. Maybe it wasn't because of 39 escaping. Maybe they had found the nukes.

To add to her apprehension, Grey ships had started to enter the thin atmosphere above the city. They docked at different platforms around the fort, and the increased number of Heaters made the risk of detection greater.

More Heaters entered the main building.

If they had found the nukes, then they might be able to disable them before time ran out. But she would not set off the bombs before she saw 39, no matter what her orders were. Only ten minutes remained on the timer. Each second that flashed by felt like a stab, a slice, a puncture in her heart.

"If anyone can do it, he can," 30 said. It was like he could read her mind and was trying to reassure her. Maybe he was just trying to reassure himself. 30 and 39 had grown closer, she had noticed. They had been friendly during training, but now they were more than that. She didn't have a family, but from what she knew of the subject, the two men had become like brothers. In the short time, they had been on the planet, they had bonded somehow. She supposed that a series of near-death occurrences was a great catalyst for loyalty.

Something blurred her vision, and she cuffed at her eyes,

but her visor was down. How did she get something in her eyes? She felt liquid running down her cheek til it met her rebreather mask. Crying. This was crying. She hurt. She couldn't explain it. It felt deep, somehow, inside her, a pain so intense at the thought of losing 39. She didn't realize how much she cared for him. It was ludicrous. She hadn't known him for long, and yet she had known him her entire life.

Five minutes. She willed the time to stop, for all to go quiet, for 39 to emerge from the distant building and be clear of the blast zone, and yet it continued, mocking her. The thud of her heart in her ears drowned out 30's words.

"What?" she said.

"We've got to take cover."

She couldn't. If she hid, then she wouldn't see if 39 had made it out, and to do that would mean that she had given up on him.

"I can't," she said. Mother begged to differ. She throbbed in the back of 20's head like a concussive grenade. The control device knew what her orders were. Well, maybe it was that she knew what her orders were, and mother simply interpreted and passed on pain to accompany any guilt she should feel at disobeying them. Either way, the throbbing intensified.

It seemed right. She should feel physical pain to accompany the tears.

Finally, as the pain began to be unbearable, she allowed 30 to pull her away from the roof's edge and down the ladder at the rear of the building. She sobbed now, uncontrolled and uncaring of how it made her appear. They crossed the street and ran the short distance to the lake. They submerged themselves. They had figured that the openness of the lake would be the best protection they could get from falling debris.

She was nearly hyperventilating as the last few seconds flashed by on her HUD. For a few seconds, she hoped that she would not be forced to follow through with the orders she'd been given, that maybe, by some strange twist of fate, the Control

Device had stopped working and that she would be able to wait longer for 39 to escape. Her hopes were dashed as mother ramped up again, signaling to 20 that she was disobeying 39's orders.

She held out. Sobbing now in her helmet. She knew that 30 would hear her crying through the comms since he patted her hand comfortingly. He knew that the time had run out, he had been given the same orders after all, but he rejected mother's insistence right alongside her. Finally, the pain stabbed at her and made her fall to her knees.

30 knelt next to her in the murky swirl of biological debris that floated around them. He gently pulled her wrist computer over to him. It flashed an insistent plea to explode the nukes in time with her heartbeat as he took her other hand and rested it atop the computer. He did not force her finger to press the button but waited with her through the agony that crippled them and threatened to kill them soon.

20 screamed. She screamed a wordless shriek of agony, pain beyond explanation both inside her soul and that which rendered her body immobile fed the yell. She pressed the button. Mother ceased her torment, and then she felt it. The earth trembled, and then a wash of detritus and mud slammed into them. They held hands as they tumbled end over end through the water until they slammed into the city's wall and were held there for what seemed like minutes, but which was probably a handful of seconds. Slowly the force that pressed against them subsided, and gravity reasserted itself. They fell to the lake bottom once more.

20 worked at the seal on her rebreather. It had pulled off partially and was leaking water into the mouthpiece. Foul water, smelling of decades-old dead things and the organic muck that lived off it made her want to gag.

Finally, she was able to refit the mask and purge the water, though the smell lingered. She couldn't see anything except 30's light that flicked on and swirled in a circle, letting her know where he was. She made her way over to him.

They slowly felt their way around the lake floor, searching for the tunnel. After a long time of trudging through the knee-high loose silt and mud, they realized that the drain must have been buried by the muck from the explosions that had flung against the wall.

They decided they should leave the lake and look for another way out.

Carefully as they could, they exited the lake, 20 first so that her cloaked form would protect her from detection. She was shocked by the destruction. This was more damage than the tactical nukes could account for.

She searched her memory of the uploads for any reference to compounding explosions when Grey facilities were targeted in the past. No, this shouldn't have happened. Not this bad. A huge crater was all that was left of much of the city, and most of the buildings outside the crater were reduced to rubble. This was a far larger yield than they had been led to believe. They were never meant to survive this. The Brass just wanted as much mayhem as they could inflict, regardless of casualties. She shouldn't have been surprised, and she shouldn't have been angry, but she was. She felt betrayed.

39 and the rest of the team had given their lives for this.

She still felt tears running from her eyes. She wondered, in the back of her mind, how much of that stuff was in her. She looked out at the Grey's city and no longer feared being spotted by the enemy. She decloaked and just stared out at the wreckage. A true succeed or die mission, only Brass was banking on the "die" portion, it seemed, a little too heavily. This seemed like a S.A.D., she thought...Succeed And Die. She smiled at her own cleverness.

She realized that the smile would look at odds with the tears if anyone could see either through her mask and visor. 39. Why did he have to be the one to die? Because he would not put that burden on someone else. He was a born leader. Born. Not true born, but destined nonetheless. He was a man that people wanted, needed to follow.

"I'll be damned," 30 said behind her.

She turned and saw the direction that he was looking, expecting that he was looking at the massive crater, but instead, he was looking toward the wall. Well, it was where the wall used to be. There was a massive breach and, through it, streamed a mass of humanity. Terrans, dirty and nude, save for a few that wore what looked like scavenged articles from the enemy, approached. They were led by a huge man wearing nothing but pants and his rebreather. 39. His well-muscled chest bore a large red handprint on it. Her heart skipped a beat, and she ran to him.

39 opened his arms and embraced her, laughing. They both laughed. They laughed through the punishment that mother dosed them with. Their feelings for each other were obvious. Obvious to themselves, obvious to each other, and obvious to mother. They didn't care. They were alive. And soon, after their promotion, they would be free. The pain was sweet. Nothing could cloud this moment.

CHAPTER 28

The troop carriers started showing up before 39, his team, and the prisoners could make it far from the alien city. They climbed to the top of a hill devoid of trees from which they could watch the Terran Marines do what they did best.

Exo-suited warriors fast-roped down from hovering transport ships while the gun teams covered the ground forces from above. This was no longer a battle. It was an extermination, a massacre. What Heaters remained in the city were wounded, cut off from reinforcements and were quickly overpowered and destroyed.

The Grey ships that hadn't been destroyed by the nukes attempted a half-hearted counter-attack, but the Terrans now outnumbered the Greys, and they quickly drove off the enemy ships.

Marines cheered excitedly as they cleared the streets. It was a bitter-sweet end to the days of stress and overexertion. 39 felt cheated somehow. Like these Marines had the easy work now that the blood price had been paid. His men, the men of the Red Hand, had paid that price.

Logic told him that the price had been remarkably low for such success. The uploads, with all of their infinite knowledge, would probably be hard-pressed to find a more resounding victory. And yet...he felt used, like a hammer. Pushed to one side when not needed. Many of the prisoners collapsed to the ground. They were clearly not used to the exercise after being locked up in cages for months. Looking at them, 39 realized that he should take consolation in the fact that he had saved far more lives than he had gotten killed in his short stint of command, but the thought felt hollow. Hollow like his stomach.

He was hungry, tired, and filthy but alive. He looked at 20 and smiled. They were alive.

He sat down on the cool grass and watched the Terran Marines mop up.

A troop transport made to land on the hill, and some of the nude wretches had to move quickly out of the way or be crushed by the ship's massive landing legs. The ramp lowered, and Major Grant ran down it before it was fully extended.

"39! You devil you, what a show." He came walking over with such exuberance that he looked to be on the verge of running. 39 stood back up and saluted as Grant came closer.

"As you were, son. As you were." He motioned for 39 to sit back down on the ground, but 39 didn't feel comfortable doing so with the Major standing, so he simply relaxed his posture.

"When I got your ping, I didn't dare hope for success, but despite all the advice I received to the contrary, I readied the company to move. I knew that if anyone could pull it off, you could."

39 almost flinched as the Major came closer and embraced him in a most uncharacteristic hug. Officers never talked to Grunts this way. Why, officers didn't talk to Grunts at all if they could help it.

The Major's staff officers looked on uncomfortably, trying not to make eye contact with 39.

"Do you know what you did, boy?" Major Grant said, pulling back to look at his face.

"Blew the hell out of the enemy, sir?"

Grant laughed. "Indeed, you did," he said between stubborn chuckles. "More than that, 39. You saved every single Grunt, officer and civilian in Fort McIntyre. You saved thousands of stranded Terrans. When the enemy fleet came in, we thought we were all done for. If it hadn't been for you, Terra would have suffered grievous losses in this campaign."

In 39's opinion, the campaign had already suffered grievous losses. Was humanity always so callous to the loss of life that they now experienced in due course? Had they always been so cold and accepting of the incredible loss of life that they now fed into the meat grinder? Somehow, 39 knew that they hadn't. After all, officers and civilians were mourned when they died. Funerals were held, and memories shared. At least, that's what he had heard. He had never been invited to one, of course, being a Grunt and all. Would that change with his advancement? Or would the other officers treat him like he was still a Grunt? In a way, he wanted them to. He felt that if he was accepted by them, then it would mean that he rejected his roots, shallow as they were. He felt that it would be a betrayal to those Grunts whose respect he valued higher than any officer.

Mother attempted to correct the direction in which his thoughts were going.

Major Grant read the discomfort 39 felt on his face as sadness for those fallen comrades he'd lost. "I'm sorry you lost men, son. How many did you lose? Our pings didn't give us a full picture because it appeared that some were taken captive, and it appears." He looked around at the nude bodies around him. "They were stripped of their exo-suits and clothes by which we could track their vitals."

"I lost all but three," 39 said, knowing that the Major wouldn't care what their designations were. As kind as Grant seemed, he would not degrade himself that far.

"We also weren't able to find C30. It seems that the Greys were using biology to, somehow, fuel the creation of their Heater soldiers."

Grant's hooded eyes looked pinched together in a scowl. He undoubtedly didn't know who C30 was. Gunnery Sergeant or not, it was too much to ask that a Major remember a single unit's designation.

"Gunny was a good man and a better soldier," Major

Grant said. 39 realized that pain caused the scowl. Pain at losing, if not a friend, then a valued teammate. The Major had known Gunny. The revelation startled 39. He had assumed too much. Perhaps the Major was truly different from the rest and not just superficially so.

The corpulent officer from the tunnel came over and inserted himself into the conversation. "Captain Ivanov, 3rd Marine Logistics." He saluted the Major.

"Captain, good to see that you've come through in one piece," Grant said.

"Thanks to this...man." It clearly pained the Captain to admit that he was only alive because of a Grunt. "None of us would have made it without him, and to be honest, I'd thought that command had forgotten about me."

The pencil-pusher Captain had delusions of grandeur if he thought that 39 and his team had been sent to destroy the enemy city and essentially win the war for Eridani B all to free him. The man would probably break down and weep if he knew the truth. If he knew that command had forgotten him. If he knew that his freedom was owed solely to the fact that 39 had taken advantage of the situation. Luck, pure dumb luck, had saved the man, nothing more. Command had written the Captain off. 39 was sure of it. Maybe being one of them wouldn't increase the value that he had in the eyes of the True-born. Maybe this was all there was left of human caring. Had humanity "advanced" its way past compassion?

Mother had not weighed in on the deep thoughts that 39 was having. It surprised him. Perhaps mother was conflicted between the praise from Captain Ivanov and his somewhat rebellious thoughts.

"Of course we didn't forget you, Captain. Let's get you some clothes. That breeze can be cold, can't it?" Major Grant walked the shorter man away toward the transport.

Grant called back over his shoulder.

"I've arranged another transport for you all. It'll be along shortly."

39 sat back down and waited.

CHAPTER 29

39 had been surprised at how fast they were moving forward with the removal of his control device. Hours from when he and the rest of the survivors had arrived back at Fort McIntyre, they were being prepped for surgery. He, 20, 30, E18 and A21 sat in a sterile room. They wore white gowns that would probably be removed once they were unconscious.

They had been rushed through debriefings and sent to the lab coats to get washed up. Now they waited. 39 was exhausted, as was everyone there. He nodded off twice before finally allowing his body to give in.

He awoke with a start and looked around him for the source of what had interrupted his sleep. The metal door, which he had assumed led to the operating room, opened. Around him, his team was bleary-eyed and startled as he was. They had also clearly been sleeping. The surgery staff motioned for them to stand. They did so, obedient as ever.

The surgery staff and doctors were all suited up in the protective gear that covered them from head to toe. It was uncommon for a Grunt to be looked after like this. Normal Grunts were taken care of in a rush of blood and cold, calculated reason. No consideration of possible infection by foreign bacteria or viruses for them. Surgeries done on the Marine Grunts were a quick and dirty system where the soldiers with wounds that would cost too much time and energy to fix were shuffled off to the corner where they could die somewhere out of the way. This surgery room was obviously meant for civilians or officers. The surfaces gleamed and sparkled with reflected light. 30 was joking with one of the nurses. He was nervous and attempted to hide it with humor thought 39.

39 was nervous too, but more than that. He felt worried. He didn't know if the two were that different, but they felt different. He tried to reassure himself. Moments ago, when asked what percentage of success would be acceptable to him, he would have said any. He wanted to be free with every fiber of his being. At least he thought he did. There was something wrong.

Something tugged at his brain, a feeling not unlike the Grey Brain back in the cavern. It pulled, and the more he tried to understand it, the more it pulled. Some instinct warned him of danger, and the logical side of his brain was trying to calm him by rationalizing that it was natural to feel this way before an altogether new procedure was attempted on him.

30 was talking. Rapid-fire questions interspersed with nervous laughter emptied out of him like a deflating weather balloon. A tray sat in the middle of the room, surrounded by their five beds. Was it strange that all of them were being operated on at the same time? He wasn't sure. Only needles...syringes, that's what they were, sat atop the tray.

39 looked around the room. There was nothing else.

They had E18 and A21 strapped down and were working on 30's straps. Something was wrong. 39 felt it now more than he could reasonably explain.

Two of the syringes were gone when 39 looked again. He looked down the row to E18. They stabbed it into his arm.

"Wait!" 39 said, but he was too late. The man depressed the plunger.

Two large men were attempting to put 39's wrists in the restraints, but he was tense, his arms bent into rigid angles that the men couldn't extend. At his outburst, they looked at each other with nervous eyes.

That was it. These were corpsmen at best, not surgeons. Rings of thinned hair gave them away. A soldier's helmet was the most uncomfortable piece of equipment they wore. The helmet's interior had mesh carbon-fiber bands that held the helmet securely to the head. The bands worked great for keeping the helmet on their heads, no matter the fight, but the designers gave no concessions to comfort, and a veteran could easily be identified by the hairless red band around the back of the head.

Every one of these "doctors" had the band, as did the orderlies. Corpsmen were low ranking officers because a medic in the field had to make a lot of difficult decisions that mother would not approve of.

39 looked around wildly. Nothing. "It will be difficult to do surgery without any equipment, won't it?" 39 said.

All of the hospital staff stopped what they were doing and looked at him. A more glaring confirmation could not have been asked for. The two corpsmen that stood over him tried again in earnest. They grunted as they tried to restrain him. A third man came running over to help.

39 closed his eyes against the pain in the back of his head. He tried to clear his mind as he struggled against the men. Mother would have him go willingly to his death. He did not know what a sheep was, but he knew he was not one. He fought as hard as he could. Fighting three men and a machine in his brain seemed too much. They would win this fight. There was no hope. They had his left arm down and the strap around it and were attempting to buckle it in place.

He told himself to calm down. His thoughts were losing this for him. Mother was draining his strength. He could feel the lights going out, and his vision swam.

20 screamed.

20 screamed, and a new force took hold of him. It was no longer self-preservation that spurred him on but the life of another, one he held in greater esteem than his own. She was more precious to him than his own pain-wracked mind. He heard her scream again and opened his eyes.

He looked over at 20's gurney. She fought with the

Corpsmen over her, the man had both legs and one hand restrained but struggled with the last. The man backhanded her.

39 raged. His anger was all he felt. It was all-consuming, and he no longer felt mother. He no longer cared about anything else. There was no conscious thought. He acted.

He ripped his right arm out of the grip of one of the men and sat up on the gurney. He slammed the fist into the man and sent him to the floor.

He used the fist again. Some stale thought percolated through. His hand as a hammer. He had been called the Hammer before. He felt like one now.

Swinging his fist like a sledge, he sent another man to the floor. Mother was nothing but a faint buzzing in the back of his head.

He kicked the third man in the face. The man's nose didn't just break. It exploded. he fell back, completely out of the fight.

Three more Corpsmen came running over to help, but 39 was up now, and he moved through them with contemptuous ease. These were not Heaters. He smashed the last one's head against the wall with a sickening thud. He roared out his rage. For some reason, he was furious that these men hadn't fought harder, that there weren't more.

He stepped over to 20 and undid her restraints, then 30, who had been forgotten in the tumult.

E18 and A21 were motionless, however. 39 could tell that they were dead. Maybe it was that he had seen so much of it in such a short time. He didn't know why he could tell, but they were gone. He checked their pulse to confirm his instinct. Instinct, it had been what had saved him.

He worked from the adrenaline that coursed through him. He pulled 20 to her feet, and he led them to the rear door.

When he opened it, he was surprised to see real doctors scurrying away like frightened forest creatures. They looked over their shoulders as they ran away.

He cornered one. 39 recognized her as the one that oversaw

his punishment, and his anger was rekindled.

He pushed her into the corner and tied her hands with a torn piece of the lab coat for which all Grunts referred to her kind. He put another strip in her mouth as a gag.

39 grabbed a med pack and signaled the lab-coated woman to proceed in front of him.

30 gripped his shoulder in trembling hands. "How...how are you doing this?" he said in shaky gasps.

"They broke me," was his only response.

30 and 20 were clearly coping as best they could, but they would not be able to maintain consciousness for very long with the pain they must be feeling from mother.

39 walked down the corridor, pushing the scared lab coat in front of him. Suddenly, an alarm sounded from speakers in the ceiling. He had to hurry.

They made their way into a foyer of sorts. The doors to the outside were in front of him. He tried them, but they were locked.

He looked around wildly and saw a room off to the right marked as equipment. He pushed the woman into the room.

There were several exo-suits waiting for their owners to be fixed up. A couple of the units were in shambles, and 39 thought that if the man that had been in this had been a Grunt, then they wouldn't have gone through the effort to bring him to the hospital. He found one that had blood on it, but it seemed in good working order.

He put rebreathers on everyone, including the woman doctor, and lifted himself into the suit.

This was not the Heavy that he was used to, but the bladders on the inside of the suit adjusted to his bigger size, and he walked around the room experimentally.

"Go back out," he told the woman.

They entered the foyer again, and this time he punched the door's control panel on the wall next to the wall and then ripped the wiring from the inside. He then pried the doors open with his suit assisted strength, first one set, then the second.

He turned back around, and 20 was laying on the floor, unconscious. 30 looked like he would follow her lead soon. He fastened a harness around 20 and clipped her tiny body to his chest clip, then he picked up 30 and threw him over his left shoulder. He picked up the doctor with his right hand and ran out into the bright light of day.

He paused when he exited the shade of the hospital eves and looked around to get his bearings, then he launched into a full run toward the closest exterior wall. This suit, though shorter than the Heavy he was used to, felt faster, and he rocketed toward the outer defenses.

He could hear the alarm klaxons echo off of the buildings around him. He charged through a group of Marines, scattering them like dried leaves in the wind. They were off-duty, and none of them wore tech. He heard one shout a curse at his back.

The street opened up to his right, and he passed by a field that was set aside for training. A Group of sentries, all suited up and looking grim, were crossing the field toward the hospital. He swore under his breath when he noticed they changed their bearing to try and intercept his head-long charge.

Based on his rough estimate, he would clear the field before they caught him, but they would be hot on his heels. He still had another quarter mile of street before the wall. Once there, he wasn't sure what to do. He knew there would be guards. Could he kill another Terran to save himself? He supposed he already had. It wasn't to save himself, though. He did it for 20 and 30.

He could see the wall through a gap in some buildings ahead. He needed a distraction, or even if they did make it over the wall, their freedom would be short-lived.

20 woke up and looked around groggily.

He turned north before reaching the wall and ran two building lengths, then turned again. Coming to a set of stairs, he took them five at a time. The Stairs led to a platform upon which sat a transport quadcopter. Perfect. He dropped the lab coat unceremoniously on the deck plating of the copter. A Marine ran up the stairs. He wore an exo-suit similar to 39's, but 39 didn't wait. He kicked the Marine in the chest just as he reached the top stair, and the Marine tumbled backward down the stairs.

He turned and set his other charges in the copter and jumped in.

He set the autopilot to the southeast, and the copter launched into the air. It banked and set off in that direction. He hit a few buttons on the controls and turned to his audience. All three people looked at him. The doctor looked at him with hatred in her eyes. The other two looked like they might pass out again at any time.

"Take off your computers," he said and matched his words with actions. He removed his, then scooped up the other three and put them in the front of the copter.

"How far out are tunnels the Greys built?" he asked 20. She didn't respond. Instead, she was sick all over the floor.

He knelt next to her and rubbed her shoulder, the tender gesture awkward in the armored exo-suit.

"I need to know… we need to know," he said.

20 looked up into his eyes and, through gritted teeth, said, "Only about a mile out, just past the tree line." She sagged after as if the effort to say the simple sentence had drained her of all she had, which was probably exactly how it felt.

39 punched a few more buttons on the control panel and returned to the others.

The copter cleared the east wall and dipped down so that it was no more than thirty feet off the ground. 39 reclipped 20 to his chest harness and picked up the other two. He had set the copter to slow and skim the tops of the trees.

As soon as they crossed the tree line, he scanned for an opening. One approached, and he steeled himself. He counted it off in his head, then jumped.

CHAPTER 30

Colonel Santos slammed his fist down on his desk. "They got away? How, may I ask, did three Grunts, very much under the control of mother, get away?" The question was a good one. What 39 had been able to do was...impossible.

Grant shook his head. He had questions of his own. "Sir, might I ask you why they felt they needed to get away? What happened?"

Santos just looked at Grant with cold eyes. He leaned back in his chair and looked as if he were considering something. Finally, he spoke, "Grant, you may not agree with my decision given your...history with Grunts, but there was no way five Grunts were going to become officers. It was an easy decision to make, really. If all five died during the procedure, then our predicament would have been wrapped up rather nicely. No loose ends and no massive population of Grunts pining away the days until their chance came. We didn't need that kind of headache. Also, 39's popularity was becoming...a problem."

"You murdered two of the heroes that saved your ass and tried to murder the other three?" Grant fumed. He felt heat rush to his face and knew that he must be red with anger.

"You are out of line, Major. They're Grunts! Might I remind you, you are a Terran officer under my command, and we are in the middle of a war? I could have you shot for less insubordination than what you just showed me. If it wasn't for your father...." The Colonel didn't finish his thought, but he didn't have to.

Grant fought his emotions. He knew he was fighting a losing battle with the Colonel and that Santos would follow through with his threat. He was walking a very fine line. Grant forced the anger back. He calmed his breathing and tried to display the picture of a humbled subordinate. He bowed his head slightly. "Of course, sir. I only fear that we could have a mutiny on our hands if word of this gets out." Grant knew that there was no chance of a mutiny ever forming. Mother would not allow such insubordination let alone full rebellion. At least it wasn't supposed to. 39 had proven himself, yet again, capable of defeating the odds.

Santos scoffed at the idea of a mutiny. His face formed into a condescending smirk at the very notion. "Major, I don't know why 39 was able to attack officers and civilians, but he is obviously defective. You can't truly believe that it's a possibility."

Grant didn't believe a mutiny was possible, but the comment had derailed the Colonel's ire. "No, sir. You're right."

Santos nodded his approval like he had just scored a point in some invisible game.

"Besides, the men will not find out about this. As far as they know, all five died while having mother removed. Am I clear?"

"Yes, sir," Grant paused, unsure how best to ask his next question without damaging the Colonel's ego. "I am worried, however, that some of the Grunts may have seen the three escape with doctor Campbell in tow." He was more than worried. He was certain that a score, at least, had seen the brazen escape and that, by now, the tale had been told throughout the regiment. Without any instruction to the contrary from their commanding officers, the regiment's Grunts would be free to recount the tale to their heart's content.

Santos scowled at Grant, angry at the revelation that, surprisingly, hadn't yet occurred to him. His scowl deepened as he realized that the cleanup of this mess would be all but impossible. The information was out, and there was no getting it back. Santos swore. He rubbed his forehead with his thick fingers and sighed. Santos stayed like that for a long while.

Grant wasn't sure what to do. He hadn't been told to go, but he felt uncomfortable seeing his commanding officer in such a state.

Suddenly Santos smacked the desk with his open palm. "I've got it! We spread it around that 39 lost his shit. We tried pulling the device, but it made him go ape. That way, everyone is happy. Hell, it might even be true."

Grant doubted anything that the doctors did to 39 caused this. The vids were quite clear, but the Colonel was excited, and this was no time to draw attention to details.

"Now, do we know where they went? It's not like we don't put trackers on the damned copters. Just track them down and kill them."

"We found the copter, sir, but when we finally managed to bypass the controls remotely, there was no one aboard. We figure they must have jumped somewhere along the flight path."

"Oh, you figure, do you?" Santos raised his hands in the air in defeat. "What a load of geniuses we have." The sarcasm dripped from the words in a most undisciplined way.

Santos seemed like, maybe, he regretted his unprofessionalism. He sat up a little straighter in his chair and sighed.

"Send squads out every mile along the copter's flight path."

"Yes, sir." Grant took the order as permission to leave and turned to go.

"And Grant...."

He turned back. "Yes, sir?"

"Make sure they report anything they see before attempting to recover the fugitives. We both know 39 is more than a match for a squad of Grunts. They'll all converge on any sign of them. You got me?"

"Yes, sir." Grant had already anticipated the orders. As

a matter of fact, he normally would have sent the squads out already, but for some reason, he hadn't. He liked 39. Despite all he'd been taught, despite all the lectures and disciplinary actions taken against him for his stance on Grunts, he pitied them. He didn't pity 39, though. He pitied any enemy of that man.

CHAPTER 31

Water filtered down through the stone ceiling and dripped rhythmically on the stone floor of the tunnel. Puddles strewn across its surface reflected and refracted the light from his suit, casting the light further down the darkened space.

They had found the tunnel's camouflaged entrance only after several sessions of torturously questioning 20. Torturous for 20 because mother punished her every word, and torturous for 39 because he hated putting her through it, but they had to know. Finally, after what seemed like hours but was only fifteen minutes, they entered the tunnels. He was surprised at how deep this tunnel went. It was far deeper than the tunnel he had shepherded hundreds of naked Terrans through.

Good, maybe the extra yards of dense soil and rock would truly hide them from the various drones and scouts the Terrans were sure to send after them.

They passed a jumble of dead wood. There must have been something that forced the wood down here, maybe a flood, a powerful one to have pushed so much of it down here. There were cut pieces. It looked like the Greys had had to clear the log jam for their army to surface and attack the Terrans on that fateful night when they had destroyed the command ship.

20 trembled against his chest. He had to stop soon. She had passed out for perhaps the tenth time since their escape a short time ago, and as they descended through an ever deeper tunnel, the air grew colder. Finally, the tunnel came to a T. In either direction, the blackness stared back at him. It seemed that

the grade was now level, and the tunnel walls were round instead of square as if a giant auger bored the passageway.

"To the left," 39 said, prodding the lab coat in that direction.

The doctor clutched the lab coat closer around her and stared into the ominous dark nervously. She began to walk, reluctantly, forward, 39 pushing her onward. As they walked, 39 noticed that the diameter of this tunnel was quite a bit larger than that that had breached the surface. The sheer size of this passage was incredible. How had the Greys managed to move this much dirt so close to fort McIntyre?

A small alcove to one side stubbornly stayed dark. 39 shined his light into it and decided it was a good place to rest. It seemed drier than the rest of the tunnel. He pointed the lab coat in that direction and followed her into the space.

He set down 30 and then unclipped 20 and set her down gently. 30 groaned a tortured half sob, then fell silent again.

"Now it's time for you to pay me back for not killing you outright. Turn off their control devices." No one had ever said he was too wordy, but his demeanor seemed to terrify the lab coat. Maybe it was just the mystic of not ever encountering a Grunt that had his own will and was able to follow it. A Grunt that could kill with nothing but a fledgling moral compass to get in the way.

He removed the gag from her mouth and waited for her to speak. The woman worked her jaw while massaging it with her fingers. She stared at 39, clearly afraid to talk with this apparition of everything that people of her caste feared. 39 realized that he was the embodiment of every True-born's deep-held insecurity in their own position as overlords over their physically superior slaves. The way this woman looked at him testified to him how much power he held and how hard they would hunt him. He didn't know why he was different. He tried to remember the last time he had felt mother, really felt her, not the faint buzz that he felt now. He couldn't place it exactly, but around the time he was taken captive. Maybe the blow to the head had knocked something loose. He smiled at the imagery. A joke was there, one that 30 would undoubtedly put a voice to if he were up to it.

The lab coat shrank back, interpreting his smile as something particularly evil.

"Turn them off," he said, with all the command he could muster.

"I can't just turn them off." 39 shifted, and she rushed on. "I can't turn them off without causing severe damage to the brain."

"Can't you...re..." he struggled to remember the word. It wasn't in the uploads, at least not in the way he intended it. He had heard it once in training when the Corpsmen had come to take out the corpse that punched the instructor.

"Reprogram. Can't you reprogram them?" he said.

She shifted and looked away. 39 didn't have a lot of experience with human interaction compared to a True-born, but he recognized her expression as discomfort. Not physical discomfort. She did not like that he knew about whatever reprogramming was. She hesitated to respond until 39 growled at her.

"Okay, there is a way," she hesitated again. Clearly, her reluctance to aid a possible societal revolution was weighed against her personal safety. Her personal well-being won out. "I might be able to reduce the punishment down to its lowest setting."

"How much of a difference would it be?"

She thought for a moment. "It would be about the difference from what you felt during the lashing to, say, an indecent thought toward the opposite sex. You have felt that before haven't you? Of course, you have." She looked down at 20's sleeping form a look of disapproval on her face.

39 thought about what she said. If the pain that mother inflicted was limited to that of an errant thought for severity, then it would be an incredible difference. He felt his head nod.

"Do it." He unslung the medical bag from his back and

threw it on the ground in front of her. "And if you decide this is your best chance to kill one of us, just know that I will be completely at ease ripping your arms and legs from your body."

The lab coat's face blanched.

"Do we have an understanding?"

She nodded excitedly.

"While you get set up, I'm going to light a fire." He threw a small emergency lantern to her and walked a short distance back up the tunnel, where he had noticed another small log jam. The exo-suit's hydraulics made short work of some of the overly large pieces of driftwood, and he was back by 20's still form without ever leaving sight of them.

Despite the humidity in the tunnel, the wood was dry and caught easily with his suit's emergency lighter. He had returned before the woman had begun working on 30 and 20's control devices. The lab-coated woman laid out the instruments that she would need with meticulous care. The tools gleamed under the inconsistent light of the fire.

39 watched her every move as she bent to examine 30's control device. She used a small tool to remove the outer plate of the device. She performed the act without a tremble or any sign of trepidation. She had done this before, perhaps a thousand times, 39 reassured himself.

She performed the work so easily while it could kill a Grunt to even touch the control device with ill intent. It wasn't ill intent, though. The ill intent was solely born by the True-borns. It was not right to enslave them as they did. Fodder for a needless war.

The thought was rebellious, and yet he felt nothing more from mother than he had when he fought those officers in lab coats. He smiled. He was free, and while he had wished that the Colonel had kept his word and made him free within the life he knew, he couldn't help but be exhilarated at the idea of matching his wits against the whole of the Terran forces. Sure, it was terrifying, but he had known little else his whole life.

He could still recall the total, abject fear that was his birth. The unknown. The absolute unknown was more terrible than the familiar regardless of how impressive an army the Terrans could and, most likely, would throw against him.

The unknown. The darkness. He looked out at the pitch black of the tunnel. Black shadow swallowed his light. He knew, logically, that there was nothing inherently ominous about the darkened tunnel, that if it had been well lit, he would see nothing lurking, waiting to strike. It was that unknown quantity that pricked at his nerves. Anything could be out there.

He tried to force his attention back to the doctor and her work on 30, but the darkness felt heavy on his back. He didn't know why, suddenly, he had this feeling, but he was too old to be afraid of the dark. Actually, he wasn't. He looked back out at the darkness.

A stone fell from the tunnel's roof and clattered at his feet. Then he felt it. The floor of the tunnel vibrated, then rumbled, growing stronger. Something was coming.

CHAPTER 32

39 stood in the tunnel and looked first in one direction, then the other. There, the sound seemed to come from the left. The rumbling steadily increased. Pebbles rained down from the ceiling, while fine powdered dust that coated the tunnel floor rose from the vibrating ground. It soon became harder to see.

Whatever it was, it was far too big to be taken down by anything he carried on his suit. He ran to the alcove and stamped out the fire, then pushed everyone bodily to the back of it. The depression in which they sheltered had seemed comfortably sized, with enough room to sit around the fire with some space left over, but now, hiding from an unseen danger, the alcove seemed small and exposed.

39 placed his back to the others and spread his arms wide, trying to block any debris that might fall on them. The rumbling grew so intense that 39 thought it would be impossible to stay standing, so he sat and pushed himself and those behind him farther back into the depression. He hoped he wasn't hurting any of his suitless charges while trying to protect them.

He looked down the tunnel as far as his beam could cut through the darkness and dust-filled air. A mouth appeared and then was gone so fast that 39 wondered if he had imagined it. Teeth lined the inside gaping maw. Then the side of a grey creature tunneled past. Its huge segmented body passed only feet away.

The passage of the beast tore up the sides of the tunnel, and loose debris began to fill the depression in which they hid.

Rocks and the finer dust from pulverized rock began to cover 39. Soon, he could no longer see the creature as its long body ground past. Too much had fallen atop him. He could hear nothing, not even the yell that he knew was coming from his lips, nothing but the grinding of stone and the rasp of chitinous segments scraping past.

Finally, after what seemed like an eternity, the beast had passed. 39 could feel it recede. The rumbling lessened, and the weight of the debris atop him began to slow its terrifying accumulation as they were buried alive.

39 shifted, careful not to crush anyone beneath him as he got his feet under him and lifted. He kept his arms spread and did his best to keep the rocks and soil from falling back behind him. He pushed for the surface and spilled out of the new wall of the tunnel, feeling relief at the sensation of cool air on his face.

He turned and unburied the others. Everyone seemed no worse off than they had been, just dirty.

Luckily, the doctor hadn't started the operation before the massive creature passed, but the tools she had laid out with painstaking care were now buried under dirt, stone, and dust.

39 began digging immediately. He forced the lab coat to help, but her progress was minimal. She had obviously never grown used to working with her hands, and she picked at the pile of rubble like a particularly picky Marine at his rations.

"Ah hah!" 39 exclaimed as he reached the tools. All of them had remained relatively close to each other, and he was able to fish them from the debris. "We need to move on in case one of those things comes back."

The lab coat didn't argue. The look on her face betrayed a grudging acceptance of her situation.

39 picked up the two currently unconscious bodies and prodded the lab coat forward once again. They walked in the wake of the giant thing that had torn up the tunnel in a patchwork of fresh scars and tilled soil. Eventually, after an hour or so of plodding along nervously, they came to a stone outcropping. The

tunnel seemed to skirt around it to the left. Apparently, the giant worm things didn't like going through some rock.

39 set down 20 and 30 and felt their necks for a pulse. He was growing increasingly worried for them. He had to get their control devices fixed soon, but he needed to find a safe place to perform the surgery.

"I'm going to explore this." He signaled the massive stone to the lab coat. "If I come back and you aren't here...I will track you down, and you won't like it when I find you." He felt somewhat foolish making the threat. It felt hollow somehow, but it had the desired effect.

She rushed to assure him. "Where would I go?" she said.

39 walked around the edge of the huge stone, searching its craggy surface for a reasonable shelter. A few spots seemed promising, but he kept searching, hoping for something that they would all fit in easily.

39 paused in his search. Was that light? He couldn't be sure, but it seemed like there was a faint glow in the near distance. He turned off his exterior lighting and waited for his eyes to adjust.

Yes. There was a faint blue tint to the air. He activated his suit's 8 gauge shotgun, which was undoubtedly loaded with cold shot.

39 slowly rounded the edge of the stone. The light grew steadily brighter, but he still had to grope with his free hand as he made his way toward the light.

On the opposite side of the stone outcropping from where he had left the others was a hole in the stone. The light emanated from the hole. The opening was big enough for him to pass through standing up. A cave. What was a cave within a cave called? He slowly walked into the opening and saw the source of the light.

A blue light sconce was mounted to the wall at about eye level. 39 turned a corner inside the cave and saw a small room. The Greys must have set this up as an early warning system for those giant worm things. Or maybe it was a forward outpost for their scouts that spied on the Terran fort. Either way, this was perfect, at least, if it was truly abandoned.

39 searched the interior. It didn't take long. The entire cave, room, and outpost were only about twelve feet square. Alcoves that appeared to be sleeping pods lined the far wall, each with a few shelves for the storage of personal effects. All in all, the place was surprisingly similar to something he'd seen in a Terran outpost. It was jarring to think of the aliens that every Terran feared passing their time much as Terran soldiers did. Recording pings to loved ones or lacking that, as most Grunts did, to colleagues in other units engaged in the fight. A few strange tokens lay on the table. Odd markings were inscribed on the surface. The things reminded him of dice. He wondered solemnly if the Greys feared Terrans equally. It seemed hard to fathom for some reason.

He pushed the thoughts out of his head and crept back out of the outpost. He returned to his pathetic team, two-thirds of which were unconscious and the other third an enemy. At least she'd stayed. He conveyed his sorry bunch down the slope of the tunnel and around the edge of the stone outcropping to the outpost.

"Are you sure the Greys have left?" the lab coat said. She trembled as she looked at the lighted interior of the cave.

"I'm not sure of anything except that your main concern should be your patients. This place is as safe as I can manage. Now work." 39 threw the tools down on the table.

"Careful with those. Some are delicate, you oaf." The scorn in the rebuke was more intense than when she had been taken captive.

"Fine, just get it done."

She sighed and put her hands on her hips. "Okay, let's get him up on the table."

39 lifted 30's limp form onto the table with gentle hands, then began stripping off his exo-suit.

"He's lucky," she said as she examined the opening in the

control device. "I kept my hand over the opening, and little got in." Referring to the debris as they were buried. "Regardless, the interior is self-contained, so he should be fine." She worked as she talked, poking around the inside of 30's head with different fine-tipped tools. "What is your designation?" she asked, suddenly.

39 looked at her and realized that she meant it. She didn't recognize him from two weeks ago when he was lashed for saving his platoon. She had stood as the presiding lab coat. The one and only person that had the authority to stop the punishment other than the Colonel himself. If she had felt that the unit's long-term function was in jeopardy, she could stop the lashing. She had not.

"You have got to be kidding me," he said. She paused in her probing and looked at him. "Do you really not remember me?" he said.

She turned her attention back to 30's head. "I don't make it a habit of remembering Grunts," she said, "Grunts" like it tasted bad.

"Maybe this will jog your memory." He lifted the shirt that just an hour ago had been white up over his head and turned around.

When he turned back, he saw that the sight had impacted her. She focused back on her work with purpose. "I wanted to stop it," she said almost in a whisper.

"Why didn't you?" he asked. "If you wanted it to end, all you would have had to do is say the word."

"The world is far more complicated than your newborn mind can comprehend," she said.

"Enlighten me." He put his hands on his hips and sincerely awaited the wisdom from this woman who was one-hundred times older than him.

She paused in her work. She looked at him, and she seemed surprised that he was serious. "If I showed pity on you or any Grunt, I'd be ostracized. My career would suffer." She glanced at him, abashed.

"I'd hate for you to suffer professionally for my sake," he

said, with obvious sarcasm. This new freedom could get him into a lot of trouble if he wasn't careful.

She went back to work on 30, ignoring his jibe. "Almost, have it," she said.

A half a minute passed in silence, and then 30 sighed. He was still unconscious, but something had clearly changed in him. His brow, which had been creased with worry, was now smooth, and his breathing was more regular.

"Can I wake him?" he asked her.

"Best to let him sleep. He's been through a lot," she said it with something approaching sympathy, a characteristic he didn't know existed among the lab coats. He picked up 30 with a grunt and laid him in a vacant sleeping pod, then went to the sleeping pod where he had laid down 20. He had decided, perhaps unconsciously, to let 30 go first just in case the lab coat needed to practice. The realization shocked 39. He had not been okay with sacrificing 30, but when given the choice, he couldn't imagine losing 20, not after how he felt was blossoming with the loss of mother.

He picked up her small but muscular frame and laid her on the table. The lab coat moved to begin the procedure, but 39 reached out and grabbed her hand, forestalling her.

"What is your name?" He looked hard into her eyes.

Her face betrayed worry. She hadn't expected physical contact, and it frightened her. "Campbell. Doctor Campbell," she said.

39 nodded. "If anything happens to her other than the promised outcome, I will think of the slowest, most painful way to kill you.... And I am very creative...for a newborn Grunt."

CHAPTER 33

39 made a mark on the tunnel wall and turned right down a new tunnel. It was obvious now that the Greys didn't build this labyrinth of subterranean corridors. Worms did. At least that's what 39 was calling them. He had never seen a worm, but its description from the uploads seemed to fit, only a thousand times bigger.

Now, 39 had forced himself to explore the warren of the passageways and was attempting to map them. If he had still been a part of the Corps, he would have employed mapping drones to do this, but his list of scant supplies didn't include such luxuries, which was why he had ventured out, alone, to search for safe exits to the surface where he could attempt to find food.

It had been two Terran days since 30 and 20 had had surgery on their control devices, and they were still weak from the trauma inflicted by both the mother and the lab coat, Dr. Campbell. They were well enough, however, to keep an eye on Campbell while 39 was away.

39 was worried, being so far from the outpost. He told himself that he would be able to run to the closest irregularity in the tunnel wall at the first signs of a worm's approach, but he would increasingly grow more anxious as he walked. Occasionally he would come to a cave-in or a vertical section that would force him to turn around and back-track.

There were things that 39 could swear were moving at the periphery of his beam of light, the instant he moved the light, flashes of movement, a hint of color, then nothing. 39 switched his light to a red light.

Red light was harder for the enemy to pick out on a dark night. At least, that's why the suits had been equipped with the function. He thought that maybe the red light would be less harsh for Eridani B's tunnel-dwelling creatures as well. Maybe some of them would be good to eat.

He came to another intersection of tunnels and crept around the corner, keeping his light low. He raised it quickly and saw a red snake, an eel...a thing protruding from a crevice in the wall. It bobbed there, unsure, it seemed, if the slight change in light was a danger to it. 39 raised his shotgun and blasted the thing. The sound of the weapon echoed off the tunnel walls and threatened to overwhelm 39's ear protection.

The massive 8 gauge round took the thing's head off, 39 was pleased to see. There was no way he wanted to get too close to the jaws of one of these. As he kicked what remained of the thing's head, he realized that he had probably walked past a score or more of the things, his only protection, the light that he now had diminished.

He turned the light back to full and picked up the snake's body. It was massive, and he doubted he would have been able to lift it without his suit. He threw the thing over his shoulder and retraced his steps, following the markers he had left on the tunnel walls back to the outpost.

He threw the snake's bright red body down on the table of the outpost.

"Does anyone know if this thing is edible?" he asked.

30 looked at the thing with disgust. "I don't think I'm hungry enough yet to try," he whined.

20 looked at the creature. "My last upload included known edibles on this planet. This doesn't fall in either the edible or inedible column. I don't think any Terran has been hungry enough to try it," she said.

Campbell looked appalled at the prospect of eating it.

"Well, I guess I'll be the first."

He took the thing outside and started to clean it. He pulled out the guts and washed the thing with some water from the outpost's cistern. Apparently, Greys used water too. Made sense why they wanted Earth all those years ago.

Once he was done, he filleted the thing and built a fire. He ripped a metal door off one of the sleeping pod's cabinets and placed the door over the fire to use it as a grill.

30 and 20 came out and watched as he slapped a large steak onto the hot griddle. He over-cooked it, not having any experience with this type of thing; he figured it was better burned than raw. The meat stuck to the improvised griddle, and 39 worked at the meat with his knife to get it free. He put the meat on a cleaned piece of slate that he found and stuck a steaming piece of snake meat into his mouth.

20 and 30 looked at him anxiously, as if he'd keel over then and there. The most probable scenarios would be far more drawn out and painful. He took another bite, then set the slate to the side.

"Well, I guess we'll see how that feels in about an hour." He knew his voice sounded nervous. Wouldn't it be poetic if he had survived all manner of violence only to be killed by poisonous snake meat?

30 nodded, and 20 looked at him with a creased brow.

"Those bastards," 30 said, for perhaps the hundredth time since he had woken up. He clearly enjoyed being able to express his feelings so freely.

"I mean, after what we did for them." 39 just nodded. He had heard all of this in all of its versions, but the pain was still close to the surface for all of them. It somehow felt right to complain. He had never done it before. It felt like putting a cool ointment on a burn, and so he understood 30's need to vent.

The fire lit up 20 and 30's faces as they both looked at him.

"Thank you," 20 said. She looked at him over the flames through tear-filled eyes.

39 felt uncomfortable and waved his hand as if brushing

the thanks away. Like 30, 20 had said this before.

"No," she said, emotion evident in her voice. "Thank you. Don't just brush that away. You saved us. Us. Not some thought-controlled versions of ourselves. Despite the Colonel's promise, I think I must have known that he was lying. At least, I don't think I truly thought that it would happen. It seemed too good to come true. And it was." She motioned to the surrounding dark. "This... feels real. It feels like the only way we could be free. I don't know how you did it, but I am so glad you did." Tears now streaked her face, and she lifted herself from the ground and came around the fire to sit next to 39. She gripped his hand and put it to her face. "Thank you."

He felt a wide grin split his face. 20 reached over to the slate and picked off a piece of meat, then slowly put it in her mouth. "Let's hope that thing isn't as hard on our stomachs as it is on the tongue." She took a drink of water, trying to rid her mouth of the oily taste.

39 couldn't help but smile even wider.

"Oh, hell," 30 said and stood. He came over and picked up a huge piece of the steak, and began gnawing on it with gusto.

"It would almost be cliche if you all died from eating that," Doctor Campbell's voice said from behind 39. He turned to look at the woman who stood in the doorway to the outpost. "I'm not going to try to revive you, idiots. My oath was only intended for True-born."

"And we wouldn't want you to," 30 said, raising the meat as if in a toast. "Can you imagine *that* giving you mouth to mouth?" he said to the others as if Campbell wasn't there.

CHAPTER 34

Santos threw the digital pad across his office. It hit the far wall and shattered in a satisfying crash of broken glass and electronics. He knew it was unseemly, flying off the handle like this, maybe even childish, but he couldn't help it.

The only news that he had received for days was bad. Since that rogue Grunt had vanished into the forest with his tiny cadre and Doctor Campbell, nothing had gone right. Despite having the Greys all but mopped up, their lack of fleet ships meant little, if any, supplies. Their victuals were dwindling with little sign of resupply. The fleet had gone, probably on its long voyage back to Terra, to inform the government that the campaign was lost. Those Navy bastards could never stick it out in a fight. He thought.

They didn't have the communications on-planet capable of sending FTL communiques. Unless the fleet sent a scout ship back to check up on their stranded Marine contingent, there was little hope of getting back to Terra. At least not for years.

It would take about five years, even at faster-than-light speeds, to reach Terra, then another five to return if they ever did. Ten years. Ten years to try and maintain the order of an increasingly disgruntled body of Marines.

Since 39's incredible escape from the medical facility, the men of the fort began to voice their objections. The Grunts didn't "voice" their objections, of course, but they found far more subtle ways to skirt mother's disciplinary reprimands. Even so, there had been a rash of hospitalizations of Grunts experiencing "corporal exhaustion," a nice way of describing debilitation in some form or another caused by mother. When a Marine had one too many negative thoughts, he could suffer severely. To the point that he was incapable of performing his duties. The hospitals were filled with such cases despite the regiment's depleted numbers. Santos knew that it was the legend that had sprouted from 39 spreading through the ranks that had caused the increase in insubordination. He had to admit what 39 had done was unprecedented.

Other officers, those not keen on the idea of a mutineer Grunt, came to him and asked, nervously, for reassurances that he would be captured and dealt with. They had the right of it. 39 had to be brought in and seen to pay for his actions. It was the only thing that could quiet the growing tumult among his men.

Colonel Santos pushed his bald head back into the cushioned headrest of his office chair. If the fleet didn't return, did it really matter if there was a complete breakdown of command? Maybe it would be better if the Grunts were culled now. It was possible that 39's ability to ignore mother was accessible to all Grunts if the right circumstances were present. The thought scared him as it should all True-borns. If the populace under his command gained their freedom, he and all True-borns in the fort would probably be massacred.

Santos didn't really understand why, but he knew, deep down, that the Grunts would kill them in imaginative ways. Grunts were generally treated quite well, in his view. It made no sense to treat them harshly. It only caused the Grunt to be less useful, their control device working overtime trying to correct the thoughts that the harshness created.

"Margo!" Santos called to his aid.

"Yes, sir." A moment later, she stood in his doorway.

"Bring me a replacement tablet."

"Of course, sir," she said, and bustled out.

He leaned forward and put his head in his hands. He waited like that for Margo to return. Finally, she returned with a new tablet. He hurriedly pressed his thumb into the sensor, and the device came to life, his settings exactly as they had been. He scanned through reports from the search until he came to the one that had begun to grow in his mind blotting out all other thoughts. "Yes," he said. "This is it." A report mentioned a tunnel. It was on the other side of the fort from where the copter had flown, but he was sure that this was significant.

"Margo, get Captain Gerrard in here. I've got a job for him."

CHAPTER 35

Doctor Campbell mumbled something that 39 couldn't make out. She was doing that more and more, and as she became less intelligible, he became more concerned.

"What?" he asked.

"I said, I haven't seen anything like this," she said. 39 felt another dull ache deep in his cranium as she prodded.

She had been insistent that she examine him. At first, 39 had thought that she wanted to see what was wrong with him so that they could safeguard against it in the future, but as she pushed, she had convinced him that her interest was entirely scientific. They had been underground now for three weeks, and his "condition" hadn't changed. She said that she had anticipated a reversal of mother's failure and that when the device started back up, it would probably kill him. They had failures in the device before, never with the regiment, but early on in the program, units had been relieved of mother's correcting influence for a time, but then the device would inevitably surge back to life, and the shock would kill the Grunt. With that in mind, 39 had consented to allow the examination with the caveat that 20 and 30 watched her every move.

"It looks like mother is still functioning normally. It isn't a control device malfunction, at least it doesn't appear to be." There was a long pause while she repositioned the light over the opening, and she continued to search for the source of the "problem."

When she had finally contented herself, she pulled off her

gloves and leaned back from him. "There's nothing wrong. I can't find a single defect in your device."

"So, I should be safe from what you talked about earlier? The...shock?" 39 asked.

"Well, yeah." She shrugged in defeat. "Mother is still, very much, alive and kicking." 39 made a face, and she rushed to explain. "Mother is shocking the hell out of you. From the levels I saw, you should be dead already," she said.

"How is that possible?" 30 asked.

"It's not. At least not in a normal person," she paused, thinking. "I think I know what is going on." She shifted. Her discomfort with the conversation was clear, but her excitement for the science won out. "I've heard of Grunts that grow used to the device."

"I call B.S. on that," 30 said. "There's no way someone could get used to this bitch." He tapped the metal plate on the back of his head.

"As unlikely as it sounds...." she continued. "Some Grunts, usually the unruly and troublesome type, grow accustomed to the pain, at least their brains do. The human brain is one of the most complex things we humans have encountered, second only to the Grey's brains. It can do amazing things. For example, did you know that because of the way our eyes are shaped, the image that we see is actually upside-down? Our brains turn it the right way. I think this is something similar. You have obviously been in almost constant pain for some time in order for this to happen. How do you feel now?"

All three of them looked at 39.

"Pretty good, actually, better than I have in a long time."

Doctor Campbell passed the light over his eyes as she spoke, looking at his pupils. "No pain at all? Do you have any sensations? Anything?"

"I wouldn't call it pain, especially compared to what I've been feeling...more like a buzz."

Doctor Campbell pursed her lips in thought.

"Can you turn it down like you did to 20 and 30... you know, just in case," 39 asked.

She tapped her lips with her left index finger. "Honestly, I think you'd be better off if I didn't touch it. I'm not sure how it would affect you. It could throw your brain into a different kind of shock. There are just too many unknowns."

39 nodded, almost relieved.

"That's what the bastards get for creating someone so hard-headed." 30 laughed at his own joke and punched 39 in the shoulder.

20 wasn't laughing. She had a concerned look on her face. She was worried. 39 wasn't. For some reason, the thought of dying unexpectedly with no knowing when or where seemed almost comforting to him, like a responsibility lifted off his shoulders. It would be a shame to die so soon after gaining his freedom and so soon after gaining 20 in earnest. Even now, she reached forward and took his hand in hers. The feeling of her skin against his made his heart race.

She squeezed his hand and smiled shyly at him. Apparently, the touch was as soothing a balm to her as it was to him. He returned the smile and the squeeze.

Suddenly 20 gasped and let go of his hand. She was staring past him.

30 cursed.

39 turned around. A drone sat, hoovering in the doorway, scanning them.

No one reacted as fast as 20. She had jumped to her feet and lunged at it. It dodged and retreated out of the opening. She stayed after it, picking up the rifle and leaning against the doorframe as she went. She sped through the darkness in reckless pursuit of the flying machine. If she could get it before it made it to the surface, they might be safe. In these tunnels, it would be difficult for it to transmit any information back to its Terran handlers.

39 followed as close as he could manage with a light for 20,

but she out-distanced him quickly. She plowed forward, heedless of danger, her sights fixed on the one objective.

39 rounded the curve in the tunnel and could just make out 20 as she kneeled and shouldered the weapon. A second passed, then another before the discharge of the rifle crashed out in the confined space, making 39's ears ring.

Either she had hit it, or it was too far away for her to try another shot because she stood and waited for him to catch up.

"Did you get it?" he yelled to her.

"Either that or knocked out its light," she said.

39 fell in with 20 as she started walking toward where the drone had been. Sure enough, the drone was down and out of the fight.

"Nice shooting, especially considering your uniform," he said, shining his light on her slippered feet. They were the slippers that they all wore and were from the hospital. The slippers matched the white coverall jumpsuits that were now far from white.

"Glad you're on our side," he said. She only smiled at the praise. "We're gonna have to pack up. They're sure to investigate their missing drone."

"I think I might have an Idea," she said.

CHAPTER 36

"Where did you learn how to do that?" 30 asked her, looking over her shoulder. 20 stopped what she was doing and looked at him as if he'd said the stupidest thing ever uttered. "It's a figure of speech," he said apologetically.

Obviously, she had learned it where all of them had learned just about everything in the foul-smelling liquid of the upload pool.

"I was given the operating procedures of all scout drones on my last upload, just before that suicide mission we were sent on."

"I see," 30 said.

20 cut two wires and stripped the insulation off two ends, and twisted the two together, opposite of how it was wired before. She stripped the insulation off of the other two and hesitated. She looked up at 39. He stood ten feet away, wearing their only tech.

"When I do this, the alarm will sound. Are we sure they're in the tunnels?"

"Not absolutely sure, but I would be. Suppose we'll find out soon enough," he said.

20 mentally shrugged. Men seemed to not think these things out as far as she would prefer. It was her plan, but 39 would be doing the brunt of the heavy lifting, and he always seemed to go by the seat of his pants, to quote an old Earth colloquialism. It was both frustrating and exhilarating. He always seemed to succeed despite his disinterest in fine-tuning strategies, but it was unnerving to her. She trusted him, though. More than any

other person in the entire universe.

She steeled herself and twisted the wires together.

The drone didn't do anything at first, and she wondered if she had made a mistake, but then a blaring alarm blasted out of the thing.

39 nodded to them, and then he climbed into the hole they had dug into the tunnel. The hole was just past the exposed rock, and the shadow of the jagged surface hid the hole. At least, they hoped it did. 20 and 30 hid behind a boulder on the opposite side of the tunnel armed only with syringes of Midolazam X, a knock-out drug that the lab coats used to quickly subdue unruly Grunts. The medicine was in the medical bag they had taken from the hospital. 20 gripped the cylinder in a sweaty palm.

There was so much that could go wrong with this plan. Maybe she shouldn't have. Maybe they would have been better off to try and escape the tunnels. Maybe they should have just run.

No, they weren't created to run.

The only light came from the intermittent red strobe that accompanied the alarm of the small drone, and the sudden violent light cast lurid shapes on the tunnel's walls. 20 imagined seeing half-hidden enemies in every flash from the drone.

They waited for what felt like an hour. She had no way of telling time down here. They were out for long enough that she started to fear the reappearance of a worm. In the time they'd been underground, they had counted five of the giants rumble past the stone walls of the outpost. There was no way for them to know if it was the same worm or different worms each time, and there was no pattern to their passing.

20 was about to voice her fear to 30 when she caught a faint light reflecting off the jagged tunnel walls. She sucked in a breath and held it, nerves suddenly on edge.

The light drew steadily closer. The light separated into three, no, four. She had expected two. A two-man team was standard for something like this. Four. There was no way. She hoped that 39 would stay hidden. They had agreed that if the odds were too high, they'd attempt to stay hidden and let the danger pass. She knew 39, though. She knew that he saw danger differently than most people. It was almost like he craved it. She only hoped that he would practice restraint now. There was no way he could take four.

Shadowy shapes could be seen now, approaching cautiously forward like wild beasts approaching a suspiciously inviting carcass. One was a heavy. The hulk brought up the rear of the group of Terrans, and he towered over the others. They must really be paranoid if they brought a heavy.

20 was breathing again, barely. She didn't dare move a muscle as she watched the four approach the drone. Finally, a scout stepped up to the drone and bent to examine it.

20 sucked in as she saw a faint shadow separate from the surrounding darkness of the tunnel behind the four. The flash of the drone light reflected the light of a syringe just before it was plunged into the heavy's carotid artery. The only sound the heavy made as he crumpled to the ground was almost entirely swallowed up by the alarm blaring its protest. Even so, the men's training kept their heads on swivels, and the next man in line turned just in time to get a fist in the face. His head snapped back alarmingly, and 20 wondered, distantly, if 39 had killed the man.

The next man in 39's path of destruction was an officer. 20 could see his silver bar indicating a first lieutenant in the thrashing light. He had enough time to get his gun up, but 39 raised his shield, and the rounds ricocheted down the tunnel. 39 charged the man and used his shield as a plow. The scout had turned and swung his gun around, but 20 was moving now. She stalked, unnoticed, to within feet of the scout as 39 struggled with the officer.

Because the scout was kneeling, 20 could reach the man's neck with the needle and pushed in the drugs. The man coughed and began to turn but lost control of his large muscle groups too quickly and went down. Hopefully, the dosage wouldn't kill the man. Doctor Campbell had been surprisingly helpful with the medicine. Maybe she was in favor of anything that would keep them from killing any more people.

39 had the officer against the dirt wall of the tunnel, and a cloud of dust had been stirred up by the commotion. The Lieutenant was trying to bring up his rifle around 39's shield and was almost at an angle that 39 could be hit when 39 moved with lightning speed, reached down, drew his knife, and rammed it with all his strength into the man's heart under his ribs. 39 stepped back and let the body fall to the ground. He was breathing hard. He looked for the fourth man and nodded at 20, who stood over the downed man.

"Oh man, are there not anymore?" 30 said from over by the boulder. "I was so ready to use this thing." Holding the tiny syringe in his meaty hand.

CHAPTER 37

The first thing they did was disable the men's wrist computers. They then carried or dragged the men and their equipment back to the outpost, where Doctor Campbell was still tied up.

"That was the last one," 39 said as he released Dr. Campbell.

Campbell was bent over one of the men, using her tools like she had before. Hopefully, she would perform the surgeries with the same steady, capable hand she used on 20 and 30.

30 was out in the tunnel digging graves for the two men that had died of the four that they had ambushed. Apparently, 39 had hit the guy too hard. After his adrenaline had come back down, he examined the poor guy's face. It had caved in with the force of his blow.

39 stripped out of the normal sized exo-suit and began to don the heavy's suit. It felt good to be back in a heavy. He pulled the breaching axe from its spot on the right leg and began helping 30 dig. "You can take that other suit," he said to 30.

30 grunted his reply and climbed out of the hole, and began pulling on the tech. "Where is 20?" 30 asked.

"I sent her out on patrol. She wanted to make sure that that bunch was the only group in the area. Plus, I think she wanted to try out her new tech as soon as possible." 20's excitement over having a set of scout tech was evident. She hadn't said anything about it, but she didn't need to. Her beautiful smile lit up 39's thoughts even now.

30 grunted.

"I hope she doesn't find anyone else. We can't stay down

here now that they've lost men. They'll send the whole army down after us."

"Unless they think the men were taken out by a worm," 39 countered.

"And how would they get that idea? They might not even know of the worm's existence. They definitely weren't in any of my uploads."

"I don't know, but maybe we shouldn't bury them," 39 said.

"Do you have any ideas?"

"I'm working on one, I think."

"You think?" he said. "Shouldn't be that hard to know if you are or aren't having an idea."

"Since you've never had one, I'll have you know it is far more difficult than it looks," 39 said.

"Well, it looks painful. Hopefully, I never have one then."

"Maybe it's time to feed the worms."

"You mean…." 30's face screwed up in disgust. "Oh, that's just nasty."

39 climbed out of the hole they'd dug, his heavy sank into the soft soil they'd piled around the hole. They walked back to the outpost in silence. When they entered, Campbell was working on the second man's control device while he was unconscious, and the one she had already worked on was laying on his side in one of the vacant bunks. He sat up as 39 walked in.

"You're him," the big man said.

39 motioned for the man to lay back down.

"Please, you have had a hard day. Lay down."

"You're 39," he said it so softly that 39 barely heard him.

"Yes. I am. What is your name?"

"Name?" He laughed. "My designation is D42. Never been asked what my name is." He sat as if a stiff breeze could knock him over. "What did she do to me?"

"She changed mother's settings. The worse you will experience now is a headache," 39 said. "The weakness will soon wear off...with rest."

"It's like I've been born again, but without all the pain I experienced the first time."

39 looked away, uncomfortable with the reverence in 42's eyes. "Sorry for jumping you. If there was any other way, we would have done it."

"There was none. I would have killed you. There is no grey area to mother. Orders are orders, and I was ordered to shoot you on sight."

"I see. What else were you told?"

42 lifted a hand, forestalling his answer. "Before we get into that, where do I stand with you?" 39 must have looked confused because 42 rushed on nervously. "I mean, am I gonna be exed as soon as you run out of uses for me? Or would there...perhaps... be a place for me here?" He looked around at the sparse interior of the outpost.

"Is that what you would want? To be a part of us... wherever that leads?" D42 nodded his head before 39 finished. "We will take whoever wishes to be free from mother's torture, but the road won't be easy. Can I trust in you? We may all be dead before we see the sun, any sun again. Santos cannot idly sit by and watch as his men, few as we are, desert. He will come after us hard. Are you up for it?"

"I am," 42 said. He looked into 39's eyes when he said it, and 39 saw his own eyes staring back at him. Some unknown quality they shared, determination maybe, shone out from his eyes like a beacon, and 39 knew he could trust this man.

"What I'm first going to need from you is your tech. We'll get you a replacement heavy as soon as one comes available," he said the words so matter-of-factly that he surprised himself. From the look of this man, he'd been on the planet for years, a veteran, and yet 39 gave orders to him without thought. "Don't worry. I doubt we'll have to wait long before we get another one." 42 simply nodded his agreement as if the loss of the equipment was a trifle.

"Now, lay down. Get some rest. You're going to need it."

42 stood up suddenly on wobbly legs and saluted 39.

39 glanced around the room, uncomfortable. "You don't need to do that. I am not an officer, and we are no longer Marines."

"Begging your pardon, sir. Always a Marine, and you're an officer more than any I've ever served under. Those bastards deserve all that we can dish out after what they did to you and your team. Absolute criminal what they did, sir. Especially after saving all our asses."

"Yes, well. Thank you, Corporal. As you were." 39 helped the big man sit back down.

"Anything happen that I should know about since I tore up the hospital?" 39 asked.

"Well, besides the fact that every Grunt has heard the story, and in spite of brutal retribution from mother, they are behind you. Loads of Marines are taken to the hospital every day because of it, but the story continues to spread. I have never heard of such dissension in the ranks, sir. I think Brass is on to your hiding spot," 42 rushed on at an apprehensive look from 39. "He doesn't know where it is, just that you must have gone underground. I think that, maybe, if we can take some patrols that are above ground, it might confuse them a little."

"Good Idea," 39 said. "In the meantime, we've got to make sure that nobody comes looking for your team."

"Oh, I wouldn't be too worried about that, sir. Comms are practically useless down here. We couldn't even get pings out, and from where we came in, it was quite a march. To be honest, I think the LT was lost. Glad you rid us of him. Too bad about 22, though. He would have been a good one to be on our side."

"Yes, the fewer fellow Grunts we have to take out, the better. I'm sorry for your friend."

"Yeah, well, he would have killed you, same as me, sir…. Mother's a bitch isn't she?"

"Yes, she is."

It didn't take long for them to be able to implement 39's

plan to get rid of the bodies. They felt the first trembling of an approaching worm only five hours after 39 began to come up with the idea. 39 had 30 help him drag the bodies out to the center of the tunnel with the odd piece of equipment. They had scrapped the suit 39 had taken from the hospital and parted it out, keeping most of the parts for future repairs; the rest, those too damaged to keep, were thrown in a pile in the center of the tunnel. A piece of armor with a hole pierced through it, a broken visor and helmet, a defective hydraulic arm, and even an inefficient rebreather was added to one of the corpses for authenticity. 39 was sure that the chunnelling teeth of the worm would destroy most of the equipment completely, but he hoped that a few of the wrist computers would survive long enough for them to be discovered, hopefully somewhere far from the outpost.

If the digested remains of Terrans and their equipment were found inside one of the giants, then maybe Santos would assume that 39 had been killed as well. 39 threw his wrist computer in the pile and ran back to the protection of the outpost. He turned and watched as the worm slid past with a grating sound as its tough scales scraped along the rock. Dust clouded the air, and he retreated inside the safe room and slid the door shut. The grinding tremble of the passing leviathan drew curses from their two newest colleagues.

"You get used to it after a while," 30 said.

They both nodded, though they didn't look convinced.

CHAPTER 38

They lay low for the next couple of days, waiting to see if their ruse worked. Although 20 was the best candidate to hunt and forage for the rest of them, 39 was reluctant to let her go. He felt... worried? Nervous? Every time she left the outpost, he stressed about her safety. With each day that passed, they grew closer. Despite the cramped quarters of the outpost, they somehow found time to talk, just the two of them, every night. At least according to their schedule, it was each night. It was impossible to tell exactly what time it was since everyone sacrificed their wrist computers, and they were stuck underground.

20 was, even now, out looking for food. With more mouths to feed, and everyone's reluctance to eat the oily red vipers, 20 had to venture farther from base to feed them. Last time she had come back with a kind of fruit that was edible, and it tasted good, but everyone had eaten too much of it, and they had all suffered for it. 39 didn't like that 20 had gone above ground, but he didn't say anything. Of any of them, she was the most capable scout. Actually, she was probably the best scout on Eridani B, If anyone could be trusted to go unobserved, it was her.

They had set up a guard rotation, assigning two members of the team, one in each direction from the base, to give advance warning of any intrusion. As a result, 39 was on guard when 20 appeared, as if the offspring of the cold, dark earth and stone around her, no more than twenty feet from him. He had a distinct feeling that she could have gotten a lot closer if it had been her goal. He cursed at her sudden appearance and clutched at his heart with only slight exaggeration.

"You're gonna give me a heart attack," he said.

She smiled and walked closer, swishing her hips and stepping with natural grace.

"I doubt a man that can take on the entire Grey army one day and the Terrans the next would have a heart attack from little old me." She reached up and touched his face, tracing the outline of his jaw with an index finger, at least as much of it as she could with the rebreather there. She had removed her graphene mesh gloves, and the sensation of their skin touching sent a thrill throughout his body.

Suddenly desire overcame him. There was no other word for it. Pure animal desire. He didn't understand it, didn't want to understand it. He just knew he had to touch her. All of her.

He tore off his gloves and reached for her face. She didn't flinch from his touch. In her eyes, as he stroked her cheek, he saw a reflection of his own feelings in her. He needed to feel more of her. He began pulling on the emergency release levers on her suit. She did the same to him. They soon stood before each other devoid of their exo-suits wearing only the thin material of their jumpsuits and their rebreathers.

39 reached up and pulled off his rebreather.

They were said to have several minutes' worth of oxygen before they passed out on this planet, but 39 needed her more than air.

20 looked at him questioningly for a few seconds, then slowly undid the straps of her own rebreather. Seeing her entire face only made his desire for her increase. He pulled her into his arms and felt the contours of her fit body against his. He was breathing hard. He was unsure if it was caused by the lack of oxygen or his complete excitement over this new, unexplored aspect of life.

He looked down into her upturned face. Then he did something that was completely illogical. Later he would evaluate what he did and think it odd, but right now, in this moment, it was the only thing to do. He lowered his face to hers and pressed his lips against her lips. She reacted instantly and hungrily pressed hers to his. They continued this for some time, exploring each other with their mouths.

What was this called? Why hadn't this been part of their uploads? This was amazing. 39 cursed the Terran Brass one more time, somewhere in the recesses of his mind, for banning this.

39 picked up 20 and gently lowered her slender body to the ground below his. He needed more of her. They pulled at each other's clothes until both were naked. After that, all 39 would remember were snatches of extreme pleasure and the absolute thrill of this thing they were doing. He didn't have a name for it and wondered if there was one. Maybe they were the first to ever do this. No matter what it was called, no name did it justice.

Afterward, they lay content on the cold soil of the tunnel in each other's arms. Suddenly 39 jerked up and searched around in the dark on the floor of the tunnel.

"What is it?" 20 asked. "What are you looking for?"

"A rebreather. We should have been dead long ago," he said

"You're just now thinking of that?" 20 laughed lightly.

"Well, uh...yeah. I guess you've probably already figured it all out?" he asked.

"Of course I have." She smiled at him. He could just see the gleam of her beautiful teeth in the reflection from one of their headlamps on the ground.

He broke his attention away from the search, telling himself that they would have been dead if it was dangerous.

"I figure that It must be the roots," she said, matter-of-factly.

He waited for her to continue, but she didn't. "Can you explain it for those of us that are a little slow?"

"You're not slow, dearest. Your attention was focused right where it was supposed to be," she purred, rolled over, and grabbed the lamp off the ground. She panned the light to the tunnel wall and ceiling high above.

"I figure that the air stays down here in the tunnels and soil. It's the only way the trees and plants above us could survive on this planet. According to the jump upload, the solar winds blow the atmosphere away quite often, so the plants get the CO_2 through their roots instead and expel the oxygen down here into these tunnels. The worms and vipers breathe it and expel the CO_2 that the plants use."

"You figured all this out while we were...uh," 39 said.

"Maybe women are just better at multitasking than men?" she said, with another of her brilliant smiles that made his blood run hot.

"See, look," she said, and shone the light on a large root in the tunnel's wall, far enough down that they could see it clearly. It looked hollow, like a tube or hose.

"I think it sucks up the CO_2 through the hole in the end."

"Amazing," 39 said. He wasn't looking at the root.

"I know. Pretty cool, huh," she said.

"I wasn't talking about that," he said.

She turned and saw him staring at her and flashed another incredible smile.

She grabbed his hand and pulled him back to their pile of clothes and exo-suits.

"I want to show you something."

They got dressed and, hand in hand, set off in the direction she indicated.

Even the warm feel of her hand in his was almost too amazing to be real. They walked for some time, and 39 began to wonder if they should have checked in with the outpost before the hike, but he was enjoying the solitude with 20, perhaps too much.

They made another turn down a branch, and 39 realized that he would be completely lost if he got separated from 20. He started to worry that she was lost, but she walked on with all the confidence that she always had. That confidence was part, a major part, of what attracted him to her, he realized. That knowing smile was always at the very corners of her perfect mouth.

He had to get a hold of himself. If he wasn't careful, this new thing between them could get them killed. It was a distraction that they could ill afford on a planet where absolutely everything wanted to kill them, a sweet distraction, but a distraction nonetheless. Holding each other's hand wasn't too distracting, though, he reasoned. It was only prudent, really. What if one of them fell into a hole?

He was about to ask if they were lost when he noticed a faint blue light in the distance.

39 let go of 20's hand and cycled to his M4.

"I don't think you'll need that," 20 said.

He didn't lower the weapon, and he proceeded slowly. He didn't live to the old age of four months by letting down his guard. He trusted 20, but everyone makes mistakes.

20, to her credit, didn't object to his caution. She, instead, swung her railgun around and switched her HUD to heat vision. 39 could see the telltale blue light reflected off her skin around the visor.

The dirt walls of the tunnel were replaced by reinforced concrete of the type used by Greys. There was a set of blast doors that were open, and as 39 crossed the threshold, a Heater stood right in front of him. He jumped and jerked the trigger, spraying bullets into the alien. It just stood there. Then 39 noticed more Heaters. He was in a giant room filled with them. He took a step back and swept the gun around, searching for a threat, but there was none.

All of the Heaters stood, motionless. They stared ahead, big black eyes devoid of life, which was how they always looked, 39 thought.

CHAPTER 39

30 reached up and poked a heater in the eye. The big glassy black membrane gave a little, then the thing blinked vertically instead of horizontally.

"That is so weird," 30 said. "Who's to say they won't all just turn on?"

"I can't be sure, but I think it's safe to assume that the Brains that were controlling these are either off the planet or dead...probably dead," 39 said.

39 looked around at the rest of the group. 20 sat in the corner, free of her exo-suit, knees pulled up to her chest.

Doctor Campbell sat with her hands tied in front of her. She had protested being tied up to be moved to the new, larger Grey base, but 39 still wasn't taking any chances with her. For all he knew, she could be just biding her time until an opportunity presented itself, and he wouldn't give her one if he could help it.

D42 and his colleague D30 stood, watching the Heaters suspiciously. D30, having the same number as 30, went by D.

"At any rate, I think this should be our new headquarters. It's further from Fort McIntyre, and I like the idea of having a pair of heavy blast doors between us and anyone or anything that comes calling," 39 said.

The rest nodded their approval.

30 poked the Heater in the eye again.

"Stop doing that. It's creepy," 20 said.

"I can't help it. It's kinda fun," 30 said.

42 laughed, and D just shook his head.

"What if They do wake up?" Doctor Campbell said. She stared at the motionless aliens with undisguised fear.

"Then we'll all probably die within seconds," 39 said. He meant it as a comfort, but the doctor didn't look comforted.

"Well, can you at least untie me? It's not like I would even know the way out of here. Besides, with those giant worms out there, I wouldn't risk it if I did."

39 nodded and pulled his field knife. He slid the blade between her wrists and severed the restraints. "Be honest, Doc, the real reason you'll stick around is that you love the taste of those red slimies," 30 said.

39 was surprised to see a genuine smile flit across her face at 30's jest. It was gone in an instant, but it had been there. Of late, it seemed that this cold, distant woman had begun to warm ever so slightly.

"If we can figure out the security station over there, then maybe we can control the doors and any advance warning systems they might have in the tunnels. Does anyone have any uploads about captured alien tech?"

"You're in luck, sir," D said. He stood up and walked over to the security station. It was a low bank of buttons, similar to the one that the Brain had been using when 39 had smashed its head. He still felt bad about that. He wasn't sure why. He'd never felt anything when killing the Heaters. Maybe it was the intelligence that the creature had, or maybe it was the feelings that it had tried to convey through their connection. Even now, that memory sent a chill down his spine. Feeling that foreign thing inside his head was disconcerting.

39 followed D to the station. It was low to the ground, obviously meant for the Brains to use, not the gigantic Heaters.

"How old are you?" 39 asked. He was curious. For someone to have been given a big upload like alien tech, he would have to either been on some need-to-know mission or had been old enough to have saved up his chits for extra uploads. Alien tech would have been one that 39 had paid for, gladly. There were many instances where knowing which button to push would be helpful. As it was, D pressed a series of buttons until a holographic display rotated into being above the console. It looked like a spider web. Big and small lines intersected, seemingly at random. D did something with a twist of his hand, and the perspective of the web changed. 39 suddenly realized what they were looking at, a map of the tunnel system. A blinking light indicated their position.

"I'm five, sir," he said.

"Five?" It surprised him. Few Grunts made it past their first year.

"If you don't mind me asking, how are you not a sergeant by now?" As soon as he asked it, he wanted the words back. They sounded far more offensive out loud. "I'm sorry. I don't mean to pry."

"No, it's ok," D assured him. "I was a sergeant...two weeks ago," he paused and looked at 39. "Me and a squad were sent out, like many other squads, in search of you. When we got back from a long day of humping it through the bush, the L.T. broke the news to all the non-comms that they were being busted back to private. Not a single Grunt commands another in the entire army." D stared into 39's eyes until the significance of the news broke through. 39 couldn't help but widen his eyes.

"Why would they do that? What does that benefit them?" 39 asked.

"They're scared, sir. They know the Grunts are mere 1s and 0s away from open rebellion. They want to take away our command structure and make us report directly to the officers. They think that it will make it easier to obey them that way."

"Is it really that bad? I have a hard time believing that my escape could have caused that much dissent among the army."

"It has never happened before. If you think about it, they have every right to be worried. Their whole system is based on mother's control. If we somehow figure out how to overcome mother, then they would have to cede freedom to us. Suddenly the entire Terran empire, built on the backs of Grunt slaves, would be gone."

39 found himself nodding in agreement. "But I don't know how it happened," 39 said.

"They don't know that. For all they know, you have it figured out and will share the knowledge with all of the Grunts. Which, in a way, you have. Or at least as close as it makes no difference. I bet they never imagined a Lab coat helping free Grunts."

"Probably not," 39 agreed.

D nodded and turned his attention back to the station. "This is a schematic of the mapped tunnels in the Greys database."

"Can you access the doors?"

"Maybe," D said. He bit his lip, thinking. "Here." He punched a key on the panel and waved his hand in a downward motion. The massive blast door slammed shut with a metal echo. 30 hadn't been paying attention and wasn't ready for the sudden boom. He swore caustic threats at D, who just smiled his response.

"Excellent," 39 said. "What about food? I know these things don't need it." He motioned to the hundreds of surrounding Heaters. "But maybe the Brains stockpiled some for themselves. From everything I saw in their city, they had planned for a far larger population than what was present. I can only assume that they use the Heaters like we use drones. If that's the case, then Heaters are not part of the species, and the accommodations that I saw were intended for Brains or some other caste that require the niceties of life."

"I'll look, sir," D said.

"Thanks, and don't call me sir. I work for a living."

D smiled at the age-old joke among soldiers. "No offense, sir, but you deserve the respect that the word implies more than any officer I have ever served under."

39 was embarrassed by the comment and shifted his gaze away from D's penetrating gaze.

"Well, let me know what you find," he said lamely and

turned away.

CHAPTER 40

39 crooked his finger and motioned for Doctor Campbell to come with him. He had D route a simple toggle control just inside the door so that they could quickly close and open it. He pushed the button, and the door slid up. Campbell followed him hesitantly.

"I thought you might want to get away from those Heaters for a bit, and I have some questions for you," 39 said.

"I'm not sure that I like it out here any better. Like I said, those worms scare me." Their way was lit somewhat by some dim lights surrounding the door, but as they walked away from the door, 39 switched on his headlamp.

"I don't think any worms come down this tunnel anymore, or else they would run into this dead end." He waved at the blast door. "Anyway, I wanted to get you away from everyone else so that you can answer me truthfully." He turned and looked at her. She stopped and looked up into his hooded eyes, waiting.

"What is your stance on what we are doing?" he asked.

She looked annoyed for a second, then schooled her face to a wintery calm. "You mean to tell me that you want to know my stance? My stance?" her voice had risen with every word. "You kidnap me, jump out of a copter with me in tow, drag me down to this dreadful underworld, and you want to know my stance?"

Her voice lowered to a mumble, and 39 couldn't make out what she said, but he would put money on an insult of some kind.

"I mean, where do you stand on Grunts." She made to

talk, anger evident in her eye, but he forestalled her with a raised hand. "Do you honestly believe that we are lower-class humans? That we deserve the subjugation that we are forced to live under? In all your time operating on and dealing with Grunts, have you never found something to pity in our plight?"

She wanted to deny it, he could tell, but she paused. She hesitated, and in that instant, he knew that she had, at some time, in some way, she felt something for them. A glimmer of sympathy.

"I don't think you are lesser humans. On the contrary. You are engineered to be better. You have been created to be superhuman. The fact that I, in some small way, have contributed to that development makes me proud." She looked away from him. "At least it did.... I don't know what I feel anymore." She strode away from him and sat down on a small boulder by the tunnel wall.

He judged it would be a mistake to speak, so he let her sit for a time, head in her hands.

"Before you took me, I was certain of the system I had been a part of all my life. Grunts are slaves. Sure we come up with nicer words for it, but the truth remains that that is what you are, and I was fine with that. But when you took me, I began to see you all as something more. Mother had always influenced my interaction with Grunts in the past, but now that you are free of her, you experience life more fully than ever I have witnessed. The way you all talk now as if waiting for mother to punish you, and delighted when you aren't. The looks you and 20 give one another. You take nothing for granted. You are not jaded as True-borns are. Every moment that you are alive is a gift. It has been... instructive."

"What if I offered you a life with us? A life that is free from the savage restraints of a corrupt system. Free of the guilt that must soak deep into every True-born's soul," he said.

"And free of the niceties I have come to appreciate." She waved vaguely at the dark tunnel surrounding them. She looked up at him, and 39 was surprised to see the glisten of tears on her cheeks reflecting the light from his headlamp. "Do you want me to live in a hole for the rest of my life? I don't think I'm cut out for that. Besides, Santos will never let you live. He will never stop. He will find us and will kill all of us, including me."

39 realized that she was right about Santos killing her. He would kill her now just because she had adjusted mother and aided the enemy. It didn't matter that she was forced to do it. She had already made the choice. She just had to be convinced of it.

"He won't, not if I have anything to do with it."

She squinted as she looked into the light of his headlamp. He moved it so that it pointed away from her. She looked at him for a while.

"I need some assurances," she said.

"I can give none other than those I have already given. You will be free of the corrupt system that has so stained Terran life that all suffer for it, not just Grunts. I see it in all of the Trueborn, but few recognize it in themselves."

He crouched down in front of her and reached for her hand. The feel of her hand in his did not send shivers of excitement through him like it did when he held 20's hand. The doctor was attractive, to be sure, but this felt different. He gently squeezed her hand.

"I would not make this offer if I did not see the recognition in you. You know we are people, every bit as precious as those we call True-borns. How we came into being doesn't matter."

She met his eyes again. She stared at him for a time, tears running down her cheeks freely now. Slowly she nodded. "It's amazing...." she said softly.

"What?" he asked.

"You are. Somehow you draw loyal followers like a flame draws moths. A true leader. I wonder now how many such leaders have had their lives prematurely ended or their true abilities squashed just for being a Grunt."

He patted her hand and rose to his feet. "Maybe we'll have

the chance to ask Santos that question." He turned away, ready to go back into the bunker.

"There's a way to beat him, you know." He stopped and turned. She looked up at him, still seated. "There's a way to beat all of them," she said.

Her tear-streaked face glistened once more in the reflection of his lamp. She was smiling.

He waited. His mind screamed at him to rush to question her, to wring every secret from her, but he quelled the thought. He sensed that this was extremely difficult for her. Her life, after all, had taught her something altogether different than what her heart was now saying. Difficult though it was, she pressed on. "There is a control station on-planet that controls all of the control devices in all of the Grunts."

Again, 39's excitement almost forced him to interrupt her. This information had been completely hidden from all Grunts, and for good reason. Every Grunt had always been told and believed that each unit's mother was self-contained. That each correction was calculated and delivered from the very device at the base of each person's skull.

"They have always needed additional computational power than what each individual device can deliver, so there must always be a central control station within range of the Grunts, or the units go offline, at least their mothers do."

"But, the control ship was destroyed," 39 objected, assuming the control station would be best positioned on it.

"True, there was a control station on board, but there is another on-planet for just the very situation that the Greys inflicted on us."

"What happens if the control station goes down?"

"Then each control device loses sync with the commands and shorts out. It can't maintain all of that information. At the very least, they'd be overwhelmed with critical errors and will shut down, leaving the host free of mother."

"Are there any risks? I know that before you said that for

cases like mine, some died." In fact, she'd said that they all died, but 39 tried to ignore that fact as often as he could.

"Far fewer casualties. I'd judge ninety percent would be fine, while five to seven percent would have some negative side effects. Neurological problems like Bell's palsy, slurred speech, and retardation. The other three to five percent would die," she said the estimates coldly, as only a lab coat could, but 39 didn't blame her. It was a self-defense mechanism. A clinical detachment to insulate her from the horrors of life and death.

Despite the possible negatives, he was sure that, given the opportunity, every Grunt would gladly, exuberantly, volunteer given those odds, but could he make that decision for them?

39 punched his fist into his open palm. This changed everything. New possibilities bloomed in his mind, like the explosions around the control ship on the fateful night when the Grunts on Eridani B were brought one step closer to freedom. He thought back to that night. He remembered being devastated, along with everyone else, that the ship had been destroyed. They looked at the ship's destruction as a death sentence when in fact, it was one of two leashes being cut. One more leash needed to be severed. One more tie to that all-powerful hegemony needed to be removed before they could be free.

In the short time he had known freedom from mother, he had grown immensely. He felt it. He experienced more emotion than ever before. He spoke with more conviction, more vigor. His mind felt sharper, able to grasp more nuanced language from his fellow freedmen. With such potent feelings never before experienced crashing upon him as a wave cascades over a rock, he knew that it had to be shared. He had to set his brothers and sisters free.

CHAPTER 41

The "bunker" was huge, and throughout its corridors and rooms, Heaters stood motionless, living still, if, in fact, these things lived. Maybe they didn't. Hell, their blood was molten rock. What living thing has stone skin and lava for blood?

30 took it upon himself to put all the Heaters in one locked room. He felt uncomfortable with them standing there, making him jump a mile every time he rounded a corner or glimpsed the hated creature's silhouette in a darkened room. He had had enough, so he had started "guiding" them to their new lodgings. He found that they automatically righted themselves when he pushed them. It was actually one of the first things that he'd done amongst the angry mutterings of his human cohorts. He didn't understand it. They were still an enemy. Not *the* enemy, but he still held every bit as much ire for them as he had a month ago.

He found that he could push them, and they would walk, robot-like, wherever he wanted. He'd had some fun with them at first, of course, placing them in random places and odd positions. He'd crossed a line when he had put one just outside of 39 and 20's quarters. They had started spending the nights together. 30 didn't know why but was intrigued all the same.

When 39 had opened his door early one morning, he'd about had a heart attack and nearly broke his hand punching the stony-like skin of the Heater. He knew instantly that 30 was the one to blame, and his anger only flared when he saw 30's half-hidden smirk. 30 felt bad about that one and quickly apologized and swore he wouldn't do it again. He then had to sit through a harranging like he'd never before experienced.

Chastened, 30 decided to refrain from such stunts in the future. It had taken him three full days to place all of the Heaters in the locked section of the bunker.

30 was in the room they called the mess since they had found captured Terran foodstuffs there. He never would have thought that the tasteless MREs would have been missed, but when he had taken his first bite of the stuff after weeks of eating only red viper and strange fruits, he savored the flavor and texture. Amazing what a little deprivation did to one's appetite.

He didn't know why the Heaters had kept the supplies. As far as he knew, they didn't eat. After all, what would a living stone do with food? Something pricked the hairs on the back of his neck in a completely foreign way. Something told him to turn around. He did, slowly. There, standing in the Heater-sized doorway to the mess was an alien-made stone.

The mess was dark, and the Heater was back-lit, so 30 couldn't see any facial features. After an involuntary jump that spilled most of his MRE on the floor, he looked around the poorly lit room, waiting for some troublemaker like 42 or perhaps even 39 to reveal themselves. He realized that he wanted someone to. He looked back at the Heater and swallowed.

"Guys?"

Nothing.

"Guys, good joke."

Nothing. No one jumped out, laughing at their witty revenge.

The Heater just stood there. This was more than worrisome. This was terrifying. If the thing came at him, 30 was sure it would do more than merely poke his eye. There was another door into the room, and 30 made for it, never turning his back on the Heater. When he finally turned away from it, he all but ran from the room. He ran to the main room that had become their unofficial headquarters.

"Guys. A Heater!" he yelled as he slid to a stop.

"Yeah, we know. There are hundreds of them," 42 said. He chuckled.

Maybe 30 had taken his pranks too far. When he needed them to believe him, it seemed that his previous behavior had a negative impact on their judgement.

"I'm serious. There's a Heater. It was just standing there," he pleaded.

"You really need to stop with these jokes, 30. One of these days, it's going to get us in trouble," 39 said.

30 felt his mouth gape. "I know, but I am being serious. There was a Heater in the mess."

"And...." 39 said, not even looking up from the holographic subterranean map he was studying.

"And, what? It was standing there in the doorway."

"So you missed one," 39 said.

"I missed one in the doorway to the second most used room of the bunker...sir?"

39 looked up from the hologram and stared at the wall, thinking. "Let's go check it out," he said.

It took them two minutes to get rigged out in their tech, during which time 30 felt sweat break out across his forehead. D and D42 remained behind at the HQ with Doctor Campbell, while 20 and 39 went with him to investigate the rogue Heater.

When they got to the mess, the Heater still stood, motionless. They approached the thing with caution. 30 was glad they were taking this seriously now, but he was afraid they would still think he had done it.

"It looks like it's deactivated now," 39 said. 39 lowered his M4 and stood up straight, the full height of his heavy suit bringing him to the thing's chest. "Maybe we should post a guard outside the Heater room," 39 said.

30 nodded. "Yeah, that sounds like a good idea," he said. He sighed in relief.

The Heater's great black eyes blinked. Such a simple thing, yet it made all three of the Terrans shift uneasily.

"Take it back to the room and lock the door. We'll have to see about creating some additional barrier to give us more notice if these things all start to wake up," 39 said.

30 moved forward and slowly pushed against the Heater until it took a step backward. He was on edge the whole way back to the Heater room. 39 and 20 stayed with him, guns at the ready. When they got there, the door was open, but none of the other Heaters seemed to be out of place.

30 pushed the giant into place and closed the door quickly. He pressed the lock function on the door, and a metallic clink sounded. He pulled on the handle to test that it was secure.

"I'll take the first watch," 20 said.

30 didn't think he would be able to sleep, but he nodded and walked with 39 back to HQ.

CHAPTER 42

They had found a few scout Greys in the massed ranks of immobile Heaters. The scouts were every bit as motionless as the rest, and once their suits were removed, they looked just like Heaters, only smaller, just as the one that 20 had stolen the suit off in the Grey city had looked.

Everyone had practiced with the new suits, even Doctor Campbell. 20 had been their instructor since she had the most experience. As she had anticipated, D had been the quickest to pick up the basics of the suit. Being trained as a scout sniper himself, the ability to move silently was already part of him, an almost natural grace that manifested itself in his every move.

39, though she loved him more and more each day, was still a clumsy bear by comparison. He struggled with the training and decided that the training was best utilized on those most likely to be using the suits.

Surprisingly, Doctor Campbell was learning quickly. They had risked going above ground with the suits so that they could train in the open. There was only so much they could do in the uniformly dark tunnels.

Right now, 20's senses were strained, trying desperately to hear, smell or even feel the presence of one of the trainees. The suits made her job difficult, but even as she sat silently on a rock, letting the sunshine on her face, she heard the faint rustle of foliage that wasn't easily attributed to some vagary of wind.

"42, I can smell you," she said. Pinching her nose dramatically.

"Seriously?" he said, somewhere behind her. "I can't smell that much worse than 30," he protested.

"You're right. You both stink. You just smell different," 20 said.

"That's incredible," 42 said. He appeared next to her as he decloaked.

The brilliant sun glistened on the dew moistened vegetation around them. A distant call of some kind of alien animal echoed through the small valley that they sat in. She didn't know why she still thought of the things on this planet as "alien." They were all that she had ever known. If anything, the Terran animals she was mentally more comfortable with were the alien creatures.

42 sat down on the log next to her. It shifted with his weight. "So…what's the deal with 39?" 42 asked.

20 was confused by the question, and she looked at 42 to judge his expression. "What do you mean?" she asked. She was worried that he might be talking about her relationship with 39.

"Well, I know the story, at least the basics of what happened, but what is he like?"

"We're both young. 39, 30 and I are from the same unit in training…five months ago?" she said the last as a question. Time had been hard to track while they were underground.

42 nodded and waited for more. She didn't know what to say. What was he looking for?

"What makes him tick? One thing I've learned in my years of life is that everyone, including Grunts, has something that drives them. What drives 39?"

20 thought about it. She sat silently for a long time, thinking about the man that she had grown to, if not love, then she didn't know what…adore? Admire? Crave? All of these were not strong enough, and so it must be…love. She thought He must be driven by aspiration. But for what? Freedom? Yes, but more.

Finally, she spoke. "He yearns for more. He hopes for more to life than just fighting battle after battle and, if by some miracle you survive, you still are just a minor piece. He was offered something more. His hopes were to be realized. A chance to be part of their world was all he hoped for, and they took that from him. He is driven, now, by the need to right that wrong. He is an unstoppable force. I almost feel sorry for Santos," she said.

42 looked down for a moment, looking at a scar on his hand, then back up at her.

"You learn a lot about a person when you fight alongside them," he said. "I hope that he does teach Santos a lesson. That would be worth everything." 42 looked off into the distance, a contemplative look on his face.

20 suddenly sprung up from her seat and launched a kick into thin air, except she connected with something...D30, clad in his cloaked suit thumped to the ground and resolved into sight. He clutched at his stomach.

"Why didn't you kick him?" D gasped, pointing at 42.

42 was laughing, a low rumble with undertones of a stone landslide.

"Take it as a compliment," 20 said. "He didn't startle me like you did."

D was still rubbing at his abdomen.

"Remind me never to scare you."

CHAPTER 43

"But why didn't they just send a signal to all of our control devices and kill us?" 20 said.

She traced designs on his open palm in the dark. He had his arms around her as they lay on the hard surface that he couldn't justify calling a bed.

"Doctor Campbell says it's because the station can only transmit general orders. According to her, there is far too much for the station to process to be able to send out individual orders like that. The individual judgement calls are handled by mother, not the stations. If they sent out a death order, then a third to a half of all of the Grunts on the planet would go down."

20 shifted so that she could look up into his eyes. There was just enough light for him to make out her beautiful features.

"We'd better be careful. If we push them too hard, then it might just become worth it to them."

39 had thought of that, and he still wasn't sure where Santo's line would be. They might be skirting that line now. He'd asked Doctor Campbell if the kill order would come through after she had all but disabled their devices. She said that it would. So they were forced to walk a fine line. A line they couldn't see.

It was possible that their ruse with the worm fooled the Terrans and that they would think they were dead. He had to go about their plans with the assumption that the Terrans were still searching for them despite not seeing any signs of Terran patrols. "Yes, we will have to be careful."

"Did she say how many guards are around the station?"

she asked.

"She said that secrecy is their best defense and that they can't have Grunts protecting it, so the few guards there are officers." He couldn't help but imbue the last word with a measure of contempt. No Grunt, who has seen more than a week's worth of fighting, respected the officer class for their prowess on the battlefield. In general, the commissioned Terrans were soft. They were born to the niceties of Terran abundance, not the hardship of imminent war.

"Can we trust her?" 20 asked.

"I think so," 39 said. He thought that her weeping openly to him would have been too hard to fake, but he supposed that someone who had been alive ninety times as long as he had been would probably know how to do a lot of things that he hadn't learned yet, namely deception. Now that he thought of it, weeping in the dark didn't seem that hard to pull off. "I don't know," he amended. "But she seemed sincere. Maybe, I wanted to believe her."

20 reached up and pulled his head down, and kissed him softly.

A distant thud and a metallic echo reverberated down the corridor outside their quarters. Another.

"Everybody up!" 30's voice came on the heels of a third thud that sounded louder than the others.

39 and 20 hurriedly pulled on their clothing and rushed out into the corridor. 30 was backing toward them. He was fully equipped in his tech, but he looked terrified.

"What happened?" 39 asked.

"They woke up!" 30 yelled over his shoulder. "I swear I didn't do anything."

"We've got to get to the HQ and get our tech," 39 yelled at 20.

"Close as many doors behind us as you can," he said to 30. "Buy us as much time as you can, but don't be a hero." 39 and 20 rushed to the main room.

Doctor Campbell had been in the corner dressed in the Grey's scout suit. She must have been asleep because her face had sleep marks from where she'd rested her head, but she stood quickly enough when they entered. "What's going on?" she asked.

39 scanned the room and saw D42 enter from a different corridor. D was already there suited in the alien scout suit, and he readied 20's equipment, recognizing, perhaps, that 20 was the better scout of the two.

"I think our roommates finally woke up," 42 yelled from across the room.

39 was glad to see that he didn't have to tell the Doctor to get her stuff. She was already going through the motions of packing her meager medical supplies taking a page from the rest of them as they geared up.

"20, I'm going to need you to lead us to the closest opening to the west side of Fort Mac," 39 said.

20 gave him a knowing look and nodded her understanding.

They were suited up in less than two minutes, but those two minutes seemed to last hours. With every crash and echo of tearing metal that reverberated down the corridor, they looked to the doorway with apprehension contorting their faces. Sweat ran down their faces despite the cool, subterranean temperatures. Finally, when they were all ready, 39 radioed 30, calling him back to the main room.

30 came rushing in, his exo-suit making a sharp clang with every step. "I'd say we have no more than three minutes. We'd better get going," 30 panted.

"Do you know the way back to the outpost?" 39 asked him.

30 looked confused. "Yeah, I think, but why...No. No, you can't. It's suicide," he protested.

"I've been wishing for a good diversion. Now that we have one, I intend to use it," 39 said.

"But those things will tear you to pieces. They're fast,

you're...not," 30 said.

"I don't have time to argue with you. 20 and I will lead them to the west of Fort Mac. You need to take everyone else to the outpost. Once we've dumped the Heaters, we'll circle back, and we'll continue with our plan. Got it?" The command in his voice gave little room for dissent. 30 looked at his feet, then nodded, somber.

"Now, get out of here before they break through." As he said it, a particularly loud shriek of tearing metal sounded through the bunker.

30 stepped over to Doctor Campbell and unceremoniously picked her up. 42 picked up D, and as they passed, 42 patted 39's shoulder. Although they had the Grey's scout suits on, they wouldn't have the added speed that the Terran tech would provide. "See you in a few hours."

39 nodded his agreement.

The four of them took off into the dark. The sound of their metal-encased feet slowly faded while the sound of the Heaters grew louder.

39 didn't want to think of what it meant that the Heaters woke up. He didn't have time to wonder if the Greys were back or if the Brains had resumed control of the Heaters or not. Right now, it didn't matter. His plan had to stay the same. There was no alternative for him.

"Are you sure you can make this run?" 20 said. She was concerned.

He could see it in her eyes. Strange how you could read a person that way. "I'll keep up. I have to."

She nodded and returned her gaze to the single door that was now the only thing that separated them from the horde of Heaters. A Heater slammed into the door with amazing force. 39 was surprised that the thing had stayed on its hinges. Even so, it had folded in considerably. One more hit like that, and it would be gone. 39 readied himself to move.

20 stood there, nonchalant and unafraid of the challenge

before them. She could probably outrun any Heater without breathing hard, but 39? 39 was a different story. Maybe he should have let 30 go with 20. He was a better runner than 39 was. He had to stop thinking like that.

He cycled to his grenade launcher and pointed it at the door. Another hammer blow against the door ripped it halfway off its heavy bolted hinges, and 39 could see the blue glow of Heater blood on the other side. Maybe 30 had injured some of them? Or maybe they had just hammered into the doors with such force that they had drawn blood. The kind of force that would take to draw blood past their thick stony hide was scary.

39 aimed for the gap in the door and launched right before a Heater's fist smashed into it. The explosion knocked the Heaters back and finished tearing the door from its hinges. 39 didn't wait; he turned and ran right on the heels of 20.

39 heard the door slam open behind him. He heard the angry chittering behind him, not like he'd heard it before. This was somehow more feral. He craved to turn around, to see what kind of progress the Heaters made through the door, but he forced himself to go as fast as his exo-suit would take him instead.

They were out of the bunker in an instant, threading their way through the dark corridors. They came to an intersection, and 39 saw 20 turn to see how close their pursuers were. She quickly crouched, bringing up her railgun.

"Down!" she yelled.

39 threw himself down. He heard the massive rifle discharge and felt the heat of newly exposed Heater blood. Luckily most of the blood was blown backward, and little landed on him. He picked himself up and glanced over his shoulder, even as he began to run once more.

The railgun had done a marvelous job, taking out at least five of the brutes, the lead of which was mere feet from 39, a smoking hole straight through its head. They were going full speed again, twisting through the massive worm tunnels. He hoped that one of the huge creatures didn't choose now to roam this portion of the network.

39 was glad they had remembered to strap on their rebreathers because the opening to the planet's surface came upon him sooner than he anticipated.

The sun was up, and it was blinding in its brilliance. After being underground for so long, it was almost debilitating, but he knew he had to keep running whether or not he could see. "We've got to lose them now," 39 yelled.

"Way ahead of you," she called back. She had, at some point, found the time to climb a low ridge that broke up the land in front of 39. She stood aiming her railgun down into the opening in the earth that they had just exited. She slammed round after round into the front ranks of Heaters as soon as they became visible. The melting corpses piled up in the mouth of the tunnel and soon blocked the way out for the Heaters.

She motioned to 39, and he followed her until they came to a gap in the ground that she scurried down out of sight. He climbed down after her. The whole experience had somehow made him feel far less capable than she. He felt like a baby by comparison. Well, a True-born baby.

She sat, lounging in the darkness of the narrow trench. He was breathing hard, and sweat trickled down his body. She looked like she could have done it all in her sleep. He sidled up beside her, and they waited, silent for any sound of the passing Heaters. She reached over and gripped his hand. He squeezed gently and looked into her eyes. He realized that, despite her nonchalance, she was nervous, scared even.

They sat for another minute, time enough for his breathing to regulate, then they heard it. The chittering growls of approaching Heaters. They crashed through the trees above without any finesse. They were enraged. Heaters stumbled about above, angrily chuffing, but the noises soon lessened and altogether stopped as the creatures passed them by.

39 and 20 waited another fifteen minutes, which felt like hours, before they extricated themselves from the small ravine.

As they walked back to the tunnel, they were careful to watch for any rear-guard actions or stragglers that might stumble into them. While they were picking their way through the smoldering remains of Heaters in the mouth of the tunnel, they heard the distant alarms on Fort McIntyre.

39 stopped and looked toward the fort even though it was impossible to see through the trees.

"We've got to hurry."

CHAPTER 44

Major Grant stood at the top of the fort's high walls panting from his run. The reports hadn't been exaggerated. If anything, there were more Heaters than the lieutenant had indicated.

There was something wrong with these Heaters, though. Instead of the well-ordered ranks that the Terrans were used to, these Heaters materialized from the forest in a more haphazard way. Also, many of these Heaters were missing pieces or even full suits of the armored clothing he was used to seeing on them.

Grant was suited up in the standard tech, and the press of the still cool metal was comforting to him. It was a blanket of protection that he gladly draped around him. The fact that he had to dress in it at all was disconcerting. They had all but written off any threat to the Fort by way of the few remaining Heaters on the planet. Where had these come from? Their scouts and patrols had finished off all remaining packs of Heaters, and those they had found were somehow disabled. They had been nonresponsive, and the lab coats had said that it was some kind of mental stress.

It was fairly well understood that the Heaters were controlled in some way by the Brains, but the level of control was still nebulous. Most of the lab coats assumed that it could only be partial control at best. They rationalized that the amount of cognitive ability to manage only a portion of a single Heater's actions would have to be immense. All Grant knew was that there were far more Heaters than there were Brains, so they had to be able to manage more than one Heater at a time.

But why were they awake now? Did it mean that the Greys

were back? Did a Grey fleet arrive and even now were amassing their forces to finish off the beleaguered fort?

Major Grant looked toward the HQ building. Colonel Santos was nowhere to be seen. The man had become despondent and talked with Grant less and less. He also stayed in his office most of the time and left Major Grant, being the senior among the other majors, in charge of the fort's day-to-day operations.

This was hardly day-to-day. This was serious. This attack could spell the end for the Terrans on Eridani B. He squinted toward the low building. The doors remained closed. In the front of the building, Gallows stood with four swinging Grunts. Relations between officers and their Grunts had never been worse. As a matter of fact, Grant couldn't think of a time in history when it had been this bad, not that the Terran council would let such stories perpetuate among the populace.

Colonel Santos had left his office for the executions. He even seemed to enjoy them. It was a way for the man to vent some of his growing disgust for the lower caste. The executions sickened Grant. Men were put to death for the grave sin of being hospitalized for punishment fatigue. Mother had done the real punishment. The men had been dried out husks, unable to speak and bleary-eyed. They were hanged without fear or understanding of what they had done wrong. Grant supposed that they had been put out of their misery. The sentence was still repugnant to him.

Grant turned back to the problem at hand. Heaters slowly approached the fort. There was something else not quite right about these Heaters. The low rumble of grating stone reverberated up the side of the plateau to Grant's ears. It sounded as if the planet's surface had suddenly opened wide, a multitude of loud pops and cracks of breaking rock. The aliens were talking, but not in the form that they had heard before. The subdued chittering that was the usual language of the Heaters was replaced with this chorus of grumbling stone. Suddenly Grant was reminded of a War cry. That's the feeling that this noise instilled. Barbaric in its simplicity, these Heaters voiced their anger, frustration, and promises of death in this basic noise that was communicable across the language divide.

Never before had there been any reports of this behavior. He looked to the Marines that surrounded him. They had made the same connection that he had. The undisguised hatred emanating from the enemy was intimidating to witness. Heaters, on their worst days, were a force to be reckoned with, but now, with the added resolve that these obviously had, the Marines were afraid. He could see it in the eyes of the men and women around him.

"Are there any signs of the Heaters anywhere else?" Grant asked his staff officer. The lieutenant consulted his wrist computer.

"Aerial surveillance doesn't show any heat signatures other than those on this side of the fort."

This attack didn't make sense.

"Have Dog company form up as a reserve ready to reinforce any location along the wall, but I want all the rest of the companies on the wall. They will not gain a foothold, understood?"

The lieutenant nodded as he worked on sending out the orders. "Yes, sir."

CHAPTER 45

39 was dripping with sweat. 20 ran ahead of him and would stop occasionally to wait for him to catch up. On those occasions, 39 was disgusted to see that she breathed normally and only had a sheen of perspiration that added to her beauty, in his opinion.

They were getting close to the outpost, and 39 was beginning to recognize their surroundings. When, finally, they skidded to a stop in front of the rock outcropping, 39 felt like he would pass out. He bent double and sucked in air. He felt like his rebreather was suffocating him, so he pulled it off and gulped the cool air.

"You look like you are about to die."

39 recognized 30's voice instantly and smiled. "I feel like it," 39 gasped. "We've got to go. Are you ready?" he asked.

30 nodded. "Yeah, just waiting on you."

39 grumbled something under his breath. He wasn't even sure what it was, just a general complaint of some kind. He straightened.

"Okay, are you ready for this?" he asked Doctor Campbell, who was crouching beside 30.

She looked nervous. He didn't blame her. He was nervous too. "Yes," she said. She visibly steeled herself and stood.

"We may need your help when we get to the station, but if you don't want to go, now's the time to speak up."

"I'm going. Seeing you all grow and learn once mother was disabled has really shown me how wrong the system is. It needs to change. I'm in," she said.

20 nodded her agreement to the sentiment and patted the True-born woman on the back.

"Let's go then. 20, you know the way best."

They set out at a jog, and 39 was grateful that 20 hadn't started at the hellish pace that they had been at earlier. Despite the slow speed, 39 was worried that Campbell wouldn't be able to match the superior genetic, tech, and training of the rest of them. Sure enough, thirty minutes into their run, she began to flag. 30, without pausing, scooped her up into his suit-strengthened arms.

Campbell gasped something about being able to keep up, but even she didn't believe it, and her complaining was limited to the single protest. Finally, 20 halted and put on her rebreather. The rest of them did the same.

She set out again, slowly and worked her way around a bend in the tunnel. She was looking at the dark, and he saw her HUD brighten, and he knew that she was scanning for body heat. He rounded the bend at her nod, and they proceeded to the end of the tunnel.

As they approached, their headlamps illuminated the end of the tunnel. A wall of concrete blocked the opening. They must have come across the tunnels in the construction of the fort and walled them off. The wall wasn't solid, however. A large fan turned in the center of it. The Terrans must have realized that there was air down here and decided to utilize it. That must have been how they got air into the network of buildings within Fort McIntyre. Efficient, but it was a weakness. One that was about to be exploited. 39 hoped that the Terran's fear of the worms would make them overlook this weakness in their defenses, and it looked like he was right. No sentries stood guard, and, he was surprised to see, no drones patrolled the opening either. There must be additional defenses inside that they would have to contend with, but by then, hopefully, they'd be fully invested in defending the outer walls from Heaters to worry about his small team.

The fan was large, but even stopped, they wouldn't fit with their tech. 39 pointed at 30 and swung his arm toward the concrete wall. 30 moved forward. He let his gun hang from the sling and grabbed a few sticks of explosives from his pack. He stooped, and when he stood, he motioned for everyone to clear the area. The team backed back around the bend and waited for the explosion.

The blast was loud. It had to be to get through the feet thick concrete. 39 hoped that those above wouldn't hear the blast with their attention monopolized by the Heaters.

39 peeked around the bend and searched for any signs of a waiting enemy. Nothing disturbed the dark but the occasional spark from severed power lines. He moved around the bend and closed on the opening. He heard his team behind him move with him.

He shone his light into the hole. Clear. He checked that the rest of his team was ready, and he signaled 30 to go ahead of him into the hole. 39 followed on his friend's heels. He could hear an alarm in the distance, but he wasn't sure if it was because of their diversion or because they'd just made a new door. He shone his light around and saw they were in a ventilation room. It was filled with machines and ductwork that forced air throughout the facility.

39 went to the only door in the room and waited for 30 to open it. He rushed through it, gun at the ready.

Nothing.

An empty barracks greeted him. He walked to the far end of the large room, and the sound of his metal-encased feet clicked on the concrete floor. 39 turned to Doctor Campbell. "The control station is east of here, correct?"

Campbell came to the door and looked out of the window. "Yes, it's in the center of that group of buildings there," she said. Pointing to a cluster of what looked like generator buildings. Maybe that was their camouflage. No one would suspect the heavy transmission lines that the control station probably needed if they thought that it was where the fort's power was generated. 39 poked his head out of the door and looked around. He quickly ducked back inside the barracks as a Marine ran by.

He stuck his head out again, making sure the coast was clear, and motioned for the rest of them to follow him. The strategy they had agreed upon was to "act natural." If they had approached the control station like the infiltrators they were, then they would be recognized and stopped or killed instantly, but if they moved as Marines on duty, then they hoped to avoid suspicion.

As they walked briskly through the Fort's streets toward the control station, the sound of battle echoed to them. The crash and thud of munitions hitting both Heater and Terran defenses alike grew in intensity. Even from this distance, 39 could smell the acrid smoke of battle. He peered through openings in the buildings they passed, trying to see the battle. He feared their "distraction" was going to cost the lives of innocent Marines. They were walking away from the battle, and yet the noise from the fight became louder. Suddenly an officer skidded around the corner of the street leading to the headquarters. He was fully teched, and his armored feet gouged divots in the concrete walkway. He paused when he saw them.

"What are your orders?" he yelled at them. Then he paused and truly looked at them, eyes squinting. His eyes went wide in recognition. 42 raised his fifty cal pistol and shot the Captain in the face.

39 winced. He would have preferred to club the guy over the head. He hated killing more Terrans than necessary, even officers. 39 sighed.

Behind them, a massive explosion sent shockwaves through the fort. When the concussion passed over them, 39 staggered with its impact. He turned and saw a massive plume of smoke. Debris, carried high by the blast, floated lazily in the air for a second before falling back to the ground.

39 peered through a gap in buildings and saw an opening in the wall. Marines were strewn everywhere. Pieces of tech rained down with bloody appendages hanging out. 39 felt a lump

form in his throat. As he watched, Heaters, despite grievous blue wounds gushing lava, charged into the breach.

A company of Marines that 39 realized must have been placed inside the fort as a reserve scrambled to pick themselves up off the ground and rush to meet the threat. There wouldn't be enough. The Heaters were too numerous, and their fervor carried them through the breach like a river crashing through a broken dam.

39 felt sick. Disgusted with himself. He had been selfish. He hadn't considered the consequences of drawing the enraged Heaters into open battle with the fort. The dead Marines that were scattered around the hole in the wall were weighing heavily on his shoulders all of a sudden. He nearly collapsed with the weight.

CHAPTER 46

39 took a step toward the chaos. He was drawn to it. He felt a hand on his arm holding him back.

"The best thing we can do is to turn off their mothers so they can escape this madness." It was 30. 39 wanted to agree with him, but in his gut, he felt that that was wrong.

He turned and looked toward the waiting control station. Though it was still hidden, he could see the unguarded entrance to the outer building that, according to Campbell, acted as a disguise for the all-important control station.

"Will there be any problems when mother goes offline? Will they get knocked out or anything?" 39 asked Campbell.

"Probably twenty-five to forty percent may lose consciousness when the control station is shut down," she said.

He had already asked this of Campbell before, but he needed to hear it again. "That's too high. We can't...not when we have already set the Heaters on them," he paused and then turned back to the chaos of the fight around the breach. "You don't have to follow me. If you want to go back to the bunker and wait this out, I won't blame you, but I can't leave them to die. It's my fault." He began to walk toward the breach.

"How do you know the Grunts haven't been given direct orders to shoot you on sight?" 30 yelled after him. It was a logical concern. If they had been given such an order, then he would be attacked by the Terrans as readily as the Heaters.

"I don't," 39 replied.

"Why do I feel like this has happened before?" 30 said and

then gave an exaggerated sigh.

39 heard footsteps behind him and resisted the urge to turn and see if anyone was following him or if they were leaving. After thirty feet, he could resist no further and turned. The whole team, his team, followed.

They came around the end of another barracks and saw the full scene for the first time. Carnage littered the ground. Whatever had caused the explosion had also dug a crater where the majority of the fighting was taking place as they watched. Marines still atop the walls on either side of the breach poured gunfire down into the crater. Occasionally one atop the wall fell from a Heater's plasma rifle, but they were doing well compared to the poor company that had been held in reserve. D company it appeared to be.

Little could be seen of the fight inside the crater from where they were, but as they ran forward, Heaters fought to the near side of the crater and pushed the overwhelmed Marines back. The Heater's snarling faces were strange and terrifying. Such emotion had never been seen on Heaters before.

As 39 watched, a Heater opened its stony jaws wide, gripped a Marine's arm with its teeth and pulled the arm free of the poor Marine's shoulder. The Marine screamed and thrashed.

39 pushed forward and was soon amongst the rear-most ranks of Dog company. He could see over the top of most of the Marines in front of him to where the Heaters tore into the Terrans with ruthless savagery. He saw, over to his right, Marines rushing from the wall to reinforce Dog Company, but he knew they would be too late.

He sucked in a breath and pushed his way past the first few Marines. He half expected them to shoot him in the back any second. There were disturbingly few Marines between him and the Heaters. The ranks that were at the rear of the group a moment ago were now fighting for their lives.

39 grabbed the breacher's axe at his leg. The Heaters were in too close to use anything else effectively.

A Heater swung a silvery blade at a Marine in front of him, and 39 pushed the man out of the way just in time. The blade carved through the air right where the man's head had been. 39 thought that he felt something coming from the Heater. A sense of frustration emanating from the thing. He shrugged the feeling away and equipped his graphene shield.

The Heater stepped forward, past the crouching Marine and swung the massive blade at 39. He raised his shield to block that side and stepped in, swinging his axe in his right hand. The Heater had wounds that oozed blue blood, and 39 buried the axe head in one on the thing's chest, opening the wound wide. The Heater gave a shriek, and simultaneously 39 heard the cry in his head. It was faint, but it was clearly there. Burning its way into his brain. 39 stumbled back into somebody.

"You okay?" 30 yelled at him.

"Uh...yeah," 39 responded. He still felt the agony of the Heater in front of him. He didn't know how, but he was connected, somehow, to the Heater. He shook his head and yanked the axe free of the Heater. A wash of anger hit 39. A half dozen Heaters seemed to be pushing their hatred at him. Suddenly 39 was reminded of the Grey Brain that he had communicated with.

39 backstepped and brought up his shield as a Heater swung another long blade at him. He was confused by the strange emotions that careened through his head. It was difficult to concentrate on the fight. The Heater slammed its shoulder into the shield, and the impact sent 39 reeling. His head slammed into the shield edge, and he tasted blood. He felt dizzy and swung his axe wildly, trying to keep the thing back while he caught his senses.

The Heater swatted the axe away and plunged his blade into 39's left thigh.

39 screamed. The world swam before his eyes.

He felt like he was falling, yet he remained standing. The Heater yanked the blade free. Pain exploded and radiated from the wound. The blade was dripping with his blood.

Darkness crowded in on his vision, and he realized that, in addition to his wounded leg, his rebreather wasn't working. It must have gotten damaged when he got hit in the face by the shield. He reached up with his left hand and pulled the thing off.

30 jumped past him and parried a blow that would have decapitated 39.

He felt like he was closing his eyes, and yet they were open, weren't they?

He realized at some point he must have laid down because he was looking up. Suddenly he breathed, and there was air. 20 was holding a rebreather to his face. She adjusted the thing to fit him then she was working on his leg. She pulled out an injector of wound seal and shot the opening in his leg with the stuff that instantly filled the wound and sealed it closed. He felt rough hands pull him up and drag him away from the fight.

It felt like a lifetime had passed. His vision started to come back, and his head was less fuzzy. The sound of battle was still very loud, and 39 sat up enough to get his bearings. Men and Heaters fought just feet away.

20 put her hand on his forehead, pressing him back down.

"I've got to get back into it," 39 said.

"You lost a lot of blood," she said.

"I'm going to lose a lot more if I don't get up," he said, motioning to the Heaters that seemed about ready to break through the thin line of Marines.

A yell from above drew his attention to the wall. Heaters seemed to have scaled it and were even now throwing Marines off it like they were nothing. If the Heaters took the tops of the wall, then Dog company would have no hope of holding off the Heaters in the breach.

39 cursed. "We need to get some help up there."

"I'll take care of it," 20 said and ran off with D and D42 in her wake.

39 wanted to follow them, but when he tried putting weight on his leg, it screamed its protest. He forced himself up

anyway. Looking around, he saw 30 fighting in the hole where 39 had been. The crater was beyond, and it was filled with Heaters waiting for their turn at the Marines.

Was what he felt before real? He decided to try something. He reached out with his mind as he had before in the Grey's city fort with the Brain. He instantly felt a wave of emotion surge from the mass of Heaters. He closed his eyes, trying to concentrate. He felt a hint of individuals now, but they were all a jumble. He tried picking one out, but it was too difficult among the torrent of communication and emotion that threatened to overwhelm him. He pushed his own thoughts out like he did before with the Brain.

All of a sudden, he felt the focus of all those individuals focus on him.

He opened his eyes. An eerie calm pervaded the fort. The Heaters had stopped their headlong charge, and the Terrans stood, confused, looking at them, unsure if they should resume shooting at the motionless Heaters.

A voice without words drummed inside his head. It did not speak, and yet 39 understood it clearly.

"Are you their leader?" the voice said.

39 was struck by the awesomeness of it. The words were translated by his brain, but they were given their meaning through pure emotion. It was raw and difficult for him to mimic, but he did his best. "No, only a slave that wants to be free," he said.

"Why are you different from them?" the voice asked.

"I no longer have a device that allows them to control me." The emotion was hard to transfer, and he hoped he was saying what he thought he was.

"Then why do you fight for them?" it asked.

"I fight for the slaves, not the leaders."

There was a pause, and 39 thought he could feel they were discussing what he'd said.

"How is it that you come to speak our language?" 39 was

taken aback. He had always been told that the chittering noise that they made was their language.

39 did his best telling the story of him and the Brain. He hoped that the parts with him killing Heaters wouldn't enrage them again, but to his surprise, they didn't react to it. When he was finished, there was another long pause while they consulted.

39 looked around at the Marines. Most looked on the verge of firing their raised weapons into the Heaters.

"Lower your weapons," 39 yelled.

Terrans turned toward him, but most kept their weapons trained on the enemy.

"Do as he says," Major Grant stood atop the wall looking down at him. 20 stood next to him.

The voice thundered in his head again. "It is because of you that we are free," it said. "Because of this, we will allow you to choose a champion to face ours. This way, we limit loss of life."

"Why do we have to fight? You can leave now, and we will not follow," 39 said.

"You cannot speak for your leaders, and there are many of us that believe that we should finish you off here and now, or we will live to regret it."

39 understood their logic. They held all the cards.

"We have agreed, however, that because you have killed our overseers, we will grant you the right to be numbered among our ranks for the purpose of resolving the conflict. Fight for them as their champion, and perhaps you will prevail. If not, you will die with the rest."

Little choice, then.

He stepped forward. The pain in his leg made him limp badly. He picked his way over and around dead bodies, Heater and Terran alike, until he stood in the center of the crater. He felt the eyes of the Terran men and women stare as he walked in among the Heaters. The heaters inside the Crater pushed dead bodies out of the circle and retreated to the edge. Marines did the same, unsure why, but following the alien's lead anyway.

The Heaters started making a low rumbling sound that could be felt in the ground. They rocked back and forth slightly. Marines looked nervously around the crater.

39 looked up at 20 on the wall.

"Whatever happens to me, don't intervene," he said. He looked at her but was speaking to every Marine. 20 gave him a look that he couldn't define. He settled on concern, but it was more than that. It had love, but it also had anger there behind her eyes. Maybe Terrans weren't so different from Heaters. So much could be said with a simple look.

Slowly, the Marines that looked down at him nodded as they began to comprehend. They didn't understand fully, of that 39 was sure, hell, he didn't understand fully. No, they could not understand. They couldn't feel the emotion that transmitted through unseen chords to him. They could not know how savagely many of the Heaters planned on resuming the battle after 39 was killed. He felt himself being targeted by hate-filled Heaters bent on venting their frustration at anyone, regardless of his freeing them. There were others, however, that saw him differently. They allowed logic to temper their hate. The hate for the Greys was so intense that it spilled over, and those less vigilant among the Heaters wanted to take their revenge on anyone different than themselves.

39 was lucky that those with cooler heads prevailed, but if he lost, then the battle would resume, and vengeance would be sought from the Terrans. He turned in a circle, looking for the Heater that would be the enemy's champion. The strange rumbling chant that emanated from the Heaters was oddly comforting.

At the edge of the crater, Heaters separated, allowing a massive warrior through. It stood head and shoulders above those around him, and compared to 39, he was nearly twice his size.

He got the feeling that firearms would not be acceptable to use in this fight, so he disengaged them and threw the weapons to the side, then walked over to a fallen Heater and picked up the strange oversized swords that the Aliens preferred.

The giant Heater entered the crater, and the rumbling stopped. The Heaters stood totally motionless except for the one that 39 was to fight. He circled cautiously, eyeing 39 with those dead Heater eyes. 39 moved around the edge of the crater, limping badly but managing to stay out of the Heater's reach.

The Heater made a couple quick jabs, testing him, and 39 wasn't pleased with his own reaction speed. The Heater's face remained stoic, but his mind sent an insulting barb that pricked 39's pride. Without words, it managed to imply that 39 was weak and a poor representative of the human race. Sadly he had to agree. He didn't know how he was supposed to beat this beast with a wounded leg and no guns.

The Heater thrust the point of his sword at 39's chest, and he was barely able to knock the blade away as he staggered back. 39 knew he wouldn't last long against this Heater if he didn't go on the offensive. He gritted his teeth as he pushed off the edge of the crater with both legs. He launched himself inside the Heater's reach as the alien was swinging his sword back for a devastating strike that would have decapitated 39. He punched the Heater in the face with the pommel of the massive sword...once, twice, three times. Chips of stone broke free from the alien's face with each blow.

The Heater, instead of pushing 39 away, embraced him in a bone-crushing hug. If it hadn't been for his exo-suit, he was sure he would have died, even so, the rigid graphene titanium construction groaned under the pressure, then gave a loud pop, and his suit's leg hydraulics stopped functioning.

39 knew that just seconds more, and he would be crushed. 39 swung his sword down and into the Heater's side. The blade didn't penetrate. It was a glancing blow, but the big alien released 39 and stumbled away from him, momentarily out of the action. He hit the emergency eject function on the suit and quickly stepped out of the suit. Without the suit, the sword felt heavy,

and his legs moved sluggishly in the dark Eridanian soil.

"What is he doing?" He heard one Marine say out of a general babble of dismay. He knew his chances were slim in the suit, but they were nonexistent out of it.

39 glanced up on the wall where 20 stood, tears running from her eyes. He saluted her with his sword, then readied himself for the Heater, who had recovered from the wound enough to begin his deadly stalk once more. The alien sent more images and feelings to 39 through the strange connection that 39 had somehow developed. They painted a picture of condescension and mockery at his unimpressive suitless form. The sword he wielded was now as tall as he was and heavy, but 39 was determined to kill this giant or die trying. Wasn't much of a promise since those were his only options anyway, but he felt motivated nonetheless.

39 suddenly rushed at the Heater. The alien swung his sword in an overhand chop that would have cleaved him in two, but he ducked and rolled, bringing the point of the blade up under the giant's armpit. It penetrated, and blue viscus blood ran out onto his sword. 39 pulled the sword free. The Heater was shrieking madly. Its emotions assailed 39, but he ignored them as he had the pain in his leg. 39 danced back, out of easy reach of the Heater. He felt his boot fill with blood and knew, distantly, that his wound must have opened up again.

Marines were cheering, but it was all far away, misty like a foggy morning. The Heater was the only thing now. He saw the thing clearly, and it was almost like he knew what the thing would do next and acted accordingly. 39 moved to his left, then dove to his right. The Heater had charged wildly, swinging his sword but sliced through air. 39 had dove out of the way just in time, and the giant ran past. Both of them were bleeding freely, and 39 knew he needed to bring the conflict to a head soon, or he'd lose consciousness.

39 picked up a chunk of concrete and hurled it at the Heater. It smashed against the back of the thing's head. The

Marines' cheering grew to an unignorable level. He knew the concrete wouldn't hurt it, but he also knew that this particular Heater was extremely prideful, and 39's throw would send the thing into a blind rage.

The Heater turned and sprinted at 39, but before it could take two steps, it tripped on his exo-suit and stumbled forward onto 39's waiting blade. 39 had wedged the pommel against the ground, and as the Heater's lava-like blood poured out, 39 jumped free. The Giant body of the Heater slowly slid down the long length of the blade until it was resting on the ground.

CHAPTER 47

39 stood looking at the surrounding Heaters as if talking to them, but no sound came from them. Suddenly the Heaters at the breach in the wall began streaming back through it out and down the side of the plateau. They left the stunned Marines staring at their retreating backs.

Major Grant was just as shocked as his men. The enemy, who had been on the verge of taking the fort, now trotted out of range of the defense turrets and disappeared into the forest beyond.

Suddenly, the man who had appeared out of nowhere and saved them all again from certain disaster collapsed to the ground.

"Corpsman!" Grant yelled. "Get that man help, now!"

He rushed to the stairs and took them two at a time. Had he been another officer, he probably would have let the poor man die. It would be a convenient end to a troublemaker. If he were Colonel Santos, he supposed he would even help fate along and finish off the wounded man. But he couldn't. Deep in his heart, he knew that such an act would be contrary to everything he was. He would sooner stop breathing than betray G39.

The crowd around the crater parted to let a Corpsman through, and by the time Grant arrived, 39 was already being worked on.

"Is he going to make it?" Grant asked the young officer after a little while. 39 was unconscious, and he looked extremely pale.

"I'll do my best, sir. He's lost a lot of blood." The Corpsman didn't look up as he worked.

Blood formed puddles all around the crater. So much blood that it was impossible not to step in it. The sun was at its very hottest in its long sojourn across this alien sky. Sweat trickled down his neck and along his back under his exo-suit.

"Captain Stewart. Keep an eye on our friends out there. I don't want anyone sneaking up on us," Grant yelled up at an officer on the wall. The man nodded and ducked out of sight as he, presumably, carried out his orders.

The Corpsman was setting up a mobile IV. "Stretcher!" He called into the mic on his shoulder. A minute later, a stretcher carried by a four-legged robot came to the crater.

Grant knew that as soon as Colonel Santos learned that 39 was in the hospital, he would be marked for death, but there was little for it.

The Corpsman had 39 loaded onto the stretcher, and Grant was walking beside the robot when there was a thunderous explosion not far to his right. Grant looked that way and saw a plume of smoke rising into the air. He turned toward the wall expecting to see Heaters attacking there, but it was clear. As he watched, however, Marines began to drop like boneless dolls to the ground.

The control station. It had to be.

"Take him to the hospital. Make sure he is treated as an officer." Major Grant ordered the Corpsman. Grant didn't wait for a response but moved off toward the smoke. As he approached the door to the complex of buildings surrounding the control station, the doors slid open, and two men walked out. Grant didn't recognize them, but one was large, like 39. The smaller of the two was wearing a Grey's suit.

"Stop right there," Grant yelled at the two, drawing his pistol and pointing it at the men. They hesitated before raising their hands in submission.

"What have you done?" Grant asked, though he already

knew the answer.

The big man spoke. "We've undone the evil of your kind." The last was said with a sneer as if his "kind" was too despicable to speak of.

"If those things come back...." Grant motioned vaguely in the direction that the Heaters had left in. "We'll all be dead. Grunts included."

"If you think we'd abandon each other if the Heaters come, then you don't know us," the smaller of the two said.

"Perhaps, but if you can't convince me, then there's no officer in the army that will be."

20 suddenly appeared from behind Major Grant, and he kicked himself for not paying better attention. "Major, we have no qualms with you. It's Santos that cannot be trusted. He promised us commissions and then tried to kill us for our efforts."

Grant stood and pondered what she had said. It was true. Santos had betrayed them after delivering salvation to the whole army. If anyone deserved freedom, it was 39 and 20. He lowered his gun.

"Whine, whine, whine. That's all I hear." Grant turned toward the voice. Colonel Santos was there with two big lieutenants, guns raised.

"Shoot them," Santos said, pointing at the two men in the doorway.

"Belay that order," Grant said. For a stunned silence, no one moved. It was difficult for him to even come to terms with what he was doing.

The lieutenants looked at each other and then back at Colonel Santos.

"Don't look at me! You have your orders, you useless buckets of shit!"

"Do not shoot those men," Grant said, raising his voice. "Colonel, surely there's a way we can figure this out without bloodshed." Grant knew that with the control station down, the officers could be seconds away from a massacre. Diplomacy was needed now more than ever.

"You have got to be kidding me, you yellow-bellied bastard," Santos said, raising his gun toward Grant.

Time seemed to slow as Grant realized that Santos would shoot him down right here and now. He stared at the Colonel, unblinking, waiting for the finger on the trigger to tighten. Waiting for that bullet to pass through his brain. He idly wondered if he would feel anything.

Suddenly a bright red line drew itself across the Colonel's throat. It opened like a smile, then blood began to pump free. Instead of a bullet in the brain, Major Grant watched as Santos clutched at his throat as he tried, in vain, to keep the blood inside him. He slowly sank to his knees, then to the ground.

A person slowly shimmered into being next to Santos.

"Doctor Campbell?" Grant said. Disbelief was evident in his tone.

She stood, holding a blood-soaked dagger. She was wearing a Grey suit similar to that of the smaller of the two Grunts in the doorway.

"Hello, George," she said.

CHAPTER 48

When 39 woke. A blurry abstract resolved itself into the image of Major Grant over him. He felt his body tense, unsure of what the Major's presence foretold. He was in the hospital in a regeneration pod. He could feel the tingle of the anesthetic and the pull and tug of the little robotic hands as they tied the tissue back together on his thigh.

20 was there as well, as was 30. This surprised him. Surely they were all still on the Colonel's death list. 39 raised himself up on his elbows and looked around. Doctor Campbell was there. She had replaced her Grey scout suit with the standard lab coat, and she was looking at a tablet making notations with a stylus.

"You'd better lay back down," Grant said. "Before she looks up and sees you. I've been her patient before. You don't want to get on her bad side."

Doctor Campbell looked up from her tablet. "I doubt anything I say could keep 39 from doing what he wants. He's so stubborn that he broke mother."

39 held out his hand, and 20 took it. He looked into her eyes and smiled. Whatever came, he'd face it with her. That thought strengthened him. Though he feared for her safety, he knew that, much like himself, she would never leave his side. She was every bit as stubborn as he was.

"What happened?" 39 asked. His voice sounded dry and gravelly.

"Well, you've been out for hours. Loss of blood and extreme fatigue, I'm told," Major Grant said.

"Are the Heaters gone?" 39 queried.

"However you were able to convince them to fight a champion seemed to have worked. I have no reports of any Heaters, but I don't know that I would get any reports of such a move in any case with the chaos going on," Grant said. He glanced sidelong at 30.

"Chaos?"

30 stepped forward. "Yeah, you know how you were busy saving the fort? Well, Doctor Campbell took D and D42 to finish our mission. They succeeded, and Colonel Santos is dead." 30 shrugged as if he regretted not being the one to have done it.

30's blunt explanation brought a smile to 39's lips. "Did it work?" 39 asked. "Are they...."

"The Grunts have been freed," Major Grant confirmed. "But they're making a mess of things right now. They have the officers barricaded in HQ and are threatening to burn it down with the officers inside. Though they don't treat me with the same hatred, they won't listen to me. We need you, son."

Major Grant placed a hand on 39's Shoulder. "Your colleagues assure me that your intention was never to massacre the officers, but it is you that they need to hear it from. They won't listen to anyone else."

39 nodded.

"Doctor, am I cleared to get out of this?" 39 motioned to the pod.

"As long as you don't push it and you come straight back here for the pod to finish knitting your leg. No fighting Heater champions for you," she said, her stylus moving up and down in an admonishing gesture.

Doctor Campbell hit the release on the pod, and the door that covered the lower half of his body hissed open. He had a moment of panic as he realized he was naked underneath, but he quickly rejected the feeling. What was it? Embarrassment? He had never felt that before. He wondered what other human feelings he had not been alive long enough to experience.

30 held out a clean jumpsuit, and 39 quickly climbed into it. Everyone but Doctor Campbell left the hospital and made their way over to HQ. They walked slowly since 39 still limped, and he fought a grimace with every step.

They saw Grunts, newly freed from their control devices, looting the quartermaster's warehouse. 39 stopped them with a terse command, and the men dropped the stuff and stared at him as he and his entourage passed by. One of the men whispered to the other, and then they followed, curious.

They approached the Q from the west, and so they approached the crowd from the rear. 39 could hear angry voices toward the front of the group stirring the Grunts into action.

With help from Major Grant, 39 climbed to the top of a short storm-water diversion wall and looked out across the sea of freed men and women.

He was nervous. That feeling he recognized, but why should he be more scared now than he had been when facing an alien city full of Heaters? What would he say? Would they listen to him?

He heard voices nearer to him talking excitedly, and then some of the crowd was turned toward him, then more, as they recognized him and word spread. Soon those at the front of the mob were now at the rear, looking on expectantly.

The crowd of Marines stood motionless, waiting for him to say something. He was surprised by this. Why should what he said matter? Why should they follow him? He knew why others might say they would, but to him, the reasons seemed superficial.

He cleared his throat and winced at how loud it seemed among the silence.

"Frankly, I don't know what to say," he paused and raised his voice even louder. "I have been where you are now. God knows a part of me still is there with you. Angry, no, enraged. Enraged at a system that would allow such inhuman treatment of us. They created us to be their fodder. We sweat and die in their wars, and for what? So they can move on and conquer another part of the universe at the expense of us," he paused, looking out at the crowd. They looked at him eagerly, many nodding their heads.

"I don't know how many times, amid mother's merciless correction, I yearned for freedom. I even visualized that if Grunts were in charge, we would be more. We would be better. If we kill every officer here, as some of you insist, we will be no better than they. Our freedom cannot come at that cost. If we destroy them, we destroy our chance and that of every Grunt to be free."

Some looked angry at his words, but others were nodding. Most stood unreadable.

"The Terran Navy could be back here at any time. If they appear in orbit and find out that we massacred the True-borns, what do you think they'll do? We can be an enemy of Terra, or we can help them see the error of their ways and perhaps gain our freedom, all of our freedom, not just for the Grunts on this isolated planet, but for Grunts everywhere."

39 was worried that this line of reasoning might not work on the amped-up Marines, but as he looked at them, he knew that he had underestimated them. These men and women were scared. They didn't know what to do, and guidance was craved.

"The only way forward that doesn't automatically end in our extermination is to make peace with the True-born on this planet. They cannot help what caste they were born into any more than we can. I know that many of you, like me, have heard of the things that Major Grant has done in defense of our kind at great risk to himself. He is a good man, no matter that he is a True-born."

He paused and straightened. He was hesitant how the next part would be received, but it was the only thing he was sure about.

"We can be our own Terran colony here, far from Terra, and a strategic outpost, a bulwark against the Greys, but I think we need a True-born Governor. I nominate Major Grant."

Grant looked astonished.

"Why not you?" Someone yelled from the crowd. The sentiment was parroted by hundreds of voices.

"Red hand! Red hand!" A chant picked up among the Grunts. It echoed among the Marines long after he held up his hands for quiet.

"Major Grant has the experience that we need. He has been alive three hundred times longer than I have, and I don't know about the rest of you, but I'm still figuring things out."

"Besides, if the Navy comes and finds a Grunt in charge, they'll probably blast this place to smithereens," he paused again to let that sink in. The dissent seemed to have been quieted. "Who is with me in making Major Grant the Governor of Eridani B?"

He raised his hand in the air and waited.

39 knew there must be some kind of committee back on Terra that would normally make such appointments, but being so far away, he doubted that there would be much the Terrans could do years from now when a force was sent to the planet once again.

At first, no one raised their hand, and 39 swallowed nervously. Then a few tentative hands lifted, then, a dam seemed to break, and almost all of them were raised.

39 let out a breath that he didn't know he was holding. He turned to Grant and held out his hand. Grant took it. 39 could see the gratitude in Grant's eyes, not for the position that 39 had used his influence to get him, but for the peaceful resolution of the situation.

Grant stepped up onto the wall next to 39.

"My first act as your governor is to appoint G39 "Red Hand" as my war advisor and Brigadier General and commander of all the forces on Eridani B."

A cheer started up, and chants of "Red Hand!" reverberated through the crowd.

39 turned to 20 and lifted her up onto the wall. He pulled her close and kissed her in front of a thousand Marines. They cheered louder, and all 39 could think of was how incredible this

felt. His choices were his own. There were difficulties ahead, but he knew that with help, they would get through them together. All of his hopes had been realized.

Life, to this moment, had been a dizzying panoply of conflict and action. He knew more would come, but with his freedom, he felt all was possible.

L.J. Stubbs has always been drawn to futurism and the wonder inherent in 'what could be.' The possibilities are literally endless, and he loves contemplating the myriad paths that humanity can take. L.J. Graduated from Brigham Young University in 2009 and married his lovely wife shortly after. They now have three rambunctious boys and live along the Snake River in Idaho.

L.J. Stubbs enjoys writing full-time, which is a life-long dream come true. When he is not writing, he can be found reading a book or working on an art piece that he uses to channel what he calls his 'creative juices.' L.J. is known for putting himself into his characters and takes pride in the connection that his readers make with those personalities.